Cramming
at Randy's

Diner Days

Alex Silver

ISBN: 978-1-998885-11-4

Contents

Dedication

This one is for all the readers who see themselves in this series, Kat for putting this series together, and all the Diner Days authors for making this project so special, thank you!

Chapter One

Ray

I get off the plane feeling untethered. This is it. My first steps into being an independent adult. It's scary to heft my battered old school bag over my shoulder and drag my carryon toward customs all by myself. This and the two checked bags my parents paid for at Trudeau International this morning constitute all my worldly possessions.

Even in my head, that seems a tad dramatic. I still have all the stuff in my room at my parent's house a five-hour drive north in Montreal. It's just daunting to move out on my own for the first time. Studying abroad seemed so cool from the comfort of home, but standing here on my own with so much unbounded freedom has me equal parts terrified and exhilarated.

I tug my colorful knit toque lower, covering the long dishwater blond hair that's tucked up in a messy bun under it. How many times have I wished for the courage to chop off the wavy ponytail my parents love so much? Ugh. Soon. The whole point of coming to Boston for school is to give myself the space to figure out who I am, away from my family's smothering love.

Standing in line with the other passengers from my flight, I'm getting cold feet. I've never had to talk to the border agents alone before. The winding lines give me plenty of time to fret that I'm going to mess up my grand university adventure before it even really begins. It would be humiliating to get sent back to Canada in disgrace. I fiddle with my passport and student visa; the paperwork is all in order. My middle brother is a lawyer and my whole family helped to make sure I have everything I need. I've totally got this.

The line shuffles along slowly. The longer it takes, the more I get all worked up that my nerves are going to make the stern-faced border agents think I have something to hide. What if they don't let me through? Am I going to be stranded at the airport? Deported? Can they even deport you if you technically never clear customs? So maybe a random search is more likely? I swallow hard, bile rising at the thought of being searched.

A big, intimidating man in a uniform waves me up to his kiosk when it's my turn. He barely glances at my papers and asks why I'm coming to the US. His voice is warmer than his expression. His accent reminds me of an old cowboy movie with vowels that pour like honey.

"School." I bite back my nervous babble about my program and what I'm planning to study. He might sound nice, but he doesn't need to know my life story. I've done this before to visit my aunts, but always with my parents doing the talking. My dad rambles at the agents, and my mom always reminds him to only give them the information they ask for. No need to volunteer anything and draw out the ordeal.

The agent nods, checks my visa, squints between the picture in my passport and my face and asks me to lift my hat. I do. He nods again.

"Good luck with your studies, ma'am." He waves me through.

My gut roils with the wrongness of that title. It's not just that it makes me feel like a fraud of a grown up. A kid cluelessly adrift in a world that expects me to be a functional adult when I was living under my parent's roof just this morning. I want to correct him. Sir.

It's still scary to face the responsibility of being a grownup, but that word is less viscerally wrong. I swallow the impulse as I follow the other weary travelers from my flight toward the baggage claim. My nerves settle as I wait in the crowd to collect my things and turn to find my ride on the other side of the security cordon.

"You made it! Welcome to Boston, kiddo!" Aunt Marie-Clarie, Dad's little sister, meets me with a bone-crushing hug and helps me wrestle my suitcases out to her car. "How was your flight? You must be hungry?"

"Good, nice quiet flight. Yeah, I could eat," I agree.

She rattles on a mile a minute about how much I'm going to love Boston and how glad she is that I'll be close by for the next few years. We get into the car and pull out of the airport lot. I let her words wash over me as we drive. They're a comforting reminder I'm not entirely alone in this new life I'm starting. I have a touchstone if everything gets too overwhelming.

I tune back in when we're approaching my campus in Boston's South End. The stately Victorian homes here remind me a little of home, or at least some of the ritzier neighborhoods back in Montreal. This is going to be home for the next few years and I want to drink in every sight.

"I can't believe I'm really here," I say, more to myself than my aunt.

"You are. You know you can come to me for anything if you need a friendly face or a hug or a listening ear. Tammy says I shouldn't pry, but I want you to know we're here for you, no matter what, alright?" Aunt Marie-Claire glances over at me to emphasize that she means the offer.

I smile because it's nice to hear her confirm that I have people I trust in the city if I need a safety net. And my aunt's wife, Tammy, reeling in her more pushy impulses sounds about right. The two of them always make me feel safe.

I told Marie-Claire I'm bi before having the words to tell my parents. I just needed to run it past another queer person to make it feel real. She's a huge reason I chose Boston for university. I need the freedom from expectations my aunts give me to explore again now; the chance to figure myself out without a lifetime of assumptions freezing me in place.

"Yeah." I can't figure out how to say all that to her yet, but she doesn't make me and more of the anxiety knotted in my chest loosens. Her ability to make space for me to share without pressuring me to fill it seems like a superpower right now. "Thanks,

Aunt Marie-Claire. I appreciate it. And the ride."

"No problem." She reaches over to ruffle my hair through the knit hat I hate to take off. "Anything for my favorite niece."

I squirm in my seat at the subtle sting of that title. I know I'm supposed to laugh and remind her I'm her only niece. But it cuts, chafing even more now that I'm so close to my fresh start. My chance to just be me.

"What's wrong, ma belle?" her genuine concern, even as she uses the familiar gendered endearment, cuts like a knife. I should just tell her. This shouldn't be so hard. I trust her. I do. There's just no way she could keep something that huge from my folks and I'm not ready for them to know.

"Nothing. Just nervous about the new school." I scrunch down low in my seat and pull my hood over my hat, hiding.

"You sure?" Marie-Claire glances over, eyes darting over me, then back to the road in one of her more parentally concerned expressions. I avert my face. The piercing denim gaze so like my own is too much scrutiny to bear. At least the neighborhood we're driving through is interesting.

"Yeah. It's nothing. Just tired from the flight." I continue staring out the window. She goes back to keeping her full attention on the traffic, letting the little lie pass.

It's not entirely a lie. I was up at the crack of dawn, triple checking that I had everything I needed. We had to get to the airport hours early, thanks to the international travel rules. But it wasn't a bad flight, and I had a quick nap on the plane. I'm excited for the new student orientation on campus and more than ready to focus on that instead of family drama.

Still, I am all but certain that if anyone in my family will understand this, it's my lesbian aunt. The words still get caught in my throat. Like they've been getting stuck for ages with all three of my older brothers, even though the second oldest, Darren, is queer too.

"Okay. But you know you can tell me anything, right?" Marie-Claire pats my knee as we stop at a red light.

I swallow hard, try to nerve myself up to say the words for the first time. *I'm not your niece because I'm not a girl.*

Nope. I can't do it. Those are words I can't take back and I'm not ready to upend everything. What if it's not real? Or if nephew doesn't fit the way I think it will? What if I'm wrong? I can't even figure out exactly what I'm trying to say. I'm not a girl? It's true, but if I say that, then everyone will assume I must be a boy. For a while, that felt close enough. Still off, but at least in the right vicinity.

Except then I grew up and now calling myself a woman makes my stomach churn, like the words are a massive lie I can't keep telling. And man feels like a funhouse mirror version of the truth, an exaggerated caricature. Hence Boston. I don't have the words to describe myself yet, but I'm hoping a bit of anonymity in a new setting will help me figure it out. I just can't explain something I don't fully understand myself yet.

"Yeah, I know." I force a tight smile.

"Alright." Aunt Marie-Claire pats my knee again. It feels like the light will never change and I'll be stuck in traffic enduring her too perceptive scrutiny for an eternity. I can tell she sees right through my lies, but for now she's willing to wait until I'm ready to talk rather than prying. She points out the window. "Oh, look, that's Frisky's. Did I ever tell you that's where I met your Aunt Tammy? We danced until they kicked us out and then got milkshakes at Randy's afterward. Just down the road here." She points out a diner that looks like something out of a fifties era movie. The wide windows look in on pink and blue neon lights, chrome accents, and a checkerboard tile floor.

I press my forehead against the car window, staring at the place as the light finally changes and traffic crawls past the bustling place. I imagine a future where I can fit in with the vibrant people drinking milkshakes and flirting with their dates out in the open. It looks so unabashedly queer and I want to be like that. Open and honest, and just me.

My aunt glances over at me, assessing. Before I can open my mouth to offer any kind of reply, she pulls down a laneway and into an open spot, parallel parking like it's nothing. She pats my knee. "Come on, I'll get you some pie to celebrate being new to the city."

"Um, okay?" I slouch in my seat, not ready to go in there with my curves and long hair on full display. Everything about me feels wrong today. With the stress of traveling, it's one of those bad days where the dysphoria makes me wish I could erase my entire corporeal form from anyone else's perception.

Failing that, I've got on so many layers I'm melting in the autumnal heat.

"Don't look so nervous. It's a queer friendly diner, not an inquisition." Aunt Marie-Claire winks at me. "It's close to campus, and it's not the worst place to make friends, since you're new to the area. Introducing you to Frisky's will have to wait until after your birthday. But it's a great place to meet girls. Or guys, since you aren't picky." She winks at me.

I wrinkle my freckled nose at the idea of going to a queer club with my aunts to hook up. They might be way cooler than my folks, but that's still a resounding no to trying to grind up on potential dates in front of them. "Yeah, uh, I might see if I can make some friends to go with."

Aunt Marie-Claire gives me a faux-stern look and a finger wag. "Only once you're old enough. It's only a few more months until you turn twenty-one. We don't want you getting into trouble and jeopardizing your visa."

"Yeah. I know." I force a smile, stomach roiling at the thought of messing this chance up before I even begin. It's jarring that the age is so different here. Back home I've been of legal drinking age for years, but I can wait to go out clubbing until I turn twenty-one next month.

Any thoughts of drinking fall by the wayside as I follow Aunt Marie-Claire into the diner. I tug the drawstring on my dysphoria hoodie tighter over my toque, wrapping the oversized garment around me like an invisibility shield.

The people inside make me ache with a longing to be open about myself. Guys with stylish clothes and hair, a server in an aqua pinup model dress that matches her manicure and her coif.

A rainbow flag decal in the window and pride stickers of every sort on various patrons' belongings. I see a laptop with no less than three different flag stickers plastered over the back.

My heart beats hard against my ribs with a longing I can't put into words to belong in a place like this. Not as the bi girl I've told people I am, but as myself on every level. A place that sees me and accepts me without making demands I can never meet.

I shove my hands deeper into my hoodie pocket and wish I had more layers on to hide my curves.

A group of raucous college kids is sitting in the corner booth as Aunt Marie-Claire leads me up to the counter to order a to-go pie. My eye catches on one of the student's pulling another down into her lap. The one being pulled down laughs, the sound ringing with effusive joy. Another of their friends is wearing a Northeastern hoodie. My new school. We could be classmates.

The alluring stranger's shaggy dark hair makes me think of a rockstar and they flash a gleaming grin as they struggle up off their friend's lap. They stand and I notice their shirt has a splashy genderqueer pride striped heart across the chest. Huge letters around the graphic spell out *ask me about my pronouns*; I want to ask them.

What would it be like to be that carefree and open? What does it feel like to be yourself?

"Come on, Celeste. I gotta go for real this time. Need to grab my books before all the good used copies are gone for psych 101 with McGregor." They turn to address their friends, still laughing. "He's the one who makes you buy the book he wrote for supplemental readings and there are never enough copies."So they are a student, and they're in the same psych class as me. Or at least we have the same professor. What are the odds of that? Getting to see them again might be worth the frustration of my CEGEP psych credit not transferring even after I appealed the decision. I'm openly staring and I should tear my gaze away before they notice me creeping. But I can't seem to actually do it until my aunt touches my elbow.

"Hey, which flavor is your favorite these days, kiddo?"

"Um, I guess they don't have tarte au sucre?"

"Nope, but pecan is similar."

"Ok, that, I guess? Thanks Auntie."

"Sure, anything for my favorite local nibling." She ruffles my hair through my hat and I freeze at the new favorite label. Does she suspect? Before I can spiral overthinking it, she continues talking. "Want a milkshake or anything else while we're here?"

"No, I'm good!" I say hastily.

My stomach is roiling from being here and everything I want to try but don't feel ready for. I just want to get settled into my dorm room. My cute new potential classmate is standing behind us at the register, waiting to pay. I might combust from the electric tingle of their eyes on my back. It takes all my self-control to resist the urge to turn and stare awkwardly some more.

My aunt pays for the pie and I carry it back out to the car. I catch one more glimpse of the cutie in the pronoun shirt as they flirt playfully with the server taking their money.

I can't get the image of the diner—or my adorable potential classmate—out of my head as Aunt Marie-Claire drives the rest of the way to campus. She finds parking and helps me get all my stuff unpacked in my cramped little dorm room.

My folks had to pay extra for a single in the new student dorms, but with the way my CEGEP credits transferred, I'm technically a transfer second-year student rather than a first-year. So that made it easier to get the coveted single.

The room itself is tiny, but my aunt took me shopping to make sure I have everything I need but couldn't fit on the plane, including snacks. So now I've got cool rainbow tie-dye sheets and a colorful rag rug to cover the threadbare brown carpeting. Colorful twinkle lights hang in front of the bare metal blinds covering the window.

The sturdy, yellowish fake oak twin bed only fits in one spot, along the wall opposite the door. I've got my alarm clock and various chargers lined up along the wide window ledge at the head of it that doubles as a nightstand. The matching narrow desk and chair wedged next to the dresser fit along the other wall.

I have barely enough room to open the tiny closet, but I just need it for my winter jacket. I didn't pack any of the dressier femme-coded clothes that lurk in the back of my closet at home and only see the light of day under duress. By the time Aunt Marie-Claire declares my room habitable, I have a cozy space that looks like a rainbow threw up in here.

It's perfect, and it's all mine. Which is good, because the idea of having to share with some random girl makes my toes curl with dread. No roommate means not having to pretend, even if I am too scared to introduce myself as anything other than the legal name printed on my brand new student ID.

My aunt walks toward my scheduled orientation activities with me, stopping at the turnoff that will take her to the parking lot where she left her car. She invites me over to her place to have dinner this weekend, then she gives me one more fierce hug.

"I'm proud of you, mon chou, have a great first semester," Marie-Claire says before she walks away. She tosses me the same endearment she uses with my brothers, as casual as anything. It's not that it's just for boys, it's just not specifically for girls the way *ma belle* is. She turns for one more parting word. "Oh, and don't forget to call about joining us for dinner soon. Tammy wants to see you, and I *can* resist prying." She winks at me.

I stare after her, flabbergasted that she might have guessed the things I don't have words for. My aunt leaves me speechless, standing on the sidewalk in front of the auditorium where I'm supposed to meet the other psych majors for our campus tour.

The stately architecture looming over me makes me feel small and homesick as she drives away. It's silly to feel so cut adrift at being on my own for real. This is what I wanted, yet I'm terrified at the reality of it now that it's far too late to back out. I'm still not ready to embrace being openly trans, but after that subtle nod from Aunt Marie-Claire, I have no remaining doubt my aunts will be in my corner when I am. That gives me the courage to turn and face the new school year with renewed confidence. I can do this.

I wanted to have the freedom and space to figure out who I am. That's why I came to Boston, to find a place where I can be myself. A place to belong. Now that I'm here, it's all so daunting to actually take that first step out of the closet. I take one shaky step toward the iconic building, and then another, until I'm swept up in a stream of other students, all following the same new student schedule.

It feels like I got too much freedom in my attempt to step out of my comfort zone. Now the closet that chafed so much back home seems safer amidst so many other changes. Thinking about introducing myself at all the orientation activities with the guy's name I picked ages ago feels like biting off way more than I can chew. I'm second-guessing everything already, and classes haven't even started.

When I get back to my loud and proud dorm room, I don't have the energy to brave the cafeteria. Instead, I curl up under my fuzzy blankets and have pie for dinner. Under the cozy covers, I scroll through my social media feeds, wishing I had the courage to just tell someone who I am. Just so I can hear my name from another person.

I was so sure that coming here would be my chance to make new friends without the constant disconnect between the person I am inside and who everyone else sees. As if there's an impenetrable invisible barrier locking away a huge part of myself from every interaction. But I just can't seem to find the words. At least the pie from Randy's is as delicious as my aunt promised.

Chapter Two

Jordie

"Oh, crap. Is it really almost one?" I scramble to shove my schedule and notebooks back into some semblance of order.

I have a class in half an hour. It's tempting to cut, but it's still the first day and I should probably at least grab the syllabus. I suppose. Ugh. Psych 101 is going to be full of clueless first years, second years with no idea what they want to do, and slacker seniors who put off a required gen ed. I'm *so* not looking forward to that. But my advisor says I need it to graduate, so here I am preparing for a lecture I don't want to bother with.

"Yep. Unless my phone is also wrong." Jacob holds his phone up in an obnoxious gesture; he's such a punk sometimes.

"I gotta cut out early." I shove back from my seat at the diner. Randy's is my group's favorite late night hangout, but it's also got killer food on days when we have enough time to wander away from campus between classes.

"Aw, you gotta run?" Celeste pouts at me, stirring her coffee. I'm not sure how she manages the dainty spoon with her long lacquered nails, but they don't seem to impede her at all. Pixel, her girlfriend, cocks her head at me.

"Jords is leaving? Boo! I was going to order dessert. Wouldn't you rather stay here and have pie with me than sit around in a boring class?" Pixel has the poutiest begging face I've ever seen and I'm not sure how Celeste ever says no to her.

"Don't make me say no to that sweet face, Pix," I tease. "I really don't need an excuse to skip the psych class that fulfills a general education requirement I've been putting off for years."

"You're being a bad influence already, pet?" Celeste arches a brow. Pixel squirms in her seat and tries, unsuccessfully, to look contrite.

"I'm not! I'm just saying, Jords can probably just do the readings and spare themself the need to languish with all the newbs."

"Yeah. It's going to be a shitshow of new students." I pout, this is what I get for putting off the required class until my last year.

"Score, you can totally scope out the fresh meat and snag any cute baby queers for us," Jacob teases.

"Dude, freshman are practically actual babies; no thank you. I do not need some teenager's drama." I gesture dramatically.

Jacob winks salaciously. "I mean, they can't cause much drama if you hit it and quit it." He lets the ridiculous fuckboy mask drop a fraction, though. "But it sounds gross when you put it like that. I just meant new faces on campus—of age, legal faces. There are only so many queer and curious guys to fuck on campus. Eventually, everyone either pairs off and you're scrolling past the same sets of abs on all the apps, you know?"

"Ugh, you're such a horndog. Why are we friends with you?" Celeste flaps her hand at him in a shooing gesture. "He's got a point though. You *could* make new friends, Jords. That's how I met Pix in our second year." Celeste smiles at her girlfriend.

"She's right, you never know, the love of your life could fall into your lap if you go to class." Pixel nods.

"Yeah, I guess." I grimace, slinging my bag over my shoulder and pulling out my wallet to settle my tab. "I'm not looking to be anyone's fairy queer-mother, thanks. Been there, done that, outgrown the t-shirt."

Jacob lets his obnoxiously flirty persona drop entirely for once in a rare moment of vulnerability and gives me a sympathetic smile. "They aren't all going to be Nell. You shouldn't let your ex screw with your head forever, Jords."

I don't point out that he's being a massive hypocrite. Out of all my friends, Jacob might be the one who understands the most about what it's like for love to turn into a betrayal. He just channels his hurt into a very active sex life and I... don't date newly out people.

Teach them about queer topics, sure. Hand out condoms and dental dams like they're candy, absolutely. One-off hookups, occasionally, if we're both feeling it. I'll hold hands for STI testing or coming out phone calls, sure. But I draw the line at dating them.

Nell was my high school girlfriend who dumped me at our

graduation party with a weird little speech thanking me for easing her into gay dating. It wasn't my first round of being an experiment, but it's still the one that hurts the most since we dated for over a year. I thought Nell was really into me.

After Nell, I spent the next couple of years throwing myself into flings. Most of them I knew were casual from the start. Along the way, I let myself get too close to a few newly out friends. It took getting my heart bruised one too many times by thinking something more could develop from all those intense emotions around coming out before I learned my lesson and swore off dating baby gays.

Pixel and Celeste give me sympathetic smiles. "Well, nothing says you have to make new friends, but you should get to class if you're going. Toss me a twenty and I'll cover your tab." Pixel holds out her hand to me.

I dig out the cash and hand it to her, then I head back to campus. Randy's is less than a fifteen-minute walk away from my on campus apartment at my usual pace. So I have plenty of time to stroll leisurely away from the commercial area and past rows of stately brownstones. I scroll on my phone as I cross campus.

I catch up on an email from my younger brother. Liam sent it on his school account during study hall, asking for help with an essay he needs to write for his English class. He sends me screen caps of the assignment and a draft of his outline to correct, so I save a copy and promise to look it over tonight.

My baby sister Kara texted me a food SOS during her lunch

hour to complain about Dad's weird experimental recipes replacing her usual dessert options in her lunch box. Technically, he's her dad and my step-dad, but that's a distinction without a difference. From the start of his relationship with my mom, he's always shown he considers Liam and I as much his kids as Kara.

Mom's the one I call when I need someone to talk sense into me. Dad is the one I call for parental advice when something breaks. It was his idea, which Mom quickly endorsed, to move us to Boston when I was having a hard time adjusting to being out as a genderqueer in our more rural hometown.

Now he's on a kick about creatively adapting old recipes to use more local produce. Kara begs me to smuggle her some donuts from the trendy little shop down the street from Randy's when I come over for family dinner this weekend. Holes has the best strawberry glazed confections, so it doesn't take much arm twisting before I agree to satisfy her sweet tooth if she can hold out until the weekend.

She peppers her messages with over dramatic GIFs to the effect that she is dying from dessert withdrawal and I'm literally saving her life. That, along with her barely decipherable tween slang, makes me shake my head at her and wonder when my twenties started making me feel so ancient.

I reach my lecture hall and send Kara a *got to go. Some of us pay attention in class* text punctuated with a winking kissy face emoji to rile her up about it not making sense. I don't question why she's messaging when she should be in class. The kid takes notes on her tablet to accommodate for her dyslexia, and she has it set up to relay texts from her phone. She's a bit too clever for her own good and always has been.

My psych 101 lecture is in one of the fancier buildings with larger lecture halls. For a class that so many students take to meet gen ed requirements, it's not the biggest I've taken, probably because there are so many sections offered each term. I walk down the sloping aisle lined with cushy seats, toward the front of the hall.

I settle into an aisle seat near the front. If I don't see all the baby-faces surrounding me, I can pretend they aren't there. Or that's what I tell myself. Students noisily trickle in around me, but the seat beside mine remains empty as knots of freshmen and sophomores fill the room.

The tone that marks the beginning of class sounds out in the hallway and the lecture hall is packed with eager first years. The professor has his nose buried in his notes, waiting out the wave of noise rather than competing for our attention. I can't fault that approach; why scream when he's the one we're all paying to be here to listen to?

This is why I hate giant intro classes. But I've been putting off this class even though I know I need it to graduate. I already have ideas for the handful of short papers I know we'll need to write. Worst-case scenario, if I struggle to make it through the lectures, I can borrow Celeste's old notes. She already offered.

At least the seat beside me remains empty. If I play my cards right, I can keep my interactions with my fellow students to a minimum. It's weird how much younger the first years seem these days. I might be becoming a bit of a curmudgeon.

The chatter gradually settles, and the professor sends his TA down the central aisle, handing out a stack of syllabi to each row of the lecture hall. They're still a little warm from the printer, the familiar scent of toner lingering on the fresh pages. I take my copy and pass the rest of the stack along. There's a slight whump of air as the door behind me flings open. I glance over my shoulder at the disheveled person standing in the doorway, a heavy stack of textbooks clasped to their chest, shoulders heaving with every ragged breath. Some impulse compels me to turn and get a better look at the panting first-year.

Jacob might've put thoughts in my head, but something in their panicked gaze won't let me turn away. Their eyes frantically scan the crowded hall for an open seat. I wave them toward the one next to me.

They slump down the aisle, gawky-looking and swimming in a Dysphoria HoodieTM that obscures their figure. A big floppy beanie covers their hair, pulled down until it almost obstructs their wary blue eyes. They remain hunched over their armload of books as they shuffle awkwardly past me to get to the empty seat on my left.

I don't know the kid, but they look like me six years ago. My folks moved us to Boston when I was the newly-out-as-trans kid for my junior year of high school. I needed the fresh start after my old school—staff and students alike—didn't handle my transition well. Ugh. My heart clenches with empathy for this stranger.

I'm going to say hi and make a friend. Jacob is going to crow to high heavens about me adopting a baby freshman. Regardless, I can't ignore the lost look in their eyes as they dart from my dyed jet black curls to my single hoop earring and down to the pronoun pin on my blue velvet blazer. The kid latches on like I'm an oasis in the desert.

This kid needs something they probably can't articulate to themself. I'm nothing if not a sucker for a baby queer making that first tentative step into self-discovery and seeking community. They lift a hand from their books to give me the tiniest hint of a wave as they reach the chair beside me. And then it's like everything happens in slow motion as the professor clears his throat and turns on the projector to get started.

The kid seems to run out of hands trying to do too much at once. Wave, set down their school bag, pull open the seat on the theater-style chair, and place their books next to mine all while simultaneously attempting to sit. I reach to steady their shoulder as they stagger.

Their stack of books topples to one side, and they stumble right into my lap. Their books clatter to the floor at our feet as I wrap my arms around them so we don't both go down with the books. It's reflexive and I can't help the zing of warmth I feel when they realize I won't let them fall and they relax into my hold.

Jacob is going to laugh himself silly if I tell him my new baby queer tripped and literally fell onto my dick. I mean. Not exactly, but I can feel myself reacting to having them squirming in my lap as they gather their things. It's not really the time for a boner, so I focus on the little details that make me feel more protective than turned on.

Their shampoo in my nostrils has the same citrusy tang of the one my teenage brother, Liam, uses. And they seem at pains to conceal the curves I have no business holding as I steady them so they don't fall off my lap. So, probably not she/her pronouns if that's what they are trying to hide, but there might be other reasons for clothing that obscures their form.

"Easy, I've got you." I steady them with a hand on their upper back as they lean down to retrieve their books from the ground.

"Sorry!" they murmur. "Shit, I'm so sorry." Their cheeks flame as they snag the book, press it to their chest, an added layer of shielding, and scrabble off of me. They had to have noticed my dick chubbing up at having them wriggling around on top of me. That doesn't seem to be what has them upset as they mutter something under their breath. "Esti de marde. Pourrais-je être plus maladroit?"

I don't recognize the words, but from the tone I'm guessing that's profanity. It takes a moment for me to parse that they're speaking French. They hurriedly slide from my lap and into the seat next to me, casting me a sidelong apologetic look.

"De rien," I mouth at them. Not sure whether it's the right response at all, but dredging up my best effort. I've only had two semesters of the language so far. I need to consider a tutor if I want to pass this semester, but I think that's the right response? Or maybe it's 'you're welcome'?

The kid snorts a laugh and shakes their head at me, whispering. "Sorry, English is fine."

I have to bite my lip to keep myself from reacting to their
adorable accent as they switch languages. "It's nothing. Don't
worry about it."

"Am I interrupting?" Our professor is glaring at the two of
us.

Screw that. It's not like everyone else was paying attention,
and it's not like my baby frosh *chose* to fall. I'm not questioning
how much they light up my protective streak before I even know
their name, let alone their pronouns. They hunch in on themself, tugging their beanie down to their eyebrows. As if they
want to melt into their chair and escape the coils of mortality
or at least no longer be subject to other people perceiving their
existence. My heart goes out to them.

"Sorry, Professor, won't happen again." I give a cheeky salute.

"See that it doesn't." The professor turns pointedly away
with a displeased grunt, ignoring us in favor of reading the
syllabus aloud.

The only thing making this class worthwhile today is the
adoringly thankful grin that seals just how much the baby queer
next to me seems to have imprinted on me already.. I realize
my new friend missed the stack of syllabi, so I nudge mine
in between us so they can follow along. I bite my lip to stop
myself from asking their name and disrupting the class again,
just tapping the page to draw their attention to it.

When they lean in closer, giving me another whiff of their

clean citrusy scent, I scrawl a note in the margins.

Hi, I'm Jordie (they/them). What's your name?

The kid's eyes dart from the note to the pronoun pin on my lapel, to the rainbow enamel 'they/them' ring on my middle finger, and then back to the page. They bring their pen to the paper and gnaw their lip like their name is a calculus equation that's worth half their grade. Yeah, definitely something going on there.

I slip a blank sheet of notebook paper over the syllabus; this is going to take more space than the margins allow. I write again.

Or just a name you want to try?

They hesitate, rocking in their seat and tapping their pencil nervously against the page. I bite my cheek to keep from smiling at their adorable fidgeting and prompt them again.

No pressure, babe, I can just call you Frenchie until you pick something you prefer. They stifle a laugh and dart those gorgeous blue mirth-filled eyes to my face. I wink at them.

This time, they bring their pencil to the page and write without an ounce of hesitation.

Ray.

Pleased to meet you, Ray. I bite my lip, considering whether to push my luck and nudge them even further out of their comfort zone. Fuck it. I don't want to misgender them, even in my thoughts.

Pronouns?

Ray stares wide-eyed between me, the note, and then my pronouns printed at the top of our exchange. They swallow hard and then they write.

He?

Damn, Ray is going to have all my protective instincts firing if I'm not careful. The question mark fits with the naked longing when he looks at how loudly I wear my pronouns for the world to see. I wonder if that's the first time he's told anyone? Part of me likes the idea of being his first. The more rational part realizes what a big thing that could be. He might need to have a safe place to work through all the big feels after this lecture.

I'm totally just being a good friend when I write my next overture.

Cool, grab a coffee with me after class?

Ray gnaws his poor lip again. I'm so tempted to reach over and thumb it away from his teeth. Or maybe replace his teeth with mine. But no. I'm not thinking about kissing a freshman who doesn't even know who he is. Ray is off limits. No matter how adorable he is. I wait, trying to play it cool and casual while he writes his answer.

Yeah. Okay.

Ray gives me a sidelong glance and a cute little smile before tucking his hands under his thighs to keep from fidgeting with his pencil.

It feels like an eternity passes as our curmudgeonly professor drones his way through the entire needlessly lengthy syllabus. But maybe that's partly because I spend the time transfixed by a beautiful boy who can't seem to hold still for two seconds.

First, his foot bounces, then his pencil taps, and then his

fingers drum. I just want to watch the smile on his soft lips get bigger every time he glances at the name written in the margins of my syllabus. The more I observe him, the more certain I am that I'm the first person he's trusted with this part of himself. The weight of that feels huge and solemn and wonderful.

It's a little like the way I felt when my folks first introduced me to my baby brother and told me that I was a big sibling now. Like gazing into guileless blue eyes and realizing that this new person trusts me implicitly to protect him and be an exemplary role model.

It's indescribably heady, but with Ray, I might need to rein in the part of me that's already confusing that instant emotional spark of connection for something it's not. I need to be focused on my studies and getting into law school, not falling for a first-year baby queer. Surely I've made that mistake enough by now to learn my lesson.

Chapter Three

Ray

I might be starstruck. That's not quite the right word for it; Jordie isn't a celebrity. They're the living embodiment of why I came to Boston. The way they wear their pronouns out in the open seems like a promise that someday I can too. It still doesn't seem real that the hottie from Randy's is actually in my class. I want to know myself the way Jordie seems to.

Until I sat next to them, I was more than half-convinced I'd made a terrible mistake by moving so far from home. The overwhelming barrage of information packed into each syllabus makes it feel like I'm way behind before I even start.

I messaged all three of my brothers during lunch, totally freaked out that there is no way I can get through this semester. Adam, Darren, and even Luke all reassured me that several months' worth of work sounds like a ton no matter how it's presented.

They all promised that if I stay on top of my studies, I'll be fine. I'm trying to trust that, but it would be easier if they weren't all so darn good at school; it's always been harder for me to get decent marks. Part of that is how hard it is to focus when there's an itch just under my skin at the incongruence between who I am and my appearance.

I spend the entire psych lecture trying not to let on just how exhilarating it is that Jordie gave me the space to define myself. Stay chill, even though I'm giddy that someone so effortlessly cool wants to talk to me. I'm an enormous ball of new crush feelings wrapped up in euphoria over finally sharing my name with someone. I can't tell if I want to kiss them or be them—probably both. That's nothing new to my bi heart.

I keep glancing over at Jordie, admiring their style and their hair and their smile. Today they're wearing a preppy polo, velvet blazer, and a khaki cargo skirt for class. And they wink at me when they catch me looking a little too long. I flush and try to focus on the professor, relaxing more than I have all day. For the first time, I let myself hope I made the right choice coming to Northeastern.

Class ends and I scramble to gather all my stuff, hoping the Jordie still wants that coffee together, but not daring to ask. They stand and squeeze past me to snag a spare syllabus from the stack at the end of the row of desks for me.

"Here, ready to go?" Jordie asks, smiling at me as I take the syllabus and shove it into my bag along with most of my books. I keep out my math textbook for later since it strains the zipper on my bag and I want something to occupy my hands.

"Oh, yeah. Coffee time!" I give them a tentative grin.

"Cool, come on, I have another lecture later, so we should

stay on campus. That work for you?"

"Yeah. Me too. I have a break and then math." I wrinkle my nose at the required math credits. Jordie gives me a sympathetic look.

"Let's get going then." They lead the way out of the building.

I am freaking out as I try to match my pace to Jordie's. They're so much cooler than I'll ever be. The memory of them deflecting our professor's attention away from my clumsy tumble would be enough to have me enamored, but there's so much more to it. The way they casually wrote their pronouns along with their name was... it was everything.

It gave me the courage to finally do what I fled my home and even my country to do. Claim a part of myself that I just couldn't be back home where I was the beloved daughter and sister. The only girl in a generation. Where I could only refute that label inside my head. Not a girl. I'm not.

All my siblings and cousins are guys, and my folks have never been shy about sharing how thrilled they were to have a daughter. So how could I tell them it was a false alarm, surprise, you actually got a fourth son, not the daughter you wanted so badly? Yeah. I can't imagine how that will go over.

They love me—that's never been in any doubt. I don't think they'll be upset that I'm trans so much as it will hurt them to realize how much pressure they put on me to be something I'm not. Maybe. I hope. Unless I'm misjudging things terribly.

I shove thoughts of coming out to my family to the back of my mind and focus on Jordie. They turn toward me, their gorgeous curls bouncing with every stride and entrancing me. I like them, but I don't want to make it obvious and spoil this first overture of friendship. There's no way this is a date. Someone so confident and gorgeous couldn't possibly see anything they want in me, right? Not when I can barely stand to be seen the way I currently look. I clutch my book against my chest like a shield.

"So, my favorite spot for desserts and a chat isn't actually on campus. Randy's Diner is the best. Have you been yet?" Jordie asks, drawing me out of second-guessing what we're doing here.

"Um, yeah, my aunt took me there for some pie as a 'welcome to the Boston queer scene' thing," I say. I bite my lip, debating whether to mention that I saw them there with their friends.

"Nice." They cock their head, giving me a quizzical look. They seem to think better about prying into the details. Like they know I'm not entirely out. "It's definitely a great safe space to be queer. We'll have to hang there sometime. But since we don't have time for a proper sit-down today, there's a chain place next to the campus bookstore that will do for a chat between classes." Jordie weaves through the throngs of students with a purpose in their stride that I envy.

I have to scurry to keep up as they dodge a group of jocks tossing a ball between themselves. My arms ache from carrying all my books with me all day. Apparently that was a mistake and I should start leaving them in my room unless I actually need one to study.

Who knew we're expected to do the daunting amount of

reading listed in each syllabus on our own time? A chapter or more every week from each of the brick-like books seems totally excessive, but I'll have to figure it out, I guess. I fall behind. Jordie glances back at me with a sheepish smile.

"Sorry, bet you're dying trying to jog after me in that hoodie, huh? It's hot today." Jordie slows their pace to match mine and keeps walking. "So, what's your coffee preference?"

"I like it hot and dark."

"Ah," Jordie pulls a yuck face. "So, not with enough sugar to give you cavities?"

"No thanks. Dental work is the worst."

Jordie nods. "Yeah, but totally worth it for sweet, sugary goodness. Does that mean you wouldn't want to split a slice of lemon loaf?"

"I like cookies and stuff; I just prefer my coffee unadulter-ated," I say, flushing at the mental image of Jordie feeding me a bite a cake. My lips parting for the elegant fingers that first spelled out the question that made it seem safe to tell someone the name that's gotten stuck behind my teeth every time I've opened my mouth to share it. No cake could be any sweeter than that moment.

I thought it would be easier here. In a new city, meeting new people. That I'd be able to just write it on the name badge they gave me at the orientation table that first day. Instead, it was like my fingers had a mind of their own, writing the name I came here to escape on autopilot.

One guy in my orientation group actually introduced himself as Squirrel, unapologetically announcing that if university wasn't the place to try something different, then when could he? I wish I had half his confidence.

I didn't even dare to ask about changing the name on my school email to a preferred name. Aunt Marie-Claire even suggested that they can use my nickname instead of my full legal name if I just asked since I've never gone by my full name. I just, couldn't do it.

No matter how many times I've hyped myself up to just do it, I still default back to the name on my student ID with everyone except Jordie. They make it seem less scary to try on the name that's remained locked up in my head, like a secret. Like the illicit thrill of sneaking around to try on hand-me-down dress clothes that I purloined from my brothers and hid in the back of my closet.

"That's fair. So, yes to sharing?" Jordie bumps shoulders with me and I don't know whether to lean into the friendly touch or if that would be weird. I'm still trying to wrap my head around Jordie wanting to spend time with me. "My treat," they wheedle when I don't answer right away.

I'm so flustered that I just nod, clutching my books more tightly to the floppy chest I wish I could will out of existence.

"Cool." Jordie grins at me. "So, is this your first year?"

"Um, sort of?" I grimace, because that's proven to be a weird-ly difficult to answer question even though practically everyone on campus asks it. "I'm technically a transfer student, but our system back home is a little different?"

"Oh? Where is home? France?"

"Montreal. So, after high school, we have CEGEP before university. I did three years of a dual focus pre-university CEGEP program and applied here, so I'm technically a second-year transfer student?"

"But you already did three years?"

"Yeah, but only some credits transferred and the first year is equivalent to grade 12?"

"Huh. Here I was thinking everyone went to college right out of high school. Cool. So, is that a Canadian thing?"

"No, just Quebec. It's sort of based on the French school system."

"Ah. Gotcha. So you really are fluent then?"

"Bilingual, yeah."

"I don't suppose you'd be willing to help me study for my French class then? Last year's oral exams kicked my ass and I need one more semester to graduate."

"Oh, yeah. I can help you practice your French. Je serais heureux d'aider un séduisant comme toi."

Jordie gives me a blank look and I flush. Right. So maybe they need more help than I'm prepared for. Or they aren't into flirting with me? Either way, French tutoring would be a small price to pay to stay in their orbit.

"I'm not entirely sure what you said, but if you need to gender me, I prefer la féminin en français." They wink at me. Ah, well at least they seem to have recognized the gender of my clumsy come on, calling them a hottie.

"Le féminin, noted." I correct the wrong gendered article automatically, then swallow hard as their words sink in and I take in the femme cut of their clothing. They look good, but I probably shouldn't eye fuck my first university friend in front of a café. I swallow hard and tear my eyes back to their face.

Jordie smiles at me. "Here we are."

They sweep open the door to the coffeeshop, stride up to the counter and order for us both, tapping their card to pay before I can protest. Not like my plain filter coffee is going to break the bank or anything, but still. There's something utterly enchanting about their confidence.

The barista plates the lemon cake and pours my coffee into a ceramic mug, which Jordie hands to me with a big smile.

"Thank you." I can't tear my gaze away from theirs as our fingers brush on the warm mug. I have to hide my face in that first heavenly sip of the dark roast.

"So, Ray. What are you studying?" Jordie asks as we loiter near the counter, waiting for their caramel macchiato.

The sounds of the coffee shop are soothingly familiar. This is just like going for drinks after class with my friends back home. The hiss of a steam wand and whirr of a blender accentuate normal small talk. But it feels different here, with Jordie saying the name I could never quite bring myself to tell even the baristas who took my order back home. Maybe I could have worked up to it here, where I don't recognize any of the faces on either side of the counter?

"Oh, um, I'm a psych major. I want to do art and play therapy for kids, but it's going to take a lot of school before I can get there. My faculty advisor said I need to take the 101 class over since it's 'foundational' to my further studies here?" I pull a face.

I already took a similar class back home, so it seems silly to pay to repeat it, but I also really want to make it easier for kids like me to find their voices. Considering I'm still struggling with that at twenty. At least my dual CEGEP program paid off with enough of my art credits transferring to meet the requirements of a fine arts minor.

Jordie laughs. "So you're not loving psych 101 either then?"

"Nope. It's so many people and just skimming the syllabus makes it seems like a rehash of the class I took last year. But that was one of the credits that didn't transfer properly, so here we are."

"Indeed. I guess it worked out." Jordie nudges my shoulder playfully.

"Did it?" I arch a brow at them as the barista calls their name.

"Yeah, I got to meet you." They wink at me, then claim their drink with a flirty smile for the barista while I stare at them in a sort of amazed thrall. I can't dispute that I'm glad our paths crossed, even if my stumble into their lap might just be the single most mortifying moment of my life.

They don't seem to hold my clumsiness against me. I'm under no illusions that they missed feeling what's under my oversized hoodie anymore than I missed the erection prodding my ass by the time I righted myself. Just physical stimulation having natural consequences, nothing more, but yeah, I'd love a chance to sit on their lap in a more planned and consensual context.

I shake that thought right back out of my head. I'm getting ahead of myself. Jordie is the first friend I'm starting to make here, so my libido can chill out.

"Want to grab a table?" Jordie tips their head toward a free seat in the corner. I nod and follow them across the room.

"What about you? What's your major?" I ask as we sit.

"History with a poli-sci minor. I'm applying to law school." Jordie flashes me a wolfish grin, then sips their drink.

"So you like to argue?" I tease.

Jordie laughs. "Not really. Or at least, that's not why."

I snort and arch my brow at them. "Uh huh, not at all, huh?"

Jordie rolls their eyes at me. "Okay, so maybe I enjoy it a smidge. But I just figure it's not always easy being queer, let alone trans. Someone has to get involved in fighting for our community, so that might as well be me."

Our community. The words make me splutter and choke on my coffee. Except they felt my curves, and I told them my name. I want so desperately to be a part of that community that they just oh so casually folded me into. Can it really be that simple to find my place? My heart is pounding and my lungs burn as I cough up a spray of coffee. Jordie watches me with a wary concern in their eyes. Their curls bounce as they lean over me to pat my back.

"Sorry, not making any assumptions. I'm queer as fuck, but it's cool if you aren't." Jordie turns the patting into gentle circles once I stop gagging on my coffee. Their touch is platonic and supportive and it makes it seem like I'm not so alone in a brand new city. It's a lifeline that makes telling them everything easier. The heat of their hand sends the words fizzing out before I can contain them or second guess the instant sense of closeness they engender in me.

"I am," I rush to say. "I've been openly bi for years. But there's something else too." I barely breathe the last few words, but it's like I shed a thousand pounds of pressure for having said them. "Can I tell you something I've never told anyone else?"

"Sure." Jordie bumps their knee into mine.

"I think I'm trans." I try the words and they ring hollow. Not quite right.

I clench my fists around my mug and shake my head. I *thought* I was trans five years ago. Back in high school, when I realized I was the only one of my friends who had a passionate and abiding hatred for our school uniform skirts that went beyond physical comfort. The required skirts felt like a shining beacon of wrongness, calling attention to parts of me I didn't want the world to see as me.

After years of grappling with those thoughts, it's not a tentative thought anymore. I *know* I'm trans. It's everything else I don't know how to handle. Admitting it is going to entail so many changes; I'm not sure if I'm strong enough to smile in the face of strangers whispering to each other about whether I'm a he or a she or an it. Jordie acts so poised, but I heard the students behind us gossiping about them and pointing. I noticed the empty seats around them.

"No, that's not quite right. I *am* trans. I'm a guy, I mean," I clarify.

Jordie doesn't stop rubbing my back. "That's great, Ray. I'm glad you told me."

"Yeah?" The relief is like a cool breeze on my face in the late summer heat. Bright and energizing and right. I can't hold back my smile as I search their face for their genuine reaction. Jordie stops rubbing soothing circles and I miss the touch until they squeeze my shoulder and lean in conspiratorially close.

"Yeah." Jordie smiles at me. "Feels good to get it out there for the first time, huh?"

"Yeah." I force a tremulous smile. It is good to say the words. But I also have a sick pit of dread in my stomach at making the words real. I know from experience that this is the first of many times I'll have to tell someone. Not everyone is going to smile at me the way Jordie is, like they're proud of me for finding the right words.

"So, can I ask what's kept you from saying it before?" they ask.

I grimace and fiddle with my mug.

"No pressure." Jordie holds up their hands in a warding gesture. "I get that it's scary. A bunch of my friends didn't come out until university either. Not every family understands, that's why we—my friends, I mean—sort of made our own."

"Does your family understand?" Anxiety clenches like a fist around my heart as I bring my coffee to my lips, only to think better of that next sip and set it back down untasted. I don't want to consider someone as bright and friendly as Jordie getting rejected by the people who they love. My stomach feels sour just considering it.

"Oh, yeah." Jordie waves away my worry with a dismissive flick of their wrist. I miss their touch again as they sit back in their seat and create space between us to take a sip of their sweet coffee. "My mom and step-dad are great. They helped me do the whole social transition thing over the summer after I told them, and when my old classmates were assholes about it, Dad took a job here. He's an adjunct math professor at Northeastern, which works because him working for the school means I get cheaper tuition. That's my step-dad, not my bio dad. Sperm donor isn't in the picture. He left when my little brother got diagnosed."

"Diagnosed?"

"Yeah. Liam is autistic." Jordie watches me warily. When I don't react poorly they open up more, their love for their sibling clear in the smile on their face as they talk about Liam. "He's the best. Kid loves plants and poetry, and he's on track to graduate early. He says he wants to study botany. And we have a younger sister. Technically, Kara's our half-sister, but that's just genetics. Do you have any siblings?"

"Yep. Three older brothers Adam, Darren, and Luke." I sigh and pick at my cuticles to avoid seeing how Jordie reacts to me talking about the expectations that have been crushing me for years. The pressure to conform that drove me away from my home and family. "I'm the baby girl my folks were desperate for. So, that's kind of why I didn't tell them."

Jordie sips their drink and gives me a measured nod. "Makes sense. But you can't live to make other people happy, dude." Jordie reaches to cup my hand on the table and their warmth is intoxicating. I want to sear the memory of their hand on mine into my skin. They called me dude. The word sparks joy through me. "Is that the only reason I'm the first one you're telling?"

"No. I just—" I shrug, at a loss for words to describe everything roiling around inside of me. "I thought if I tried hard enough, I could mold myself into what everyone wants for me. For years, I got so caught up in following all these arbitrary rules of how to be a girl that now I'm not sure where to begin trying to be myself. And what if I go to all the trouble of disappointing people and telling them who I am only to discover it was all in my head? Or what if I really am a guy and I can't ever pass as one? I don't want to be a frea—" I stop myself and flush. That word has nothing to do with Jordie and I wish I could sink through the floor at even opening my mouth to say it to them. "Sorry. That isn't what I think. I'm just scared."

"Of people thinking you're a freak like me?" They quirk a knowing brow at me. Their ever present smile turns sad as they sip their sugary drink and lean back in their chair. I recognize they're creating a physical distance to echo the emotional chasm I just opened up between us with all the casual hate I know I've internalized. The word weapons I've barricaded myself behind so I could convince myself it was safer to pretend. It's not though, and I abhor the impact of those words spoken out loud.

"No!" That is *NOT* what I meant at all.

Jordie isn't a freak; they're beautiful and vibrant and everything I wish I had the courage to be. Bold and brash without being in your face about it. They take up space without apologizing for it. I wish I could be like that. But I can only stare at them. Because part of me knows that's what the world sees when they look at us, freaks. Jordie gives me hope that it can be okay to embrace what makes us who we are, but I need more time to get there. I just hope I can salvage this conversation and make them feel as safe around me as I do with them. Show them I don't see them that way.

"No?" Jordie arches a brow at me, their entire open, friendly demeanor sharpening and closing down more. I recognize the way they're preparing to protect themself from me and I can't blame them. I need to fix this if I want to see them again outside of class.

"No, I don't think you're a freak. I get that it's not quite the same, but my aunt Tammy is super butch and unapologetic about not conforming to gender norms. She's one of the coolest people I've ever met. I only meant that about myself. I don't know, just the whole closet thing messes with my head. Sometimes I think I'm going to burst from keeping it all inside. Other times, I read too many online comments about trans people, and some of the hate worms its way into my brain. Partly because if I didn't have something shameful to hide, then I'd be open about it, right?"

"Wrong." Jordie runs a hand through their unruly curls and huffs out a breath. They relax again, posture opening back up toward me. "It's okay to take as long as you need to share who you are. I wear it like a badge of honor now, but I didn't always. I get that it can be scary. Being visibly queer is always scary. The first time I held a boy's hand on a date—back when I presented more masc—we were both shaking and sweaty and just plain scared. But it felt good too."

"Did anything happen?" My nerves claw at me.

Because yeah, I was nervous the first time I went on a date with a boy too. And even more nervous the first time I kissed a girl under the bleachers at my high school. That's nothing compared to the worry my middle brother faced when he held a boy's hand in the wrong parts of town. I remember the first time he came home from a date rattled by hecklers who followed them to the metro.

It's not that I'm new to being different. It's just, everything about my early dating life felt so topsy-turvy because when I was holding a boy's hand, it felt more taboo than kissing a girl. Taboo and confusing because I was the only one who realized it wasn't the same as my oldest brother kissing his girlfriends. Like I was the only one who could see that we weren't the cute straight couple everyone assumed we were. That my girlfriend wasn't what made me queer. Queerness is a fundamental part of me that is always there, no matter who I date. That it would still be that way even if I was the girl they all thought I was.

"Sure." Jordie smiles fondly at the memory and my nerves

ease. "He kissed my cheek, and we ended up making out on my front porch until my little sister interrupted to ask if I was going to turn into a frog." Jordie laughs. "Talk about awkward first dates."

"Ah, does that mean she thinks you're a prince?"

"Sure," Jordie snorts. "We can interpret it that way. But, what I'm saying is, it's okay to be nervous. And take baby steps out of the closet. You hear about coming out like it's this onetime scary event, but it's not. It's every day, all the time, every new person you meet, and it's okay for that to be scary and overwhelming and to not be ready for it. If you need a friend who's been there, I can listen."

"I just..." I blow out a long breath. "How do I even start to be me?"

Jordie smirks and reaches over to give me a noogie through my toque, total big sibling vibes. I scowl at how much they remind me of my older brothers at that moment. Makes sense, given that they are a big sibling. Maybe that's part of the magnetic draw I feel toward them. There's something achingly familiar about the way they've taken me under their wing.

"Well, if you want to see how it feels to present more masculine, you'd be shocked what a difference a haircut and the right wardrobe can make." They wink at me. "I can come shopping with you when you're ready. And if you aren't ever ready, we can just hang out and study. You can be my secret Ray of sunshine for as long as you need before you're ready to share your light with the world. Sound good?"

"Yeah. That sounds... perfect." Shockingly amazing, if either of us is a ray of sunshine, it's definitely them. Jordie's light makes me warm right to my toes and I want to bask in it for as long as they'll allow. "So, study buddies?" I thrust out a hand, wanting to touch them as much as sealing the deal.

"Study buddies." Jordie takes my hand and we shake on it.

Chapter Four

Jordie

A month into the semester, and I'm pretty sure I'm Ray's best friend on campus. Which is fine; I enjoy spending time with him and he's as devoted to his studies as I am. His presence makes it easier to focus on my studies despite the severe senioritis rampant in my friend group this fall. Most of us are set to graduate in the spring. Even if I wasn't concerned with being a role model for my little siblings, I can't afford to let my grades slip with law school admissions riding in the balance. Ray encouraging me to stay focused on the prize is a good thing.

Ray and I both have a gap in our schedules after psych 101. It seems natural for us to study together twice a week during that interlude while most of my buddies have labs and classes of their own. Ray is struggling a bit with adjusting to university even though he says the format of his CEGEP classes was similar. He says it's just different for all his classes to be in English. He's used to most of them being in French and the larger lecture halls are another big adjustment.

On the bright side, I'm feeling much more confident in my

abilities since I've been practicing my French with someone fluent who can correct my fumbling mistakes.

"Qu'est que c'est?" Ray asks as he joins me at our usual table in the student center where we've been meeting. He's pointing at the little take out box I got at Randy's with the gang earlier. I still need to introduce the boy to the wonder that is Randy's. We just haven't really expanded our hangouts beyond an hour of studying between classes, so it hasn't fit with our time constraints.

I should change that up soon. Ray is fun to spend time with and I think my friends would like him. Celeste and Pixel have already started teasing me over how often I bring him up. Jacob has mentioned a few times, with his campiest faux-flirtatious posturing, that I should make a move or bring Ray around so that he can. It's a joke, and knowing Jacob, he's been teasing me about Ray to goad me into acting on what he sees as a crush; helping in his own uniquely Jacob way. It still revs up all my protective instincts toward Ray—yeah, that's it—I'm feeling protective of Ray's heart, not at all interested in wooing him.

"Huh? Oh! C'est un beignet. Um, voulez-vous try one?" I open the box and show him the two bacon maple donuts. They're dripping with glaze. Jacob couldn't help joking about frosting their delicious holes that had most of our table laughing and rolling our eyes at him. He's a bratty pain in the ass, but he's ours. And I thought Ray might like a treat while we study, so I grabbed a few extras to go.

"Nous sommes amis, non? Tu peux me tutoyer." Ray laughs

and switches to English for me. "What flavor is that? Do I smell bacon?"

"Yeah, Kit, one of the chefs at Randy's, is famous for their interesting desserts. They do an apple cider one that's to die for too, but bacon maple is my favorite. Want one?" I wave the box toward him enticingly.

"You and your sweet tooth." Ray smiles even as he shakes his head at me.

"I can't help being a very sweet person. If you like more regular flavors, there's a donut shop near Randy's that has them all the time—Holes. Kara, my little sister love their strawberry glazed, but Kit's are beter. Go on, try it." I nudge the box closer, eager for his reaction.

Ray hesitates a moment longer before plucking up the treat. So far he's liked most of the treats I've brought to share with him. Much as he claims not to share my love of sweets, I enjoy watching his face in the unguarded moments where he lets himself indulge.

Ray takes a small bite and his lashes flutter as his eyes roll back and he moans, the sound going right to my dick. I lick my lips, trying not to think of other ways I could make my new friend moan or wonder what he'd sound like moaning my name. Nope. Not going there.

Ray is fresh out of, well, not high school, but new to the country and university. He isn't even out about who he is. I think I'm still the only person he's told his name for all the fucks' sakes. It would be taking advantage to do more than appreciate the view. No matter how many times Jacob has teased me about 'tapping that fresh meat who I've been spending all my free time with.' He thinks calling freshman that is a funny pun, no matter how many groans it gets him.

"Oh, that's magnificent," Ray mumbles, going in for another bite of the donut.

"Right? Kit's my favorite chef at Randy's for the desserts. But everything is delicious there, really. Even Neve's weird fad diet foods usually taste good. Even if she put crickets in her energy bites last week." I make a face and Ray laughs at me.

"They're supposed to taste nutty. Did you try one?"

"No. Ew, David. Why would I try cricket protein bars when there was also peanut butter pie on the menu? And nuts are full of protein, so same thing, really." I wink at him, figuring he'll get the Schitt's Creek reference since it's a Canadian show.

Ray laughs at that, his eyes flicking over me with a marked interest. "Well, I do like putting nuts in my mouth."

His brash joke startles me into laughter, probably more than the quip deserves. He's just so sweet most of the time I forget that he's not at all tentative about being openly bi. It's just his gender that he's still exploring. Regardless, he's going to fit right in with my friends.

"Sorry, too much?" Ray asks, ducking his head, shoulders hunched like he did something wrong. I wipe amused tears from the corners of my eyes. I cover his free hand with mine and squeeze.

"No, you are just the right amount. So. I was thinking you

should come out for drinks at Frisky's with me. To meet my other friends. Or maybe we could go to a club? Some of my buddies have a drag show coming up, so that could be a good way to keep introductions low-key and split the focus away from you."

"Really?"

"Sure. We can ease you into meeting more queer friends."

"Oh." He picks at his donut, not quite looking at me. "I just…" He sighs loudly. "I don't know how to do any of this. It's like I want to make friends, but it feels so weird to introduce myself as a boy when I don't look like one. What if I never look like one? But I also feel weird about making more friends as someone I'm not."

"Hey, look at me?" I fold my hands over the notes I was getting out and lean in until he meets my gaze.

"Yeah?" Ray swallows hard. There's so much in his eyes, worry and fear warring with fragile hope, like he wants me to make his worst fears go away.

It's a heavy thing to have that much trust from someone I've only known for a few weeks. He reminds me so much of myself going to my mom scared of what it would mean to come out at school, and even more scared of what it would mean not to.

The right words aren't going to appear in my head. There might not even be any perfect words to make this easy.

I gesture toward my face. The sharp angles and blunt features feel too masculine on my most femme days and aren't ever going away short of surgery. The planes of a chest that tempts me daily to soften by going on hormones. On my most femme days, not even my favorite falsies stuffed into my cutest bras fully erase the dysphoria of my body not matching up with my self-image. I'm happy with my presentation ninety percent of the time, but I remember what it was like to worry that I'd never see my true self in the mirror.

It's still rare for strangers to get my pronouns right, but my baseline appearance is androgynous enough to keep strangers guessing. I get a decent mix of miss and sir when I put in the effort with heavy makeup and clothing and working on my voice training. That vaguely confused 'I'm not sure' look in strangers' eyes that sometimes burns with a sense of alienation and sometimes feels just right, a validation of who I am.

"Passing isn't the only thing that matters. It's okay if you take baby steps into transitioning. It's okay if you never look like society says a boy should. You know why?"

"Um, no?" Ray's shoulders hunch up around his ears, so I try not to take his ignorance personally and soften my tone.

"Because if that's who you are in your heart, then however you look on the outside, you're a boy. And if the people in your life don't accept that, then you aren't wrong; you're just around the wrong people."

Ray scrunches up his face. "I guess, but I just... don't want them to see a girl pretending."

I suppress the urge to roll my eyes and remind myself that he's just scared. My friends will be cool with him regardless, or they wouldn't be my friends. Even Jacob is a decent guy under the horndog facade. I get where Ray is coming from. That only makes me more determined to show him it's possible to keep on living his life while he figures out the nuances of living as the real him. No need to let dysphoria keep him socially isolated. And maybe if he feels more comfortable with his presentation, he'll feel more comfortable meeting the gang.

"Okay, well, I can't wave my magic wand and transform you," I say, giving him an appraising once-over. His look screams dysphoria just as loudly now as it did the day we met. "But what did I tell you?"

"The right clothes and a haircut make a massive difference?"

"That's right. And even hidden under that beanie, you're a total cutie. My friends will eat you right up." I pack up my notes and books. "You have math in an hour?"

Ray flushes at the flirty compliment. The adorable boy is so damn bashful, and it's too easy to fluster him. He's closer to my age than my little siblings, but it's so obvious that he's used to being the baby of the group. Like he just naturally looks up to me and I want to live up to the trust shining in his eyes. He's so damn sweet and earnest and I'd enjoy listening to him reciting a nutrition label in that accent of his. I have no business crushing on him when I'm off to law school in less than a year and he'll still be here. But the boy is a sweetheart and I want to help him. As a friend.

"Yeah?" Ray shifts nervously in the molded plastic seat.

"Can you skip?" I'm already shoving things back into my bag though, because I've already got our itinerary for the rest of the afternoon planned in my head. Hair first, then clothes, adult toy shop for a packer last, if he's up for it.

"Um, I guess? It's been all recap so far and I sit next to a girl from my orientation group, so I could probably get her notes later."

"Good. Finish that." I gesture to his last few bites of donut as I stand and pull mine from the box to eat on the way to my apartment.

Ray obediently gobbles the rest of his snack, licking the sticky glaze from his fingers. I sling my bag onto my back, trying to ignore the suggestive sight and the effect it has on me. Much as I like Ray, I don't want to make any exceptions to my rules about dating baby queers. Taking him under my wing is one thing. Thinking of licking him clean after glazing him in any entirely different sticky substance breaks all the rules Nell taught me the hard way.

No more horny thoughts. We are going shopping. As friends. Or queer mentor to mentee. It will be a pain to shop with our school stuff, so we should drop the bags off at my place on the way. "Ready?"

"Ready for what?" Ray scrambles to pick up his books from the table. He scurries after me when I gesture for him to follow me out of the bustling student center where we usually study.

"Like I said, you need a confidence boost. We're going shopping." I gesture expansively toward the city as we step onto the sidewalk.

Ray gives me a skeptical look, so I break through his indecision about following me off campus with a butchering of his language that I know he won't let pass. "Vasectomy!" I point toward my apartment.

"I hope you meant vas-y, because I think I lack a few requisite parts for that other thing," Ray corrects, scurrying after me. "And since we're both going, it would be allons-y anyway."

He's an adorable nerd and I'm going to help him see just how cute he can be. I pull out my phone to ask my buddies' group chat where I can get a binder for him without special ordering or breaking the bank. I've got the hair and clothing covered.

Eddie, who does my hair, is a gem and I feel more comfortable with him in a barbershop than anyone at any of the salons I've tried. I trust him to make Ray comfortable so he can focus on getting a style he doesn't compulsively hide under a hat. I'm excited to see him happy and confident.

Today is all about putting a smile on Ray's face and keeping it there. More importantly, it's about giving him the confidence to put himself out there, even if it means I don't get to hoard his sunshine smiles all to myself anymore.

Chapter Five

Ray

From the library, Jordie takes me back to their place, but we don't even really go past the entryway. They take my bag and shove it onto a hook next to theirs, right by the door. I try not to be too disappointed about not getting an invitation to come inside. Jordie talks about all the stores they want to take me to see. They scroll through different hairstyles they think would suit me as we walk from their apartment on campus to their barber—Eddie. Apparently, this Eddie is worth going to a masc space for because he knows how to work with Jordie's curls.

There's an unobtrusive pride flag decal in the front window, confirming Jordie's assurances that the place is queer friendly. The sign by the door says walk-ins are welcome, but it's intimidating to walk into a space that's so blatantly meant for men. There are two older guys sitting in chairs getting their hair buzzed and another big guy at the counter with a shiny bald pate and freshly trimmed beard paying.

I want to ask Jordie if we can even be here. But they don't

seem at all uncomfortable in this space. And when the guy paying leaves, I get a glimpse of the willowy barber ringing him up and relax the tiniest bit at his rainbow enamel hoop earring. If Jordie is comfortable here, even with their clearly femme-leaning presentation, then maybe I can be too. Even if I don't look the part yet.

"Eddie, this is my friend Ray. He needs a new look, right, Ray?" Jordie grabs me by the shoulders, like they're presenting me to Eddie for inspection.

"Um, yeah." I nod woodenly.

"Sure, I can squeeze in a cut. Can we see what we're working with?" Eddie mimes taking off my toque. I reach for it, tempted to pull it further down over my long golden locks. Hide the beautiful braid my parents love so much. Can I really just cut it off?

"Or you can tell me what you're thinking?" Eddie suggests when I stand there, frozen with indecision.

"Um—" My mouth is too dry and I can only shake my head to clear my mind.

"Blink twice if they dragged you here against your will," Eddie only sounds half-joking, but his quip startles a chuckle out of me.

"Ray? You okay?" Jordie squeezes my shoulders, grounding me. I want to be brave for them. Weird thought, but I do. "You don't have to do anything you aren't ready for. I just thought—"

"No, I'm here because I want to chop it all off," I say, snatching the hat from my head and crumpling the soft, colorful wool between my fists.

It's a daunting request. I have no idea what I'll look like without my hair. I haven't had short hair since I was a toddler playing with scissors. Dad says when he caught me trying to tape some of my hair back in place that I told him I wanted to look like my brothers.

The preschool pictures of the pixie cut my mom's hairdresser salvaged from the mess are some of my favorite kid pictures of myself. I look like a boy in those photos. Albeit one with a penchant for sparkly barrettes and swishy skirts. It's the most me I've ever seen myself.

Whenever we pull out the old photo albums, Mom laments having to correct strangers who assumed I was a boy for the next year while my hair grew back out. For the longest time, I didn't have words for the weird mix of pride and sorrow that story always fills me with. Now I do.

I bet Jordie would have had the guts to tell their parents that those strangers were actually right. I don't have their courage. But they give me the confidence to nod when Eddie takes in the braid that falls halfway down my back when I remove my hat. He gives me a kind but skeptical look. "Are you sure? That's going to take some time to grow back out if you change your mind."

"Yeah. I want it short." Like a guy. Like him and the other men who look like they belong here.

"Alright, take a seat and we can figure out how short we're going." Eddie gestures toward an empty seat in front of his workstation.

Jordie gives me a big, reassuring smile. I sort of wish I could ask them to hold my hand, but I draw strength from just having them there to support me. Whatever I look like after this, Jordie will still be my friend. They'll still see me past all the parts that don't feel like me.

Eddie sweeps a cape over me. I have to sit on my hands to keep from fidgeting and picking at the loosely draped cloth as he goes over the various options. I'm not sure how to describe the type of cut I have in mind. Jordie helps me figure it out, scrolling through images on their phone until I see one that reminds me of my oldest brother. Shorter on the back and sides, with a little length on top. It jumps out at me, a euphoric wash of longing. I can picture myself as a guy with my hair styled like the model in the image.

"This one, please?"

"Sure." Eddie nods. "We can go with a tapered look and leave a few inches on top to start and if you want it a little shorter, we'll adjust from there. And now I'm going to turn you around and suggest that you don't look until it's done if you want to get the full effect of the transformation. Are you certain you're ready?" Eddie asks, glancing between me and Jordie.

Jordie tugs playfully on my braid. "I didn't realize how much hair you were hiding under that hat, sunshine. You sure about this?"

"Yeah." I nod, my resolve firmer now that I'm so close to the point of no return.

I might look like a butch girl with short hair, but at least that's a step closer to who I am inside. It fits better than the long hair that makes me want to crawl out of my skin every time someone tells me how pretty it is. It's too tied up with being the daughter and sister my family expects me to be to feel anything but too femme for me.

"Right, did you want to donate all this length that we're taking off?" Eddie offers.

I only have to consider for a moment before I nod. "Yes, please. If that's a thing I can do."

"It sure is. Hold tight." Eddie reaches for a hair tie.

The idea of my unwanted hair helping someone else eases some of the anxiety roiling in my gut. If I somehow hate the results, I can take solace in all that long hair not going to waste. It might help someone who wants to feel like a pretty girl; that's totally worth embracing the giddy nerves sparking through me as if I swallowed a live wire over taking this plunge. And it gives me an out for explaining why when my folks see what I'm about to do. Win-win.

Eddie threads my braid through the tie and snugs it close to my scalp. He checks one more time. "I'm going to cut right above the tie. Is here alright?"

"Yeah, that would be perfect. Thank you." I force a nervous smile.

"Of course. Ready?" Eddie asks as he reaches for his scissors.

"Yeah." I nod again, and saying it makes me even more sure that this is exactly what I want. Jordie hovers nearby, distracting me with gossip about their friends when Eddie holds his scissors against my braid. I feel a pang of razor-sharp terror that I might regret this the moment he makes that first irrevocable cut.

Eddie meets my gaze in the mirror. "Last chance to back out?"

"Do it." I say, grasping my courage in both hands as I meet Jordie's encouraging gaze in the mirror.

The snick of the blades seems loud as he shears off most of my hair in one fell swoop. Eddie coils up the severed braid and stuffs it into a Ziploc bag from his workstation.

I was worried the sight of all that hair would fill me with regret, but when Eddie hands the baggie to Jordie, all I feel is buoyant relief. As if I can shed all the expectations that gorgeous long hair embodies just as easily as a single cut. Each snip of the shears as Eddie tidies the ends of my hair and reverberates through to the core of me. I'm allowed to do this. Allowed to make my own choices, even if they're wrong, and I change my mind.

Jordie is watching me with concern as my eyes well with happy tears. They squeeze my shoulder through the cape thing Eddie draped over me when he turns to exchange the scissors for his clippers.

"You okay?" Jordie asks.

"Yeah. I can really do this." The awed realization in those words is embarrassing in its naked longing.

Jordie's concern melts into another of their encouraging smiles. "You really can."

"We good to keep going?" Eddie checks in with me as he

adjusts the guard on his clippers.

"Yes, please."

I can't wipe away my smile as Eddie finishes trimming away the ragged ends of what used to be my braid, then carefully buzzes the hair at my nape. The steady vibrations remind me of my high school best friend's family cat purring on my chest. Alice always seemed so bemused that he liked me because the cat usually only likes guys. I miss my snuggles with Grumpy Gus, his rumbling purrs a loud dose of gender euphoria.

This is like that on steroids. When Eddie brushes away the last few stray hairs and I catch a glimpse of myself in the mirror, a boy is beaming back at me. Well, okay, maybe not quite. His cheeks are still too round, his chin too narrow. But at a glance, it's damn hard to tell for sure. My belly flips with delight at that. Happy squirming, like the first plunge down a rollercoaster.

"What do you think?" Eddie asks.

"I love it." I turn to get a look from every angle. Eddie grabs a mirror to show me the back and I preen a little more, floating on cloud nine as I pay and Jordie shepherds me out the door.

"This way," Jordie loops their elbow through mine as we leave the barbershop. They guide me along a bustling narrow sidewalk toward a busier road with wider sidewalks for foot traffic and cyclists.

I stuff my hat into my hoodie pocket as we walk. There's no need to hide under it anymore and the late summer weather is too hot for it. Has been all along, but I just hated how I looked without it. Now I don't. Everything seems brighter with Jordie at my side. They make learning the area around my new home seem like a thrilling adventure instead of lonely and isolating with potential threats lurking in every shadowy laneway.

The late afternoon sun is still too hot, but a slight breeze ruffles my hair. It makes me feel more connected to the world. Almost like a simple haircut let me shed a layer of the separation from reality that makes my baseline dysphoria bearable day-to-day. A promise that someday I can experience my entire life like that, free from the invisible barriers that protect and smother me.

We stroll past a mishmash of huge chains, cute small businesses in tiny storefronts, trendy restaurants, and coffee shops. In my periphery, I keep catching brief glimpses of the boyish version of me reflected in the windowed storefronts. The sight has me grinning uncontrollably. I want to just run my fingers through my hair over and over, a tactile reminder this is real. I'm really doing it. Trying to play it cool in front of Jordie, I practice as much restraint as I can muster.

"Looking good, handsome." Jordie grins at me as we walk around a coffee shop's terrasse seating.

"I really am!" I beam, running my fingers along my scalp yet again to revel in the velvety soft bristles under my palm. Sort of like petting Gus. It feels like a boy's head. Restraint might be overrated and Jordie seems to understand the euphoria is about so much more than a haircut. Then I process what they said and my face heats. "I mean, I really look more like a guy."

"Yep." Jordie grins at me. "A handsome boy." They wink,

chuckling at the heat burning through me when they praise my looks. That's a weird contrast to how I normally feel about appearance related compliments. The juxtaposition is so strange, but I want to hear more, especially masc-coded ones from Jordie. "Come on, sunshine, we've only just begun this transformation. I'm taking you thrifting and we're getting you a binder."

"School supplies?" That can't be right.

"No. For your chest so you can stop cooking yourself in those oversized hoodies you're obsessed with."

"I'm not obsessed." I scowl, getting defensive even though I was just thinking about how uncomfortable dressing to hide my dysphoria is in the late summer heat.

"Of course not. You just don't want anyone to actually perceive you?"

"Yeah." I squirm, fighting the urge to pull free of their hold to cross my arms over my chest. "Pretty much. Not if they're perceiving the wrong things."

"I get that." Jordie's tone softens with genuine understanding. "The right clothes help a lot. Promise."

"Even if I can't pass?" I worry my lip between my teeth. I'm so used to hearing how well I fit the stereotypes of who I'm supposed to be, killing myself to be that person. It's all but impossible to imagine what passing would even look like.

Jordie steers us around a crowd of younger students at a bus stop. They look and act like high schoolers with their loud voices, school bags, and fancy coffees, but there's something subtly off. It takes me a second to realize the wrongness is that back home they'd almost definitely all be wearing matching school uniforms. Another of those jarring reminders I'm in a different country here. Jordie's reply is jarring in an entirely different way.

"Even if you never pass. Passing doesn't have to be the point." Jordie tries to hide their exasperation, but I hear it in their voice.

"It doesn't?" I squeak, not daring to believe that or even let myself hope it's true. Most of what I've seen with my furtive efforts into figuring out what it means to be trans makes that *seem* like the point.

"I mean, maybe for some people it is." Jordie waves off the caveat like an annoying gnat. "But it doesn't *have* to be. The point is for you to go out into the world feeling confident in who you are." Jordie gestures at themself and then my hair. I resist the urge to touch it again.

"How do you do that?" Because I genuinely have no clue. I've only really gotten as far as the silent screaming in my head that I'm not a girl. The rest is a daunting blank canvas of trying to reinvent myself without the guideposts most people take for granted.

Jordie shrugs. "Lots of trial and error to figure out my style, and then loads of practice not giving a shit what anyone else thinks about it. And I have a feeling this place is going to help too."

Jordie stops and points to a boutiquey little shop with a discreet sign in the window.

"What do we need here?" I ask, wary of the wall of bras on

display when we walk inside.

"Binders. Pix and Celeste swear by this place. The owners are super queer and they sell gaffs and other gender stuff too, ignore the bras, okay? They'll hook us up with what we need."

Jordie leads me to a salesperson at the counter before I can protest, and true to their word, I'm whisked back to a fitting area.

"Is it alright if I take some measurements?" The matronly looking worker asks.

I nod, even though this reminds me of my first bra fitting with my mom. That was awful. It seemed like I had to smile through the entire ordeal even as I screamed internally about the wrongness of the milestone we were marking. The measuring tape makes me squirm, even though they do the sizing over my hoodie. At least it's over fast.

Then there are a few different styles of binder to choose between. I grab a couple that look comfy enough.

"Want help? The fabric can be a pain to get used to." Jordie offers.

I want to say yes. But the idea of Jordie seeing what's under my hoodie, let alone my entire exposed chest, is too daunting with the way the fitting left me reeling. Everything is too raw to handle my crush seeing the parts of me I don't want anyone to notice. "Um, not unless I need it?"

"Okay, I'll wait out here for you," Jordie offers with a reassuring smile.

I take my top choices into a changing cubicle and wriggle

into the first one. It feels like I can't breathe—the material is way too tight. The next one fits weirdly. When I finally settle on one that hugs my body and presses my chest flat without my ribs creaking, I try my t-shirt on over it. The difference it makes in the mirror takes my breath away. I reach out to touch my reflection, needing some proof it's real. I look... like me.

Jordie might have a point about this whole clothes and haircut thing. The tag on the binder makes my stomach roil in a whole new way though. I try to convince myself it's not much more expensive than a nice bra. It's not. If I use the bank card my parents gave me so I'd have spending money here, I know they won't think twice about it.

Mom is always saying that the right undergarments are important. How a nice new bra can be a huge confidence boost. For the first time, looking at the way the binder reshapes my body, I understand that on a visceral level. If I can walk out into the world looking like this, yeah. That's worth the cost. And it sells stuff they'd expect me to buy so I won't be outing myself.

Jordie is waiting when I step out of the changing booth with the binder.

"Good?" they ask.

"Yeah." I smile. I make my purchase and we leave the shop with a discreet paper shopping bag.

"Thanks for suggesting this." I smile at Jordie.

"Of course. I figured it would be good to have before our next stop." Jordie grins. "So, where were we?"

"Talking about how passing doesn't have to be the point of

transition."

"Right. Exactly. The important thing is being true to you."

"Even if people hate you for it?"

"Those people don't matter, if they can't accept the real you," Jordie insists with all the conviction I wish I had. It's obviously a philosophy they live by with their pins and rings and shirts proclaiming who they are to the world. And that's great for them, but I'm still scared.

"Even if they're your family?" There it is, the heart of my fears. I don't want to lose my family's love. I've worked so hard to be what they expect. They love me. But what if they only love the version of me I've shaped myself into for them?

"Nope. Not even them, unless it's a matter of making sure you're safe to tell them. Do you think it would screw up your school funding for them to find out?"

"No? At least, I don't think so. But they're going to be... upset isn't the right word. Disappointed, maybe? But not with me specifically. Just that they don't have the perfect family they imagined. No more visions of Dad walking his little princess down the aisle and no more mother-daughter spa days that I silently loathed. That sort of thing."

Jordie nods. "Yeah. I think my mom had a bit of that. And some confusion about what to replace those stereotypes with since it's not like I was transitioning to an easily defined identity she understood and had a societal blueprint for. But she loves me more than her ideas about who I should be, so we got through it fine."

"You think my folks will get over it?"

"I hope so," Jordie slings an arm around me, "and if they don't, then you can make a new family. But you don't have to tell anyone about anything until you're ready. You can take this as fast or slow as you want. There aren't any rules or hard and fast timelines. And if you need to stay in the closet, I can use your deadname or a nickname and different pronouns for you around them. That is assuming I ever meet or interact with them."

"I guess we'll play it by ear on that," I say.

Much as I appreciate the offer, everything in me rebels at the thought. I don't want to hear my old name on Jordie's lips. Not ever. Even if they know it from my school email address.

I still haven't worked up the courage to ask the registrar about changing that. What if my family sees it? I need to be the one to tell them. That's assuming I even *can* change it without a legal name change. Just thinking about all the logistics of transitioning makes me mildly panicky. Baby steps, and that one is way down the list.

Jordie hasn't commented on my legal name, but I had to email them for a group project, so I know they've seen it. I let the subject drop and we talk about different clothing styles. Jordie grills me about what I like and don't like as we turn onto a side street toward our next stop, a cool thrift shop.

I bite my lip and stare out over the racks of clothing, trying to work up the courage to step into the men's section to shop for myself. It's ridiculous that I can grab a shirt or something for my brothers, no problem, but picking out something for myself still seems taboo. I touch the velvety softness of my shorn scalp. I still have enough hair on the top to run my fingers through, but it feels like what I've always been told a boy's hair should be. Every time my fingers find that instead of my long braid, joy bubbles up in my chest all over again. If I can take a boy's haircut for myself, then I can take men's clothes too. I can.

I stand hesitantly at the end of the racks, still trying to nerve myself up. Jordie clucks their tongue and asks for my sizes. I stammer out my shirt size with a hot flush. I only have a vague idea of my pant size, to the extent of getting hand-me-down loungewear from my brothers over the years. The sizing is way different for their jeans, so I only have a ballpark number there.

Jordie nods. "Okay. Let's start with figuring your pants size first."

They squint appraisingly at me, then march us to a section with roughly the right waist size. "Here, hold this to your hips." They hand me a pair of ugly pants.

I do as they say, glancing dubiously at the corduroy fabric. Jordie snorts at my expression.

"Relax, I'm not saying you need to buy them, just looking for a size, sunshine." They move to stand behind me and adjust my hands, smoothing the waistband of the pants flat against my body. I hold still, every nerve ending in my body tuned to how close Jordie is standing.

They guide my hands so gently, and I savor the touch. I know they're just measuring where the outer seams of the new pants land. It means nothing. But with Jordie so close behind me and the pants tugged snug across my waist, I can almost trick myself into feeling like Jordie is hugging me from behind. Total swoony date move that has my heart pounding with want.

This isn't a date, it's just more proof that Jordie is an amazing friend. It's still trippy to be this close to them. Almost impossible to deny that I'm more attached to them than I usually get with friends.

It could just be that I don't know many people here and their kindness links them inextricably to so much gender euphoria that I've been starving to find. Regardless, I think about them all the time, and my emotions are definitely tilting more and more toward a hopeless crush. This outing and focused attention as they scrutinize my pants is adding fuel to that spark.

"Okay, so that's about right for the waist, and I'm pretty sure we're looking for a shorter inseam. Sorry." Jordie steps back and I miss the warmth of them being so close. I turn to face them.

"Eh? I'm okay with being short." I shrug. That's the least of my dysphoria. It helps that my dad and brothers aren't that much taller than me. Shortness runs in the family. "So, I just, pick stuff?"

"Yep, grab whatever speaks to you. Then we'll take it to the fitting room to figure out a style that feels like you." Jordie turns to the racks and runs their fingers over the section of clothing in my size. They start pulling out garments and draping them over their arm until I'm certain they can't carry another thing. Jeans, khakis, t-shirts, button ups and more in all kinds of textures and patterns and prints.

"I don't think I can wear that!" I protest when they grab a polo.

"No? You aren't into the preppy look?" Jordie smirks at me. They slide the hanger back onto the rack and pick a colorful short-sleeved button up next, arching a questioning eyebrow at me. "How about this?"

"Maybe?" I lick my lips. "It's not too bright?"

Jordie snorts and adds it to their pile. "Not as bright as you by half, sunshine. We're going to try a little of everything and see what makes you smile. Sound alright?"

"Yeah." I agree, licking my lips. Normally that would sound like torture, but I trust Jordie. I want to see myself looking like the guy I've been hiding under an uncomfortable cocoon of concealment.

When I'm with Jordie, I can't wipe away my smile. And when Jordie smiles back at me, I don't want to. They give me the courage to be Ray. Not just try on a name and pronouns that felt too impossible to ever really be mine, but to actually be myself for the world to see. I pick a few more items to try on, embracing this chance to figure out who I want to be.

Chapter Six

Jordie

"Is this alright?" Ray plucks at the tight black jeans I brought him to try on. I have to bite my lip to keep from hitting on him when he turns around and shows off his gorgeous round ass in the skin-hugging denim. Granted, he's looked hot in every single outfit he's tried on today, and the binder we got earlier seems to really be making a difference in his confidence with clothes. He hasn't reached for his ever present hoodie since putting on the first new shirt over the binder.

These pants are pushing his limits though. They're more of a going out look, because I want to show him off to my friends. As amazing as the pants look on him, they might not be the right look for Ray right now. I just want to figure out what about them is wrong so I can find something that works for him.

"So much more than alright. Makes your ass look fantastic," I say.

Oops, guess I can't help myself after all. Well, he looks hot. And I'm allowed to look, right? Jacob would certainly say so, but he might not be the best moral compass to follow.

"Yeah? It's not obvious that I'm... ya know?" He gestures vaguely at his crotch where there's no telltale bulge. Okay, yeah, maybe the outline of his dick would be visible in the pants if he was cis, but that's what packers are for.

It's not like most people would notice unless they were actively checking him out. Which I shouldn't be doing when he's looking at me with those wide vulnerable eyes and begging me to teach him how to do this. Step into the world as something other than what everyone's always told him he should be.

He doesn't need me to teach him how to be himself for real. He just needs someone to hold his hand and tell him it's okay. That he's perfect the way he is; no need to hide or tone himself down to fit other people's expectations.

"Hmm." I tap a finger on my chin as I scrutinize the outfit. "Is it obvious that you're hot in those pants? Isn't that the point of a going out outfit?"

Ray rolls his eyes at me, but he stops fussing with the clothing. "That I don't have a dick," he hisses under his breath, glancing surreptitiously around to be sure we're still alone in the cramped changing area.

Okay, so he's not comfortable. There's no need for him to wear something I like if he doesn't feel good wearing it. Even if he might like it some day when he's more confident in his body. Ugh. I need to reel myself in a bit, but he needs to hear this. I want to encourage him without exerting any undue influence on his style.

"If you aren't comfy, then those aren't the pants for you. But also, it's not anyone else's business what's in your pants unless you're planning to show them." I arch a brow at him and Ray snorts.

"Yeah, I guess. I just... want to be a normal guy." He picks at the tight clothes. Yep, those pants are a definite nope.

"What's normal?" I ask, his question rubbing against my insecurities. I tell most people that normal is a city in Illinois, but I went through a similar phase. Nothing good came of trying to suppress what I knew about myself to fit other people's norms. I want to spare Ray from going through that if I can. "You can be a *normal* guy with long hair, or who wears sexy skinny jeans, or one who wears baggy joggers, or whatever makes you feel comfortable with yourself. Anyone who tells you there's one right way to be yourself is a liar."

"You think?" Ray asks, those wide blue eyes of his fixed on me, full of hope. Damn, his earnestness is going to wreck all my good intentions about keeping this platonic.

"I don't think; I know. You are exactly the glorious Ray of sunshine that you are meant to be, no matter what you wear." I reach out to boop his nose and he snorts at me, then turns to pout into the mirror, plucking at his shirt now. The v-neck and snug fit seems to make him uncomfortable, so I shove a dorky sweater-vest at him. He kept ogling it on the racks, but didn't grab it himself.

"Try this on over it. Layers will make you look even flatter." I gesture toward his chest. Getting the binder to lay just right will take practice, and layering can help emphasize the more masculine look, anyway.

"It's not too nerdy?" Ray takes the soft knit with a dubious frown.

"Who cares if it is?" I challenge, shooing him with my fingers to get him to put it on already.

Ray bites his lip, but he obediently goes back into the changing cubicle to humor me. I scan the changing area as I wait, and snort when I notice a sticker of the Rock's stern face peering out from an empty cubicle. Weird place for a sticker. It reminds me of similar stickers of the same actor that appeared in one of the bathrooms at Randy's and near the back door to Frisky's tavern. I wonder what that's about.

The door to Ray's stall opens and drives all thoughts of stickers right out of my head. He makes the geek chic style work for him. There's even a hint of a smile on his face. He's an adorable little nerd, so who cares if he looks the part?

"Do you like it?" he asks, so hopeful it almost makes me laugh.

"I do." I nod. And more importantly, he seems comfortable and happy in the clothes. That's what I'm going for, not pants that make me horny. Clothes that light him up so brightly, I want nothing more than to kiss those smiling lips.

We end up finding him a bunch of clothes that suit his style. Then we pare that down to a handful of outfits with a few interchangeable wardrobe staples to bring home along with his new binder. I feel a little guilty about not checking in about a budget before this little shopping spree, but that's why we got the clothes second hand. And Ray is grinning when he pays for his purchases, so I don't think we broke the bank? I take half of his bags for him and he stuffs his hoodie and beanie into one of the shopping bags before we leave. It's satisfying to finally see him dressed for the summer heat as we step back onto the sidewalk.

"Is that everything?" Ray asks. His eyes plead to be done with the shopping.

I'm sorely tempted to have mercy on him, but our last stop will be fun. And it might make him more confident about the tight pants I want him to wear to Keith and Pixel's drag show this weekend. I want to introduce him to my friends, and maybe show him off a little. It's going to be fun to let my buddies see how adorable my little fledgling baby queer is.

I can already picture Ray in his hot as fuck new club outfit and maybe a hint of eyeliner to emphasize his gorgeous baby blues. It might be way too soon to talk about makeup as a gender neutral thing with him, considering. Still, most of my guy friends wear some, so maybe Ray has a similar view?

Either way, I can't wait to introduce him to everyone. I'm so ready to see him wide-eyed with wonder at leaving the nest for the first time. Ready to spread wings that he wasn't sure he really had until it was time to soar. I want it to go well and a packer might be just the thing he needs to boost his confidence. If he's ready.

"Jordie?" Ray interrupts my thoughts. Right, he asked a question.

"Almost done." I'm not sure how he's going to take going to a sex toy shop, but it's probably best to ease him into it. Or at least warn him before we take a bus across town during the evening rush. "Or we can do this last place another time, if you've had enough fun for one day?."

"What's the last place?" Ray asks, apprehensively.

"You wanted a packer, right?"

Ray blanches. "Um, maybe?" His voice gets all squeaky with nerves. I might have underestimated how much I've pushed him already. He might not be ready for sex toy shopping with me yet.

"If you aren't up for it, we can leave it for another time. And if you want something to help fill out your pants in the meantime, I have some safety pins you can use with the classic balled up sock."

"Do guys actually do that?" He sounds dubious.

I shrug. Maybe some guys do, but I want him to feel comfortable in his new pants, so I don't get into another chat about normal. I'm tempted to offer to make a more realistic DIY packer with him. Condoms, hair gel, and panty hose can work wonders. I swore by them until the time I helped a newly out trans masc friend make one that burst on their first night out with it. It got caught in their zipper—I'm still not sure how, but it was not a fun time. The gel made a giant mortifying mess when it popped in their pants. Socks are safer until we can get Ray the real thing.

"Sure, it's practically a rite of passage." I sling my arm around his shoulders. "Come on, let's head back to campus. I have an evening lab I shouldn't skip and you have clothes to put away."

"Yeah. I guess I do." His face falls when I mention that I have to head out. It makes my insides all warm and fuzzy to be so wanted that he's upset about parting ways.

"We can grab dinner in the dining hall first, if you want?" I suggest, because I want to draw out our time together too. Perks of living in the on campus apartments are that I have a meal plan. Saves me having to cook most of my meals, and the dining halls make it easier to meet up with classmates to study and socialize.

"Dinner?" He licks his lips. "Just us?"

His question reminds me we haven't eaten a full meal together yet, and suddenly it feels like a bigger deal. If he was one of my other friends, I'd make a flippant remark about it being a date and wink at him. Except this is my baby trans mentee who I'm supposed to keep an emotional distance from, right? Give him space to figure out who he is and what he wants?

If he was a fresh-faced teenaged first-year, I wouldn't even be tempted, but he's not. Ray is almost my age. He's adorable and sweetly naïve about some things, but he's also not new to his sexuality, just to being seen for the guy he is.

"Uh, yeah. Unless we run into friends or something. It's just dinner." I shrug with a practiced nonchalance that I don't truly feel. It's a heady thing to be looked up to like this. The weight of not wanting to let him down balanced against the glow of being able to help him find his way. I need a minute to get my head on straight.

"Oh, yeah. Cool. Can I meet you in the dining hall after I drop off my shopping bags?" Ray asks. Is it my imagination or is he hiding disappointment?

"Sure. See you there in about fifteen minutes?" I need to stop overthinking everything with him. He's clearly just latched onto me as the first openly queer friend he's made in a new city.

"Sounds good! I should grab my lab notebook anyway, so I can bring your school stuff." I give him an awkward wave and we part ways while I kick myself for fumbling with the whole super casual dinner invite.

If the point of keeping my distance is not to hurt him, I pretty much blew it. Ugh. I'm tempted to text my friends to meet us for dinner as a buffer to keep things from devolving into more awkwardness. But I also don't want to share Ray yet. My own personal ray of sunshine for just one more night before I bring him to tomorrow night's drag show.

***

After we part ways, I rush home to grab what I need for my evening lab. I don't linger for long since Celeste and Pixel usually get home around this time. Partly to avoid questions about why Ray's stuff is in our entryway, and partly just to maximize my time with him before my lab.

Meeting up with Ray in front of the dining hall goes smoothly once I remember that I'm not looking for his ever present wool beanie. As soon as I stop scanning the crowd for a shrimpy guy drowning in his oversized hoodie, I pick him out near a cluster of rowdy jocks. I lift both arms to flag him over to me. Ray waves when spots me, his face lighting up again as he beelines to my side.

I grin as I take in the sight of his tentative smile. I can't help a quick once-over. He looks good with his freshly shorn blond hair golden in the late afternoon summer sun. He's still wearing too many layers to hide his curves, and he keeps tugging the hem down to cover the front of his pants. But for all that, he's cute in an open heather blue button up over the dorky tan sweater-vest over what I suspect is probably two t-shirts, minimum. So we might need to work on less is more with his styling, but still adorable.

"Hey!" We exchange pleasantries as I hand over the school bag Ray left at my apartment earlier.

Ray gives me an appreciative up-down with his eyes, trying to be surreptitious about it and failing. I opted for bold floral print leggings and a slouchy femme sweater. The chunky yarn has just enough shimmer to it to satisfy my magpie need for color and sparkle without being too over the top. I know I look good and it's nice to be admired, but I pretend not to notice the attention so as not to encourage a crush. We fill our trays and find seats across from each other at the end of a table. It occurs to me that I'm running out of time to invite him out this weekend, so I dive right in with that first.

"So, earlier, when I asked you to come to a drag show with me?"

"Yeah? I guess I can't use not having anything to wear as an excuse now, huh?" He chuckles weakly.

"Nope. You definitely can't." I grin. "So, how about Friday night? I think I mentioned that Pixel and Bella Donna are performing?" I stab a chunk of zucchini on my fork. As if I'm not totally over-invested in his response.

"Your roommate, right?" Ray asks.

"Yep, Pixel and I share an apartment along with Pixel's girlfriend, Celeste. But it's Donna's debut show, so we're all going to support her. Keith's been a bundle of nerves all week."

"Keith is Donna?" Ray checks.

I nod, my mouth full of veggies.

Ray gives me a sympathetic smile. "I bet he has. My second oldest brother's ex is a drag artist. He didn't miss a show while they were together. We still go to support her sometimes. So, I'm all for showing up to support a friend."

"Yeah?" I try not to get my hopes up that he's going to agree, but I really want him to. I want to take the next step in our friendship from acquaintances thrown together by taking the same class to actual friends. "So, does that mean you'd want to come along? Everyone wants to meet you."

"They do?" Ray sounds unduly surprised by that.

"Well, yeah." I stuff more veggies into my mouth to give myself a minute before I give away just how much I'm coming to enjoy our time together.

"Why?" Ray's brow scrunches in adorable confusion.

"I might talk about you a lot." I hedge.

"Oh, yeah?" he asks.

"Yeah. Anyway, come to the show and meet my friends? They're all totally cool with the trans thing. Heck, half of us are trans or gender non-conforming and all of us are queer," I assure him. That's another reason I want to introduce him to my friends, so he'll have other people to talk to about his gender stuff.

"If you're sure it's alright, yeah. I want to come with you."

"Good. It's going to be epic!" I grin at him, and Ray grins back.

That genuine smile of his could easily melt away all my resolve not to get involved with a baby queer again. One-night stands and offering guidance are fine; letting my heart get involved isn't. I swore I wouldn't be anyone's long-term experiment or gay training wheels again after the ways Nell played with my heart, but Ray feels different. I definitely need a buffer if we're going to keep this friendship growing past our biweekly standing study dates.

Introducing him to the gang seems like the best of both worlds. I like him. I want to be friends. And I want him to have the same level of support that I've had with my transition. Even if it means I don't get to keep all the happy he sparks in me to myself anymore.

Chapter Seven

Ray

My folks call me after dinner on Thursday night. I've been keeping busy all day with classes and studying with Jordie and trying not to dwell on the fact that it's my first birthday away from home. I miss my family and our silly little traditions.

Dinner alone in the dining hall after my math lecture just really drove home how lonely I've felt all semester. My study sessions with Jordie have been such a bright spot, but dinner with them on Tuesday felt like a harsh reality check. I'm not as important to them as they are to me. Why would I be? They have friends and family and a whole life here.

A life that they're sort of inviting me into a little more tomorrow night. I'm trying not to read too much into the drag show outing, but I'm excited. The loneliness has been getting worse and I'm not entirely sure I can handle being so far from home for the next three years. Still, I'm not prepared for the lurching dread that hits me in the chest as I answer my family's video call with the knee-jerk impulse to jam my toque onto my head.

It sucks to hide the drastic change in my appearance, a wary acknowledgement that something that brings me joy might be shameful to them.

I had to take off my binder as soon as I got back to my dorm. It smells like I might need to wash it before the drag show. After a couple of days of wearing it around campus for a full day of classes, it's getting hard to see myself without it flattening my curves. At least the stylish layers Jordie suggested help minimize my chest more comfortably than my oversized hoodie, even without the binder underneath risking outing me to my family.

I plaster on a fake grin and wave for the camera. A fresh wave of lonely hits at seeing my family on my computer screen. I hate feeling lonely with them, like my secrets are a barrier between us and true closeness.

"Happy birthday!" All three of my brothers and our parents chorus as soon as I connect to their video chat request. I roll my eyes at them. The dorks all gathered together for this. Mom even has her traditional sloppily frosted cake sitting on the table with a huge off-kilter 21 candle jammed into the top layer.

It doesn't help allay my sense of alienation from the family that my brothers are a lot to live up to. Adam is the oldest. He's a doctor, and he married his residency arch rival, Jackie, last year. Darren is a lawyer, working for a queer rights charity. Luke just graduated as a civil engineer. He's ace and has always been indifferent toward sex and dating. I think our folks have finally accepted that he truly is happy being single.

When they take their seats at that table with the camera angle zoomed out more, I can see that my oldest two brothers have partners with them tonight. Jackie looks effortlessly serene with a hand on her perfectly round bump at six months pregnant with my first nephew. Darren's date is someone I don't recognize, but he's been talking about a new paralegal he met through work, so I assume it's zir.

"Did you get yourself a cake like I asked?" Mom fusses.

"Right here." I hold up the cupcake that Jordie brought to our study session earlier.

They hugged me when they handed it over and it felt so good to be wrapped in their arms. Like I wasn't alone and untethered in a strange new city. Their body was so soft and yielding against mine, their floral shampoo sweet in my nostrils. Jordie gives excellent birthday hugs. I'd told them about my birthday last week, but I didn't expect anything from them. I know they have an evening recitation on Thursdays. So it wasn't like they were going to show up for another dinner like the one we shared after shopping on Tuesday.

The pretty confection they gave me is a sweet gesture. The bright yellow sunflower frosted on top is almost too gorgeous to eat. It made me smile because of how well the vibrant flower evokes their nickname for me. I didn't bother with candles since I don't want to be that guy who sets off the smoke detectors and gets the entire dorm evacuated. The thought draws me out of my wistful thoughts of Jordie and back to the expectant faces of my family watching me from my computer screen.

"I'll have to pretend about the candles," I joke weakly.

It's nice to be the center of attention, even if it's only virtually. The evidence that my family cares enough to get together to celebrate with me, even long distance, goes a long way to assuaging the ache of missing home. It fills a hollow space inside my heart. Maybe they don't see all of me, but they care.

"We've got you covered, sis." Adam gestures toward the cake with its burning candles. And all the joy I felt at being remembered and celebrated by my family shrivels like a salted slug.

I tug my toque lower over my shorn hair, hiding myself from them. The walls around my heart try in vain to block out the sting of them not seeing me. It's not their fault. I still haven't worked up the guts to tell them yet. I want to, I just... can't. The words stay locked in my throat, along with the burning sting of hurt tears.

"You're old enough to drink there now, right?" Darren asks.

"You know the first thing she did was probably to grab a fake ID, otherwise what's even the point of undergrad?" Luke teases.

"Studying hard, obviously." I stick my tongue out at Luke. He rolls his eyes.

I know for a fact he spent his college years studying his ass off. All my brothers studied hard and they're all successful in their chosen fields. I struggled to get good enough marks to get into Northeastern University. And much as I'm devoted to my chosen career path, I know it's not as glamorous as what my brothers do.

My reply gets all three of my brothers started heckling me about what I'm even studying and if I've declared a major yet.

Even if I wanted to hear their well-intended teasing, I wouldn't be able to parse who was saying what as they all talk over each other. I haven't told them I want to be a therapist for kids like me because I haven't told them who I am yet. The longer this goes on, the more it feels like an invisible wall growing taller and more impenetrable between us.

"Enough of that. Sing to your sister." Dad cuts through my brothers' good-natured teasing.

Luke sticks his tongue out at me behind our parents' backs. Darren winks at me, miming a drink, as if our folks can't see them both in the little picture-in-picture square. All of my brothers obediently sing the birthday song to me and my name shouldn't cut like a knife, but it does. The words to tell them are on the tip of my tongue, but what if they don't listen? Or worse, if they hear me and it changes everything for the worse?

I pretend to blow out the candle on the screen. Luke snuffs out the ones on the table. As Dad serves everyone slices of cake, I stay on the call. I'm not prepared for the longing that hits me square in the chest as they eat the cake Mom made for me. It's an almond torte with chocolate buttercream and I know from every other birthday of my life that it tastes even better than it looks.

Mom is no baker and her frosting skills leave something to be desired, but the old family recipe is foolproof and delicious. I want to be there with my family around me eating that cake. Even the annoying parts of being the baby of the family have me homesick. I want Luke to poke me in the ribs as he jokes about the birthday kid getting the last piece. I want to be there jostling elbows with Darren because he's left-handed and always seems to end up next to me. Coming out is terrifying because I can't fathom a future where I'm permanently locked out of our traditions. My heart aches to soak in more of these moments of family time, stockpiling memories in case they can't accept who I am.

I haven't been this intensely homesick since I stepped through security at the airport and waved goodbye to my parents. The lump in my throat feels like it might choke me. I have to set aside Jordie's cupcake untasted. I can eat it later. When I'm not hollowed out and aching for the sense of belonging that I came here to find. I miss Mom and her soft hugs. And I miss my brothers' gentle teasing and roughhousing affection and Dad's awkward heart-to-hearts.

Maybe I can ease into this, one tiny step at a time.

I want to tell them. They chatter in a polyglot blend of English and French. Adam and his wife throw in the occasional Spanish. I've missed hearing more than English. The ebb and flow of conversation only emphasizes how far from home I truly am, even if it's only a five-hour drive back to them.

The hollow ache of missing my family and feeling like a ghost haunting them as they celebrate a stranger who looks like the palest reflection of their hopes for me goads me. I try to endure it, but after a while I can't take another second. My face is all hot and my throat feels almost scratchy with the burning need to just say it.

The words won't come. But I yank my hat off, the soft wool crushes under my fingers and I crumple it nervously between my hands. For a few heartbeats that stretch into an eternity, no one notices or says anything. Then my mom gasps, fingers pressed dramatically to her chest.

"What happened?" Dad says it like an accusation, and I can see in both of my parents' eyes that they hate my haircut. "Qu'est-ce que tu a fait à tes beaux cheveux?"

It's so hard not to feel like that is the same as hating me. It's not, but it hurts and I can't explain or even show how devastating their response is. I sit there, feeling numb and cut off from them by so much more than the miles separating us.

"You didn't mention wanting a new look," Mom adds more diplomatically. She sounds more hurt than angry. So maybe she's just upset that I've made such a huge change without including her.

"You loved your long hair! It's going to take so long to grow it out again, darling. Why would you let all that effort and time go to waste?" Dad gestures. And maybe he's just upset because of all the hours we spent together with him helping me put it into braids and trying new looks.

Years of laughter and tears as he learned how to style long hair on the days when Mom had early shifts at the hospital. She couldn't be there to get me ready for school most days. Maybe he just misses the way it was a part of us bonding. But it hurts to have him reject something that feels like the first step toward finding the real me.

My brothers are just watching; spectators to the latest family drama. Luke is grinning like he has a joke on the tip of his tongue. Adam looks sternly disapproving, like he wants to agree with Dad that I acted rashly. I don't look at Darren; if any of them would understand the significance of this gesture, it would be him. I don't want to see rejection from him, so I don't meet his gaze on the screen.

I want to scream that it's just hair, it will grow back. But it's not just about my hair, and I have no intention of letting it grow back out. This is about so much more than my hair. If they can't accept that I'm an adult who can make my own decisions about a freaking haircut... I'm too scared to bring up the axis-shifting changes I came here to consider, free from their stifling love.

"I just needed a change. What do you think?" I run my fingers self-consciously through the velvety stubble on my scalp. Even in the face of my family's disapproval, I can't help but smile at the giddy delight of the short hair that meets my fingers. The boyish face reflected on my screen feels like a promise.

"You love it, don't you, dear?" Mom's face softens at my smile, and I nod. My chest feels less tight and I can breathe again at the glimmer of understanding there in her face.

"I really do. It's like a literal weight off not having to deal with it. And I donated most of it, so all that beautiful long hair won't go to waste." I bite my lip as I look at Dad, echoing his words back at him. Someone who needs it can have all that beautiful long hair.

"Then I'm glad you did it. I'm sure we'll all get used to the new look, right dear?" Mom elbows Dad. He glances down at her, takes in the *smarten up* look in her eyes and nods.

"Of course, if you love it, then we love it for you, honey. You just took us by surprise," Dad says the words stiffly, but I know he means them. For a second, I think this is all going to be okay and I can say the words that might change everything without losing them.

"Ah, nice do. Bet you'll get all the ladies with the new butch look, sis," Luke teases me. And the words are like a gut punch. They land squarely on the insecure part of me that worries I'll always look like a butch girl and not who I really am.

Darren elbows him. "Cut it out, Luke." My favorite brother defends me.

"Yeah, lay off," Adam adds.

"Sorry, I'm sure you can get as many dates as you want, sis," Luke assures me, all earnest caring as he sees the emotions playing out on my face. "You'll always be our baby sis, no matter how you dress or how many hearts you break." He gives me a cheesy wink.

My stomach sours at the blatant implication that I made such a drastic change for other people. I did it for myself. Not to look the way I think other people want me to, and it hurts not to be seen. Doubly so, because I got a taste of that sort of acceptance from Jordie. Someone I've only known for a month sees me more clearly than the people who love me the most. That makes the lonely ache I've been fighting all day worse. I was right to leave, to come somewhere I can have a blank slate to figure out the man—no, that's not quite right either—the person I am inside.

"Boys, honestly!" Mom chides, turning to give all of my brothers an exasperated look.

How would it feel if that epithet included me? I want it to, not just to be included in that fond tutting, but because that word fits me. It's all so complicated and strange and I really miss Jordie right now. Wish I could talk over the subtle nuance of why being called a boy feels like liquid sunshine pouring over me, but man chafes. Albeit in an entirely different way than girl and woman. Each of them is an ill-fitting scratchy garment I can't wait to shed.

Girl is like too-tight underwear I've outgrown. Woman fits like the underwire bras I've never quite grown into and good riddance to them when I switched to wearing sports bras with tight compression exclusively. Man is more like formal wear. Too stuffy for day-to-day use and I have nowhere and no desire to wear it. Boy is like my comfy jeans that hug my body and make me feel like a million bucks, even if it isn't always the right attire for every occasion.

Dad looks into the camera and smiles conspiratorially at me, breaking me out of my weird spiral about clothing. "You see what it's like when it's all boys? We miss having you home to even things out, baby girl."

I grimace, fuck. How do I tell them how much that sort of comment hurts? I can't. I can't do this.

"Uh, yeah. I should go, I need to study for a test. Talk to you all soon."

"What? On your birthday?" Luke teases.

I roll my eyes. "Yeah, Luke, shockingly, the professor didn't consult me about the test schedule. And unlike you, I really *do* need to study if I want to pass." I stick my tongue out at him, embracing the childish teasing that makes me feel more like I'm on even footing with him again. Luke returns the gesture. Adam rolls his eyes at our antics. "Bye everyone, thanks for the birthday wishes." I wave.

My family takes my cue and waves back. It's not entirely true that I need to study. I have until next week to cram for the test, but I can't do this for a moment longer; pretend every *she* and *elle* and utterance of my name doesn't hurt.

"We put some cash in your bank account, dear. Treat yourself," Mom says, blowing me a kiss.

"I will. Thanks, Mom."

"Be safe. Stay with your friends if you go out, pour bénéficier de la force du nombre," Dad reminds me.

"Yeah, I will." I swallow the bitter lump in my throat at knowing he wasn't that overprotective with my brothers when they went out at my age. Then I hang up and swallow back my tears. I can lie to myself that it's because I'm far from home in a strange city, but I know the truth is because they're guys.

The cupcake from Jordie is still sitting there; for a second, I want to just smash it. To break something beautiful in the real world, make it reflect all the tangled up emotions I can't seem to reconcile and don't want to hold inside. I want to feel the bright yellow frosting squishing between my fingers. I reach for it and the note Jordie included in the box catches my eye.

For the birthday boy, may your day be as sweet as you! Bony feet! ;)

The butchering of the French for happy birthday makes me snort. It's so Jordie. They see me. I brush my fingers over the word *boy*. Me. Someone I just met a month ago knows me better than my family. That breaks open the floodgates; tears burn down my cheeks as I pick up the dainty cupcake and bite into it.

I want to destroy the beautiful frosting swirled on top. Tear it apart with my teeth. The sweetness is almost too much, just on the edge of cloying, but I bet Jordie loves it and that makes me smile through my tears. They have the biggest sweet tooth and they are forever bringing baked goods to share whenever we get together to study. It's time to admit to myself that I have the biggest crush on them I've ever had on anyone. Not the least because they see the real me under the socially acceptable facade I've fear of the unknown has kept me too scared to shed.

They've held my hand through the first baby steps of becoming the Ray I long to be, and I want them to hold my hand through it all. What would they have said if they were here for that scene with my family? Probably followed my lead and not corrected the deadname that I hate more every time someone says it. It's so much harder to pretend now that I've found the courage to ask for the name that fits all of me.

On a reckless impulse, I dash away my tears, snap a selfie biting into the cupcake and send it to Jordie with a quick thanks.

Then I toss my phone face-down on my bed and bury my face in my hands. I'm not ready to see their response to the picture. Did it come across as friendly? Or clumsy flirting? I rub my palms over my eyes. What was I thinking? Ugh.

Is it too late to unsend the message? My phone buzzes as I reach for it to check. I stuff my face with another bite of cupcake to shore up my nerves, then flop onto my bed to check my phone.

Jordie: Mm, looks delicious! I should have sprung for a whole box. You like it?

Ray: Yeah. It's good. Reminds me of you.

Jordie: How so? It reminded me of you too, sunshine ;)

Because they're so sweet it makes my teeth ache? That's far too flirty. I delete it and try again. Except instead of backspacing over the next coy tease I tap out, I slip and fat finger the send button on an even more over-the-top cheesy line. Crap.

Ray: Hm, maybe because it looks as amazing as it tastes?

Oh, shit. Did I really just imply that I want to taste them? I mean, I do. But that's not something you say to a friend.

Jordie: Aw, you think I'm as pretty as a cupcake?

They send a GIF of a closeup on a drag queen batting absurdly long lashes. I snort, smiling to myself as I roll onto my back to keep texting. I feel as giddy as I did texting my first boyfriend at fifteen. It feels like a first, everything brand new because this is the first time I'm flirting as the real me, nothing held back. No major secrets hanging over me or making me squirm at every well-intended compliment and gendered endearment.

Ray: You know you are. What are you doing tonight?

Jordie: I'm still in my recitation. Bored to tears. What are you doing?

Ray: Studying.

Jordie: Nerd.

Jordie: I need to finish going over this study guide so I can GTFO, but you're coming out with me tomorrow still, right?

Ray: Yeah. Wouldn't miss it.

Nerves roil in my gut. They're taking me to a drag show to meet their friends. It's not like I haven't gone to similar shows at home. I've enjoyed drag performances with and without Darren. This is different; I'm going to be meeting Jordie's friends. As Ray.

I'm going to get dressed in the new clothes we bought, the stiff binder that makes me look even more masculine than just my hair and the layers of baggy clothes I've been wearing for months. Or the more fitting layers we got at the thrift shop. I'm going out as a boy for the first time and meeting new friends and it's going to be amazing. Or terrifying. Both. Definitely both.

I roll back onto my belly, trying to block out the sick feeling in my stomach just thinking about all the ways tomorrow could go terribly. Luke's teasing about being a chick magnet now plays on repeat. I don't want to look like a butch girl, or draw the confused second glances that make Jordie smile like a Cheshire cat when people aren't quite certain which pronouns to use for them. What I want is to look like a guy. I want people to see the real me I am inside.

Jordie: They're going to love you. Fair warning, Jacob will hit on you.

Ray: Yeah? Does he hit on everyone?

Jordie: No. Just hot guys and the occasional masc-leaning enby. I'd say he doesn't mean it, but he does. He just doesn't do relationships.

"Agh." I kick my feet, because *ah!* Jordie thinks I'm hot. Or they're just being nice. Trying to boost my confidence.

Ray: I'm excited and nervous to meet everyone.

Jordie: Nothing to be nervous about. They'll all like you. Want to bring your new clothes over here before so we can get ready together? I know the dorms can be a pain if you wanted to have more space or privacy or whatever.

Ray: Oh, score. A proper invite to the inner sanctum? I'll be there!

Ray: J'ai hâte de te voir.

I throw in the French, since they always seem to appreciate the practice when I talk to them and talking with my family has me all nostalgic for the sound of home. There's a long pause and I chew on my lip, wondering if maybe they changed their mind or I'm coming on too strong.

I finish my cupcake in tiny nibbles as I skim the textbook for the first psych 101 exam that's coming up next week. It's hard to focus when I keep glancing at my phone, hoping Jordie will text again. Maybe I can finagle some extra study sessions with them out of the test. I bet they'd be down for that.

Jordie: Totally. I had to look that up because for a second I thought you were saying you hated to see me, and I was confused, but I'm excited about tomorrow too!

Jordie: Ah, my group is teasing me about being glued to my phone. I'll text you more later, birthday boy. Enjoy the rest of your treat ;) <3

Jordie: If you're up for it, meet me by the dining hall in an hour and I'll show you something cool. ;)

Ray: Oh, another surprise? Do I get a hint?

Jordie: Hm...How about it's my little brother's favorite spot on campus?

Huh, so it's a hint and a quiz on how well I've paid attention. They've mentioned Liam is into a few things. The library for the poetry? But we've been there a few times to study. They've mentioned taking me to check out the arboretum, but that closes at dusk and it's getting late. I'm stumped, but I want them to know I pay attention to what they say as intently as they listen to all my transition and coming out woes.

Ray: I'd say the arboretum, but isn't that only open during the day? Some other magical hidden garden?

Jordie: Ha! Yep, it's closed, but my botany lab's final project means I have permission and the security codes to enter after hours. We'll have the whole place to ourselves to check out cool plants. Perks of using botany to fill in my missing lab science credit, yeah?

Jordie: I snuck Liam in the second week of classes, and he keeps asking when we can go again.

Ray: Sure, that sounds fun. I'll meet you in front of the dining hall.

Jordie replies with a string of emojis that straddle the line between excited about our plans and flirty. My heart beats faster at the images. I'm reading way too much into something so innocuous. I know I am. But Jordie just makes me smile so much. And I don't want to stop.

Chapter Eight

Ray

"Everything alright in there, Ray?" Jordie knocks on their bathroom door.

My name on their lips still fills me with an unfamiliar warmth. It's indescribably right. If they didn't sound so exasperated, I might take more time to revel in that sensation. I'm already taking too long changing, and now I'm taking too long to answer, grunting as I struggle with the stiff spandex and nylon of the new binder Jordie helped me pick out.

"I'm all about being fashionably late, but Miss Donna will have words for us if we miss her set," Jordie warns me.

"Yeah," I squeak, nervous sweat prickling over my skin at the pressure to make a good impression on Jordie's friends tonight. "I know. Guess I'm nervous." I blow out a frustrated breath. I don't want to be nervous, but it's my first time. First time meeting most of Jordie's friends. First time going out for real as Ray and wearing a binder and looking more like me off campus, stepping into what feels more like the real world.

We've been hanging out a lot since I fell into their lap in

our intro to psych class. Jordie is the one who showed me the best dining halls to use my meal credits and get caffeinated for late night study sessions. They've taught me shortcuts across campus. Yesterday, for my birthday, they even gave me a tour of the campus gardens that the botany department maintains with all kinds of interesting plants. Not to mention our shopping expedition and taking me to the barber.

The best is still last night's birthday stroll along the densely planted garden's meandering paths. Stepping from one pool of pale yellow lighting to the next limned the entire evening with an ethereal air. It was like finding a magical oasis of calm in the bustle of campus. Jordie gave me exactly what I needed to ground me after how cut adrift my chat with my family left me.

I kept stealing glances at Jordie's smiling face, only to find them watching me with just as much intent curiosity. As if my reaction to their special place mattered to them. It made my heart feel all fluttery and as light as the delicate moths flitting between the flowers. It was a perfect way to take my mind off being homesick and wishing someone saw the real me on my birthday. Jordie does.

Right now, though, they're helping me decide what to wear for our big night out. It's my first time inside their cramped little on campus apartment. The friends they live with, Pixel and Celeste, are already at the club for the show since Pixel needed to get ready to perform. So it's just the two of us here now. Being alone in Jordie's personal space has me thinking all kinds of ways about Jordie. Ways I shouldn't be thinking about my only real friend here in Boston when I'm half-dressed, but I can't help it.

"Need a hand?" Jordie eases the washroom door open by the barest crack.

I glance in the mirror, instinct telling me to cover up. Except the binder is a pain in the ass to put on alone and it feels tighter and stiffer after I washed it last night and left it to air dry all day in my room. I could use the help.

It wouldn't be the first time a friend helped me change. Heck, it wouldn't be the first time a friend I'm crushing on saw me semi-nude—bi guy problems. I tamp down the squirming in my gut at Jordie seeing me vulnerable as I push it open wide with my foot, both arms engaged with the binder; trying to wriggle it down over my head and into place really isn't going well for me.

"Please?" I wriggle helplessly, no closer to getting the fabric untangled. It's mostly covering my nipples, at least. I just sort of have my arms hopelessly tangled in it somehow.

Jordie steps in, biting their lip to stifle a laugh at my predicament. They tug the hem down over my chest, then help me pull my arms through the proper holes. They turn toward the outfit they picked for me, tactfully looking away as I adjust everything under the tight compression material to lie flat. I shove my nipples toward my pits, the way the instructions I've read online say to do. It's weird, but I'm sure I'll get used to it, considering how much more comfortable it is to look like me than to hide under my collection of oversized hoodies.

"There, now put this on." Jordie hands me an undershirt,

then a casual button-up—they swear by their layers. I get dressed obediently. My boxers are a little too roomy, but I like the men's jeans that make my ass pop. Even if I am a little self-conscious about the front panel that I don't fill out properly. This pair isn't as tight as the first one Jordie clearly liked on me. It was tempting to pick them just for the heat in Jordie's gaze on me, but I don't have the guts to wear skinny boy jeans.

"What's wrong?" Jordie notices me fussing.

"Nothing, just, it looks too flat?" I prod the excess fabric over my crotch, trying to make it look less weird.

"Hm, well, it's short notice for anything that's going to pass a squeeze test, but until we can get you an actual packer, I might have something that will work. Give me a minute." Jordie ducks out of the washroom, leaving me to fuss with my outfit.

They return looking sheepish a moment later. "Here, this might help with the roominess?" They offer me a tightly balled up sock and a safety pin, then help me with positioning the faux bulge in my pants, lower than I'd have guessed.

"What do you think?"

I grimace. But my underwear no longer bunches when I move and the weird empty fold in my pants seems less obvious, so it's an improvement. "Good, I guess?"

"Good. We'll get you situated better when you're ready. Don't forget, store-bought is fine when you can't grow your own." They wink at me as they adjust their falsies in their bra to fill out their silky button-up blouse. I lick my lips, trying not to fantasize about how it would feel to cup their full chest through that silky material. That's not what this is. We're friends getting ready for a night out together. Tonight is not a date.

"Yeah. Um, maybe soon? One milestone at a time. I've got meeting your friends for the drag show tonight and my aunts are insisting on taking me out to Frisky's for a drink to celebrate my birthday this weekend. They're being weird about how I'm all grown up." I roll my eyes, but I'm actually excited about the weekend trip to the queer tavern with my aunts.

Aunt Marie-Claire and Aunt Tammy insisted on planning a special birthday outing for me tomorrow night. It feels like an initiation into a more grownup world of queer culture, courtesy of my elders. A rite of passage similar to the drag show with the first friend I'm making as Ray. Going out with the first peers to know all of me means just as much, but I need both. A community all around me that isn't reliant on any single other person.

"Fair. You let me know when you're ready for that step. For now, can I help you with hair and makeup?" They gesture toward their cosmetics cluttering the countertop.

I nod hesitantly. Darren and Luke both wear a bit of eyeliner when they go out. It doesn't have to be a girl thing. And coming from Jordie, it doesn't feel like one. "Yeah, if you think it won't make me look like a girl."

"I've got you, babe. Look at me?" Jordie selects an eyeliner and tips up my chin to stencil it along my lids. They assess their work with pursed lips. I admire the flawless makeup they put on their own face earlier, smokey eye shadow that brings out the

warm amber in their beautiful brown eyes. They grab a thing
of hair gel and slick the floppy top part of my newly trimmed
hair back for me. Their hands on me don't help with getting
my focus off the blood rushing to my groin. "Anyway, you have
nothing to be nervous about, Ray. It's going to be fine. You look
fantastic."

Jordie is full of all the confidence I lack as they take my arm
and loop our elbows to drag me in front of the full-length
mirror in their bedroom.

I keep my eyes averted as I tug self-consciously at the brand
new binder. I'm not ready to see the full results of this new look.
Jordie clucks and turns me to face the mirror. I shiver at their
forceful fingers gently pressing along my jaw to make me take
in my transformation.

My breath catches at the first glimpse of a boy staring back at
me. He looks like a stranger I desperately want to know. And all
I can do is stare at the surreal version of myself I'm not sure how
to be.

"See? You look fine, Ray. My very own twinky ray of sunshine." Jordie squeezes my shoulders in a friendly hug.

"Please, I'm not." I roll my eyes at them, but I secretly love
that nickname. I want to be their ray of sunshine for always. But
their admiration gives me the courage to face the mirror again.
And I can't help the wide grin that splits my face when I see the
lanky boy still gazing back at me. "Binder and a haircut, huh?"

"Yep. Does wonders for the confidence, right? Told you to
trust in Jordie to show you a good time, didn't I?" They jostle

me playfully. It's so easy to forget the ways they seem older than me despite a barely two-year age gap when they get silly like this. Jordie seems so secure in who they are and they're in their final year of university applying to law school. So much further along a path that I'm just starting toward our respective dream careers.

"You did." I smile at them.

"So, are you ready? Unless you want to see an angry drag queen?" They stuff their phone into their tiny golden clutch since their sparkly jeggings don't have actual pockets.

"No, thanks. Let's go."

"Got your ID? You'll need it with that cute baby face." They pinch my cheek and I scowl.

Jordie shoots me a vaguely apologetic look for what feels like a dig about my face. I know they didn't intend it that way. I've vented to them enough about my angst over appearing younger than I am. How I sometimes worry that I'll never pass as a man, even though a big part of me recoils from even wanting that. They spent a solid hour of our study time earlier today assuring me that if that's my goal, I can make it happen given enough time and patience.

"Not a comment on your age, just that you're a cutie, but you still need ID if you want to get into the club," Jordie assures me.

"I've got it, yeah." I bat their hand away, then pat the wallet in my pocket.

My aunts took me to the DMV to get a US driver's license after the first weekend I visited them now that I'm living here, to make life simpler. If only I'd dared to dress like this for the picture. It's weird adjusting to the fact that here in Boston I'm only old enough to drink since my birthday last night. I've been legal drinking age for years back home in Montreal.

It's also weird that I'm closer to Jordie's age than most of the other first- and second-year students I have classes with. I've always been on the older side for my grade with my fall birthday. Now, after completing three years of CEGEP back home for my dual focus music and social sciences certification, that extra bit of maturity compared to my year-mates seems even more pronounced. The US is subtly weird in lots of little ways, but it's still weird to wrap my head around how similar it is to home too.

"I'm ready."

"Perfect." Jordie steps into a pair of sky-high heels that I'm sure a pop diva would be envious of, like it's nothing to go dancing on stilts. I'm enamored of their grace, just like I am about everything else Jordie-related.

I tug on my worn pair of rainbow-checkered Vans. Just as we're about to leave the safe bubble of their apartment, Jordie turns to me. In the narrow entryway, our faces are inches apart, even with our height difference exaggerated by their shoes. My breath hitches. Jordie's eyes search my face. I lean in, lips parted, hoping. Is this the moment where Jordie sees me as relationship material?

"Time to let the world see you shine, Ray." Jordie kisses me, a soft—platonic—peck on the cheek. Right where they pinched me earlier, and I'm half tempted to pull them closer, turn my face and kiss their lips. Smudge their carefully applied lipstick and skip the club altogether. But Jordie grabs my hand and pulls me out the door, locking it behind us and leading me toward the edge of campus.

We hop a bus and get out at a stop a few blocks away. Even though I feel completely different in my binder and with my new hair, no one gives me a second glance. They're all too wrapped up in their own lives or their phones to pay us any mind. I breathe easier once it seems clear no one is going to bother us.

Until I have to show my ID and the bouncer looks between me and the picture of a long-haired girl for an agonizingly endless moment. Am I imagining his sneer? Probably. This is a queer club with drag queens and everything.

I let out a relieved breath when he stamps our hands and lets us enter the dimly lit club. It's loud inside. Raucous music, a thumping beat. Colored lights strobe to the beat. I can feel the anxiety creeping in on me, but Jordie wraps an arm around my shoulders and steers me to their friends. Six students sit crowded around a table that's barely big enough for all of them. They turn to face us when Jordie greets them. Four of them are white like Jordie and me, the other two are a big Black man and a willowy Latina. They all somehow shift around to make room for us to join them.

"Listen up, this is Ray, and he's our brand new baby queer. So you're all going to make him feel at home tonight, right?" Jordie levels their serious look at their friends as they propel me toward the crowded table.

"Hey, baby!" The woman closest to me waves and pushes out a chair next to her with one stiletto heel. She taps her fingers on the backrest with a welcoming flourish. I can't help noticing the long, teal lacquered nails on all but two of their elegant tawny-skinned fingers. When the probable reasons for that nail configuration occur to me, I have to duck my head to hide my embarrassed flush. "Jordie told us they were bringing us a new baby gay. Sit and tell us about you. I'm Celeste, she/her. This guy next to me is Abe; he's Bella's boyfriend. Our Jords told you we're here to watch Bella Donna's stage debut tonight, right?"

Abe is the burly Black guy in a tight Northeastern t-shirt under a denim jacket that strains against his bulk when he lifts a hand to wave at me.

"Yeah. She's a drag queen, right?" I nod and wave back at Abe.

"That's right. And when Queen Donna is out of drag, he goes by Keith." Celeste smiles at me. "My girlfriend, Pixel, is performing tonight too, but it's not her first rodeo."

I sit hesitantly. Jordie stands behind me, their hands on my shoulders while Celeste goes around the rest of the circle making introductions. Jordie's touch is reassuring. I'm not sure that I wouldn't head for the hills at the onslaught of unfamiliar names and faces if they weren't pinning me to my seat.

Jacob is the pale emo rockstar type with the movie star smile. Kale is the lanky blonde with the nerdy glasses who keeps giving Jacob puppy dog eyes. Sheila is pretty and curvy and a little tipsy already. She keeps pawing at Lio, the shortest of the group, who keeps gently redirecting Sheila's hands off their lap and back to her glass of water. I'm not sure if that's a lack of interest on Lio's part or an abundance of concern for their tipsy friend. They don't seem put off by the touching either way.

"Jords, you didn't tell us he's so cute! I could eat that scrumptious little morsel right up." Jacob, dressed in shades of black from his shoes to his shoulder-length hair, gives me an appreciative once over.

Even though Jordie warned me he's a flirt, Jacob's obvious interest sends a thrill down my spine. He's devouring me with his eyes. He extends a hand toward me across the table, more like he's showing off his own tidily manicured nails—painted black, of course—than like he wants to shake.

"Um, hi?" I say as I tentatively take his hand.

"Jacob. Charmed to meet you, dear heart," he introduces himself, even though Celeste already did that.

Jacob grips my fingers and squeezes. He holds eye contact and tugs my hand toward him until I hitch up against the table. It seems like he was considering planting a gallantly over-the-top kiss on the back of my hand until the table got in the way. I laugh as I pull my hand back. No wonder Jordie warned me about him coming on too strong. It comes off as playfully smarmy, and Jacob winks at me as Jordie loops a protective arm around my shoulders.

"Behave, Jacob," Jordie chides their friend. Then they lean in closer to me, their arm a comforting warmth around me. I like how much that anchoring touch makes me feel like I belong here with their other friends. "Will you be okay if I leave you here for a second to grab us some drinks before the show starts?"

"Um, sure." I glance up at them, my eyes pleading for them not to leave me alone even as my mouth betrays me.

"Perfect, what's your poison?" Jordie is so cute when they smile, it distracts me from the question.

"Huh?" I stare at them, mind racing with all the possible hidden meanings my answer could reveal about me. My cousin back home has all kinds of theories about what it means when you ask someone to get you a drink. She's turned the art of being bought drinks into a well-rehearsed spiel. And come to that, is Jordie offering to buy my drink? Is this a flirty gesture, or is it more of them looking out for me like my fairy-god-queer?

"Rum and coke?" I ask, because it's easy and the sweet soda will mostly cover the taste of booze. I'm overthinking what my drink choice says about me. Drink orders aren't actually some convoluted Cosmo quiz with the power to reveal my entire fate with Jordie, right?

"Coming right up, sunshine." Jordie kisses my cheek and gives my shoulders one last reassuring squeeze. Then they head to the bar, shimmying through the throng. I watch them go, trying not to lust after the way my friend's sparkly leggings frame their sexy ass. They're my first and only friend here. I shouldn't complicate things with a crush. Jacob interrupts my poorly concealed ogling with a snort.

"Don't go getting ideas. They're nice to everyone, *sunshine*," Jacob teases. His tone on the nickname I've been treasuring isn't mean, but it's not nice either.

"Knock it off, Jacob." Celeste gestures sharply with her long pointy nails. Jacob rolls his eyes, but he sips from his pink cocktail and turns toward the stage, clearly not looking to pick a fight.

"Jordie's nice to everyone because they're a genuinely nice person. You could crush on worse." Celeste cuts her eyes toward Jacob and Kale mercilessly as she pats the back of my hand. Kale—who has been watching Jacob with the same naked longing that gave away my interest in Jordie—hunches his shoulders and grumbles something I can't quite hear into his beer. So I guess I'm not the only one here with an unrequited crush on someone else at the table.

"Is this show starting soon, or what?" Jacob gestures toward the stage with his cup. Like he's hoping the performance will save him from having to confront whatever is going on—or not going on—between him and Kale.

Celeste shakes her head disparagingly at the two of them.

I get the idea that Celeste is only mostly joking about Jacob being a worse target for my puppy love crush. She's so matter-of-fact about my crush on Jordie, it's less mortifying to be so transparent about it that everyone here noticed I'm into Jordie within five seconds of meeting me. Except presumably Jordie.

Unless Jordie can tell too and is ignoring it to let us both save face. That's a bucket of cold water over all my warm fuzzies about tonight. I sigh. It doesn't matter since there's no way I'm acting on my attraction.

The show should start soon, but I'm surprised when it turns out they actually stick to the schedule at this venue. I'm used to delayed starts back home. Darren's ex always jokes that you can't rush royalty. The last notes of a Baelfire song that's been hovering in the top 100 all summer fade from the speakers, replaces by an emcee.

They announce the lineup of drag artists who are about to take the stage as Jordie makes their way back through the throng of dancers with our drinks. They set both cups on the table in front of me, then Celeste pulls them down onto her lap to watch the show.

Celeste notices me staring and winks at me. "Our Jordie is a cuddler and we're out of seats."

I watch Jordie settle into sitting comfortably in their friend's lap and wish it was me they were spending the show cuddled up with. It's just as well that the drag show is starting. I need something to distract me from watching the way Jordie's smile lights up their entire face when a song they like plays. I'm enraptured with the performance, but I can't help stealing glances at Jordie. I love how uninhibited they are as they tip their head back to whoop and cheer for Pixel along with Celeste. The spitfire of a drag artist takes the stage. Pixel steals the show with a commanding song and dance routine, but Bella Donna is good too.

The both work the crowd expertly. I get swept up in the excitement, roaring the chorus back to them when they hold the mic out to us on their suggestive closing number. It's a great show, and a perfect way to get to know new friends without too much pressure. I have an amazing time, and for once, I don't feel lonely and alone in a crowd. It's like a glimpse of who I can be when there is nothing left to hide.

Chapter Nine

Jordie

We linger after the drag show until last call, drinking toast after toast to Keith and Pixel's performance. When the club closes, Pixel and Celeste head home, both of them entirely ready to take Pixel's post-show buzz behind closed doors. So I won't be going home anytime soon if I don't want an earful of my roommates fucking.

It's just as well that the rest of my friends aren't ready to call it a night; that means I have company to stay out. Plus, it's a perfect excuse to spend more time with Ray. We bring our little after party down the street to our favorite diner. I arrange it so that I'm next to Ray. I walk a little too close to him, a boisterous joy bubbling up inside me every time his arm bumps against mine as he talks with my friends. His accent comes out more when he's tipsy and I hang on his every enchanting word.

Randy's is open all night, and it serves the best middle of the night breakfast in town. Or at the very least, the queerest. The place is popular, even in the wee hours. It's a Friday night, so we have to wait for the staff to clear a big enough table for our group, even though it's normally seat yourself.

I recognize a table of regulars who usually sit by themselves in what we affectionately call the writer's corner, all tapping away at their computers. In deference to the crowd, they've consolidated at one table tonight, though it's relatively recent for a sprinkling of scene kids to be sitting with the writers.

Archibald is holding court at the counter by the register, telling anyone who will listen that his dirigible is going to be ready any day now. A group of theater nerds are standing at their table doing some sort of dramatic reenactment.

Ray crowds closer to me, staring wide-eyed at the bright chrome and neon interior—not to mention the visibly queer clientele and staff. I flash him a reassuring smile and quash the urge to touch him. He grins at me, then goes back to feasting his eyes on the diner. I follow his gaze to one of the corner booths. From the amount of leather and collars visible at one of the large corner booths, there might have been some sort of kinky event earlier in the evening too.

I watch as one person at that table hooks a forefinger through the D-ring on another's collar and hauls them closer for a rough kiss. That's my cur to glance away from the sensual display and scan the dining room for friendly faces. I recognize a few other folks from the drag show and wave at them as they stand nearby to wait for a table.

Ray smiles and strikes up a conversation with one of them in rapidfire French that's hard for me to follow. But it's fine, because I'm a bit smitten watching Ray get all animated at the little auditory taste of home. I know he's been missing his family and Montreal. I'm glad Randy's is giving him a sense of connection to his language community as well as a queer safe space.

I try to pick out what Ray and his new friend are saying, but I only catch every fourth or fifth word. The conversation ends when Ray's new friend's companions pull them away to join their group at a table near the front window.

"New friend?" I ask, trying to act nonchalant.

"Yeah, Claude. They're new to the city too. And they've got family ties to the same tiny town in Québec as my grand-père Gagnon."

"Oh, that's cool." I force a smile.

I'm not jealous, precisely. I just don't want to be left behind so soon after connecting with Ray. Anyone I mentor outgrowing me is always going to feel like a *when*, not an *if* because of Nell. She's the reason I can't shake the sense that any friends I make early in their queer journey are inevitably going to discard our friendship the moment I'm no longer useful.

It's hard to hide my hurt over that future betrayal. Ray shifts uncomfortably from foot to foot in front of me. Ugh, I should be the bigger person here.

"You should get their number to stay in touch," I suggest.

"Oh, uh, I guess? Could be nice to have another Boston Francophone to chat with. I've got my aunts for that already though. Anyway, I'm going to run to the washroom," Ray mumbles. He points before making a beeline to the all-gender bathrooms off to the left.

I stare after him as it dawns on me that he didn't dare to go at the club. He has stuck to my side like glue all night, but that is no less than I expected when I let the little baby queer imprint on me. Encouraged him to open up to me faster than I usually let in new friends, if I'm honest. Ray stepping into himself is a constant temptation to forget all my rules for protecting my heart.

I feel a pang of guilt for not realizing Ray might not be comfortable going to the men's room just yet while we were at the club. At least Randy's makes it easy to go without stressing over which door will be least likely to result in an unpleasant confrontation.

I snort cynically at the idea of going to the bathroom being some twisted version of a vintage TV game show. Behind this door is an entire ass who might take a swing at you. Wouldn't be the first time. Well, now that I suspect Ray is getting self-conscious about it, I can pass along which buildings on campus and local businesses have the best all-gender facilities.

I can't tear my eyes off him as he navigates between the crowded tables. I'm all swoony over him, but he's just so damn cute. Seeing him like this, with the confidence to step into the world as himself with just the barest amount of support and hand-holding is satisfying. Ray makes it easier to ignore my usual misgivings about blurring the lines of friendship with a newly out person.

"You've been awfully quiet tonight; what did you think of my show?" Keith jars me out of my thoughts about Ray. I'm getting overly attached, but that's a problem for another day. Tonight, I'm supposed to be supporting Keith after his first drag show, not obsessing over a crush I'm not planning to act upon.

Keith bats his long, artificial lashes at me as we wait for a seat. He drops his head onto my shoulder and pouts up at me, waiting for the praise that is his due.

"You were radiant, darling." I shove him off my shoulder, grimacing at the wet patch that his sweat-damp short hair leaves on my favorite blouse. His hair is a mess from the wig he wore earlier, his cheeks still flushed from the rush of performing.

Keith took off his costume and most of his makeup before we left the club, but he's still positively glowing from the high of being on stage. Smokey liner and vibrantly silver shadow still accent his eyes.

"Thank you, do go on." Keith weaves his fingers together and props his chin on them to bat his outrageous false lashes at me some more.

"Your outfit was on point, the set list was stellar, and you slayed the moves. You know it was perfection." I humor his insecurity about the show by repeating the same litany of praise from the first time he asked back at the club.

Keith did great. Sure, there were a few minor hiccups. A song where Bella Donna garbled a verse and a nail-biting moment when it looked like her wig might topple off her head during a particularly energetic dance sequence, but overall she was dazzling.

"Mhm, go on..." Keith gestures for me to keep talking, twirling his fingers in front of him.

"Ask your boyfriend if you want to be bathed in flattery, you insatiable man." I laugh, shaking my head at him.

"Are you being a pest, Keith?" Abe pulls his diminutive boyfriend back against his chest and nuzzles into his sweaty hair.

"Of course not, Abraham, I would never." Keith cranes his neck to look up at Abe and flutter those pretty lashes at a more susceptible target. Abe snorts, wise to Keith's flirtations.

"Of course you would. We all loved your show. Now, be a good boy and stop fishing for compliments if you want your reward later."

Keith licks his lips and nods. He pivots the conversation. "Your new boy is adorable, Jordie. Wherever did you find him?"

"You know that psych class I didn't want to take?" I remind him, since he missed the introductions earlier.

We've talked about Ray before. According to Celeste, he's all I talk about lately, but I just like him. He takes his classes seriously and helps me to focus on mine when we meet up for our standing study dates after our psych lectures.

That's another way he isn't like so many other folks I've handheld through coming out or early transition goals. Ray and I talk about other things than how I can make his transition easier for him.

"Yeah?" Keith prompts me with a knowing smile. He's bait-ing me into rambling about my crush, and I can't even bring myself to be mad about it.

"Well, he fell into my lap while trying to sit next to me. Literally landed right in my clutches, all awkward and sweet."

"And you just had to take him in like a stray puppy?" Keith teases.

"I'd give your puppy a bone anytime, Jords." Jacob gestures lewdly, in case any of us are unclear about his meaning. His played up interest in Ray stirs up my protective instincts.

"Don't make him uncomfortable, Jacob." I wag a finger at him. Jacob playfully snaps his teeth at me. It doesn't help my mood that he's obnoxiously hot. I saw Ray staring at him across the table with all the usual awestruck signs of being addled by Jacob's charm and good looks.

"You mean back off because you've got dibs?" Jacob flicks his eyes over me, like he's sizing up the competition.

His gaze makes me uncomfortable, mostly because Ray isn't a prize to be won and even the implication otherwise makes my stomach squirm. And maybe a little because it's obvious which of us is more conventionally attractive if we were competing over a crush.

Jacob looks like he could be a rockstar. By contrast, I'm drab. My dyed black hair is in desperate need of a trim and retouch to the color, ashy brown roots growing out and the tips frizzy. My eyes are a boring muddy brown, my cheekbones are too sharp, my lips too thin, my nose too long. And that isn't even getting into my bigger issues with my body. Hips too narrow, shoulders too broad, all my softness is in all the wrong places, padding my middle.

I shift my shoulders, subtly reminding myself of the breast forms that fill out my flowery blouse and make me feel pretty. Sure, it would be nice if I had more of a chest, but store-bought works too. Maybe someday I'll have my own curves to work but that doesn't help me right now. Tonight I opted for a larger pair of falsies, a little extra helping to fill out my shirt. And I didn't miss Ray's eyes surreptitiously all over me earlier.

Bad Jordie, no crushing on the baby. Even if he is my age because his school system makes no sense. His accent makes me swoony too. Especially when he remembers to drop his voice to that lower register that has my silky panties fitting too tight. Ugh.

"No, I mean he's still figuring out who he is and what he wants; he doesn't need you playing with his heart." And he doesn't need his first queer friend at university perving on him either. I need to keep things platonic. With me and all of my friends.

"Last I checked, he's an adult who can decide for himself what he wants. And if he does want me, he'll know the score before we fuck. I'm not a total asshole." Jacob rolls his eyes at me. "You're clearly both into each other anyway, so it's a moot point."

"Oh look, Zo's waving us over to our seats!" Sheila chirps, interrupting before I can get into it with Jacob or deny my interest in Ray. Sheila waves back at Zo, bouncing in place. The movement makes her scowl and aggressively adjust her bra before starting across the diner to the corner booth that's ready for us.

Lio trails after Sheila, smiling indulgently as they gently steady their bestie when Sheila veers off course. She's totally wasted and it will be good for her to get some water and delicious diner food in her stomach.

I peruse the specials board as we walk to our seats. I skim right on past Neve's caramel crunch protein balls and narrow in on Kit's contribution to the seasonal dessert offerings. This week they've got a pumpkin spice tiramisu that sounds divine. And if it's like any of Kit's other innovations, it's going to be pure decadence.

I'm drooling already. And that's before Ray steps out of the restroom, still looking just as mouthwateringly handsome as when we left my place hours ago. I wave him over as he turns, eyes darting around the room like he's afraid we ditched him.

"We're over here," Jacob calls across the busy diner like the giant putz he's being tonight, hand raised in a wave.

Ray's face lights up in a relieved grin when our eyes meet across the room. My heart skips a beat at the sight of him, more of that giddy joy at being his focus bubbling up inside me. Ray makes his way over to us, weaving around the tables to slide in next to me. I try to act casual about how I totally arranged it that way.

"Do you all know what you want?" Zo asks once he's seated, their pen poised over their order pad. Tonight, the pronoun pin on her apron reads she/them. Her teal hair matches the

50s pinup girl dress with a flared skirt. They smile, watching us expectantly.

"Coffee, bring the entire pot," Sheila makes grabby hands. "Please?"

"Sure thing, doll. I'll bring over a carafe. How many mugs?" Zo counts as we all raise our hands.

"Magic bean juice all around, gotcha." Zo winks. "What else?"

"The usual," Sheila gestures toward Lio. "And whatever they're having is on my tab."

Zo goes around the table collecting our orders.

"Is there any more of Kit's pumpkin tiramisu?" I ask. Sometimes they run out of the more popular specials.

"Plenty. You'll love it. My kiddo is officially obsessed with the stuff since Kit tested it on the staff last week." Zo's smile brightens, looking more genuine when they talk about her kid.

"She's got good taste."

"The best." Zo nods and turns to Ray. "You're a new face; what can I get for you?"

"Umm." Ray's gaze flies over the menu. "Don't suppose I can get fries with cheese and gravy?"

"Marty can do an alright off menu poutine, but it's shredded mozzarella, not curds. That alright?" Zo gives him a sympathetic smile. "Need a minute longer while I go grab the coffee?"

"No, I'll be fine with the shredded cheese, thank you." Ray flashes her a relieved smile as Zo tucks away their order pad.

"Coming right up. I'll be back with your drinks," she tells the table at large.

"Ray!" Keith leans into Ray's space as soon as Zo leaves, eager to solicit more attention. "What did you think of my show?"

"You were wonderful," Ray says, totally earnest.

Keith grins and leans back against Abe's side, basking in the praise.

Jacob lobs a napkin at Keith. "Stop digging for compliments, oh vain one, we all saw you being brilliant. Let's hear more about Ray. What are you studying?"

Ray squirms in his seat at the interrogation as all my friends lob questions at him. He answers easily enough about his plans to help queer youth, but I can't help feeling some kind of way when he scoots closer to me on the booth's bench seat. As if I might protect him from my friends' overzealous interest. I might be reading into things, but I enjoy being his safe space to shelter from the spotlight.

Chapter Ten

Ray

"What can I get you, doll?" Our purple-haired server slides into the booth next to me.

Their blouse matches their hair. I'm almost certain their nametag said Zo last time we were here with Jordie's friends. And over the weekend when I came for brunch with my aunts, but today it reads Orchid. The purple enamel pin next to it on their vest says they/them. Come to think of it, I think their hair was teal last week too. Huh.

Jordie bats their lashes playfully from across the table. Their eyes dart to the nametag. "What's good today, Orchid?"

Orchid lean conspiratorially close and Jordie mirrors them, forearms on the table, clasped hands inches away from my place setting. Orchid winks at us, a twinkle in their eyes. "Not Neve's Paleo kelp noodle stir-fry, but don't tell her I said that. Her pizza chicken yesterday wasn't half bad."

"Pizza chicken?" I repeat, unsure I'm understanding correctly. Chicken on pizza seems remarkably normal compared to kelp noodles.

"Mhm." Orchid nods. "Basically what it sounds like. It's a pizza, but instead of a crust, she pounded a chicken filet flat and pan-fried it. Low carb and gluten-free."

Jordie and I exchange looks. That is not something I would have thought of, but it doesn't sound half bad. Kelp noodles on the other hand... I'll pass on that.

"Um, want to split an appetizer sampler?" I ask. It was delicious when Jacob ordered that and foisted his food on everyone the other night, but I'm not sure I can handle an entire order on my own.

"Sure, that sounds good." Jordie sets aside their menu and smiles at me before addressing Orchid. "We'll get the sampler plate to share, and I'll have a milkshake. Strawberry, please, Orchid. Plus whatever else Ray wants, and one check, it's on me."

"Coming right up." Orchid turns their bright customer service smile toward me. "Can I get you a drink too, doll?"

I flush at the pet name even though it's probably what Orchid calls all the customers they don't know.

"Coffee, please."

"Great, I'll be right back with that. Cream and sugar are just there." Orchid jabs her pen toward the little bowl of coffee fixings, then tucks their pen behind their ear as they stand to collect our menus. Their retro skirt flounces as they walk away. Leaving me alone, sitting across from my crush at a restaurant.

This isn't a date. Maybe if I tell myself that enough I'll stop feeling so awkward and nervous.

Well, maybe it is a *study* date, but that's not the same thing at all. We were supposed to be meeting two of our psych 101 classmates to cram for the first exam. Except they bailed at the last minute so it's just me and Jordie pulling out our notes and the study guide the prof posted.

"So, you were saying you needed to brush up on the last few lectures?" Jordie prompts me when I spend too long arranging and rearranging my notes in front of me to avoid awkward eye contact. My brain is putting way too much emphasis on the date part of study date now. It feels like we're starting to be real friends who go out and do fun things together. Like the arboretum, shopping, and drag night. Date type things.

They rest cool fingers on the back of my hand to stop me from straightening my notes for the third time. I glance up and Jordie is smiling at me, their head cocked and eyes full of warmth for an overall expression somewhere between bemused and reassuring. I take a deep breath, yeah, okay, I need to chill. This is just like the dozens of other times we've met up to study this semester.

"Yeah. Sorry, I might be getting too in my head about exams? Test anxiety. Also, I guess I'm just not getting how they got some of these experiments past ethical review panels."

"Well, I mean, most of them didn't have much in the way of ethical oversight until the 1950s, and even then, it was only because enough people got mad."

Orchid comes back over with our drinks, pouring steaming hot coffee into my mug and sliding Jordie's milkshake in front of them. Jordie thanks them by name and nudges my foot under the table so that I do the same. Orchid beams at us and tells us our food will be right out. I raise my brows in question and Jordie leans across the table, waiting until Orchid is out of earshot to explain.

"What's up? I swear they were going by a different name last time we were here."

Jordie nods. "Yeah, they typically default to Zo and she/them. But they've been experimenting with names and pronouns for a while now. Trying on different combinations to see how they fit."

"Oh." Like me. Except I agonized over what name to change to for ages before finally settling on Ray.

Even then, the first time I actually said it aloud to another soul was with Jordie. Because I had it in my head that once I let the new name slip past my lips, it would be stamped indelibly onto my soul. No going back or changing it. Which, in retrospect, seems silly. If I can change it once, I can change it again. But it felt huge and I'm attached to the name after years of using it in my head. Plus, it sounds so good when Jordie calls me Ray.

Orchid seemed so happy when we both used their name, so maybe there's something to be said for getting a feel for how a name fits before committing.

Jordie takes a sip of their milkshake and I can't help staring at them as they purse their lips and suck. "Mhm, they don't like that one; it'll be different by dinner shift."

"Huh? How can you tell?" I thought Orchid seemed happy.

"Their smile didn't reach their eyes. Mark my words, Orchid isn't the one." Jordie grins at me like we're sharing a secret. "Anyway, mind if I move over beside you so all this isn't upside down for one of us? Might make sharing the food easier too."

Do I mind having them squished in close? Uh, not by a long shot. It's a toss up whether that will be better for curbing my horny thoughts compared to sitting facing them as they suck their thick milkshake through their straw. Ugh. I'm doomed to having half my focus on keeping my attraction to myself either way.

"Um, sure, plenty of room," I pat the vinyl beside me and slide a little further down the booth.

"Cool, grab anything you need from your bag and I'll stick it over here out of the way?" Jordie reaches for my school bag. I dutifully remove a couple of extra pencils and paper, then hand it over.

Jordie settles in beside me with a happy wiggle and a sigh. "Much better," they grin as they turn their pile of study materials to face us both. We go back to comparing notes on our study guides while we wait for our food.

I guzzle my coffee every time Jordie's flirty energy gets too intense, trying to mask how flustered their focus makes me. Which happens often. They have this way of leaning in close and casually touching me. Their finger brushes my hand as they point to a line on the printout of key topics I'm filling out. Their knee bumps into mine when I hand them my notebook to ask if they caught a section I missed when my pencil broke in the middle of a lecture.

"It was last Wednesday, when we were talking about Freud versus Erikson?" I point to the missing lines where I left space to fill in the gaps.

Jordie barks a laugh, then winks at me. "Oh, Freud? He's a mess. I mean, you want to talk about psychosexual stuff, what's with men's clothing overcompensating for cis dudes' natal lack of—ahem—pockets, right?"

"Oh my gosh, yes!" I agree with a startled laugh.

It's so true. The new pants we got together have pockets big enough to swallow my entire forearm. My phone and wallet both fit comfortably, a feat unheard of with the pants I had before, let alone the skin-tight leggings and skirts Jordie wears most days.

Maybe the psychosexual model of development got debunked, but it sure feels like everything has a subconscious sexual undercurrent right now. That might have more to do with the fact I'm sitting thigh to thigh with this vibrantly delightful person I want desperately to kiss.

"I'm pretty sure he said that line from the study guide word for word at the end of last Thursday's lecture, just a second." They flip through their notes and nudge the page between us. I lean in to read what they jotted down. Jordie has really pretty handwriting, which is distracting.

I reach to tuck my hair behind my ear, only to remember that it's short now. At the last second, I change the gesture to rub at the back of my head instead. The velvet softness of my short hair sends a thrilled jolt of remembrance through me. I have a guy's haircut now. Thanks to Jordie—the first person to see me as the guy I am. Warmth unfurls in my chest at that reminder, how can I help liking them when they make me feel so right?

"Here." Jordie taps their notes. "Our prof was just outlining their theories of development and comparing them."

They nudge the page closer, leaning into my space to point at the lines in question. I lean in too. With us both bent over their notebook, I can feel their breath hot on my cheek. It's so absurdly intimate to huddle over the same papers together, our knees bumping.

It's so easy to picture other reasons for getting this close to each other. All of them have me aching to turn my face for a kiss that surely wouldn't be reciprocated. Soon, I'm gulping imaginary sips from my empty cup and wishing I had more coffee and more charisma.

"Sorry to interrupt, but your food's ready." Zo—Orchid no longer written on their nametag in magenta dry-eraser—interrupts my horny thoughts about Jordie with their return.

The smudged out letters have been replaced with Kal. The pronoun pin next to it remains unchanged. They slide our brimming platter of appetizers in front of us, along with a stack of extra napkins. I'm not really surprised that Jordie was right about them not loving the name Orchid. They have a way of seeing people that I envy.

"Thanks, Kal," Jordie says. "Orchid wasn't doing it for you?"

Kal scrunches their nose. "Nope. Destiny suggested it, so I

promised the kiddo I'd give it a try, but it's too fancy and floral for me. Maybe she can name her kitten that."

"Are you caving on the kitten?" Jordie asks, reaching for a fry.

"Maybe for her birthday. Mom suggested putting the litter box in the weird little nook by the balcony, so they're wearing me down. Who knew Grandma would side with the kid?" Kal chuckles as they roll their eyes. They jut their chin at the notes we've spread across the table. "Anyway, how are classes going?"

"Good. We can clear out after we eat if you need us to." Jordie gestures at our stuff spreading across the table.

"Pshaw." Kal waves them away. "Please, you're fine. It's quiet this time of day, no worries. Stay as long as you like."

"Thanks. Can you drop off a carafe of coffee when you get a chance? Ray keeps sighing into his empty mug." Jordie nudges me playfully. Their fingers on my elbow send a zing right through me.

I flush at the realization they noticed I've been out of a coffee for a while. And I keep forgetting and lifting it to my lips to hide my awkwardness around them. Like a total loser. I feel my face heating, and I take another frazzled sip of nothing. Real smooth. I hunch in my seat. Jordie shakes their head at me, lips pinched tight like they're trying to suppress a smile, but don't want to rub in my utter lack of anything approaching chill.

"Sure, be right back with more coffee. Do you want another mug or a refill on the shake?" Kal smiles between the two of us and points at Jordie's almost empty glass.

Jordie looks chagrinned. "Can I split the difference and get a coffee shake next, Kal?"

"Sure thing." Kal flounces away again.

"Dig in." Jordie passes me one of the tiny plates that Kal left on the table next to the food for us. I take mine and watch as they fill their plate. Until Jordie glances up at me, with a defensive hunch to their shoulders. "What?"

"Nothing." I squeak, voice going up an octave. That makes me wince. My voice is too high by half most of the time without nerves making it weird. I reach for some of the fried pickles and onion rings that are calling my name. It will be harder to be awkward if I've got my mouth stuffed.

Oh fuck, and now I'm thinking of what parts of their anatomy I'd love for Jordie to stuff into my mouth. Or other orifices. Do they even top? I shouldn't ask them that.

I mean, I know for sure they have a dick after changing in their room with them the other night. As if that wasn't clear after my accidental bout of sitting in their lap the day we met. But... ugh. No. Nope. Not thinking about my friend's genitals and what they like to do with them.

"You good, sunshine?" Jordie is watching me with concern.

"Yeah. Totally. So good. Um. Just nervous. About the test. Obviously." I laugh like a weirdo.

Jordie pats my shoulder. "You're going to do fine. Is this your first university midterm?"

"Yeah." I nod, swallowing down the lump in my throat. I really am nervous about that.

CEGEP was so different from high school and then coming

here has been different in new and not so exciting ways all over again. It's a whole new world to navigate and I'm not sure if I'm really cut out for this. Huge impersonal lecture halls and proctored exams where I barely know my professors and just—it's a lot.

Jordie is the only reason I'm not totally overwhelmed and considering calling my folks to get me a one-way plane ticket home. I don't want to give up. It's just harder being away from home than I thought it would be.

Even if this fresh start was exactly what I needed to feel comfortable being myself. The anonymity that makes me feel small and insignificant in this city and my new school also makes it feel safe to be myself with Jordie.

Jordie has somehow become my safe space in the short time I've known them. I don't want to lose their friendship by giving up and going home. Which means I need to prove to myself that I can handle the stress and the rigorous academics and all of this.

Jordie slides even closer in the booth. Their thigh presses against mine and it's like I can feel their body heat searing into me. I have to close my eyes against all the other ways I want them to touch me as they rub a comforting circle on my back.

"We are going to ace this test, Ray. Let's go over the entire study guide and then we can do my flashcards before we focus on the areas where you've been struggling. Sound good?"

"You made flashcards?" I turn to look at them, which puts a little space between us so I can clear my head of pointless fantasies.

"Yep, it's my not so secret weapon." Jordie nods and plucks up a fry to gesture with before dipping it into the dregs of their milkshake. "Usually just writing out all the main points is enough to get them to stick in my head, but they're good for reviewing too."

I grab another fried pickle as I nod. "Mhm, sounds good." I take my time chewing as I shuffle through my notes for the study guide. They wink at me, shuffling closer on the bench seat to share their stack of flashcards, our knees bumping under the table. Neither of us moves away.

Their body heat is a warm flush along my skin, making me acutely aware of their presence beside me. I'm not imagining them flirting; except what if I am and I make things weird by reciprocating something that isn't really there? Nope. Better to shove my crush way down deep inside, where it will never see the light of day.

Jordie wraps their lips around their fry to lick creamy milk-shake off the tip. They have to realize how suggestive that looks, right? I feel myself flushing hot at the sexy sight. I'm sorely tempted to harken back to our earlier banter and throw out a cheesy pickup line about them being welcome in my *pockets* any day. Except I'm way too much of a chicken to flirt so outrageously.

I've got plenty of practice with keeping my personal crap to myself. For all that I cut my hair and changed my wardrobe, my parents still don't know I'm trans. Not because I think they'll freak out or anything. Just, I can't count how many times Mom told me how badly they both wanted a little girl after my three older brothers. The last thing I want to do is disappoint them.

"Help me finish these?" Jordie suggests, dabbing at their mouth with their napkin and nudging the plate of fries closer to me.

"Sure, thanks." I take one, but my mouth goes dry as I watch Jordie drag another fry through their drink. "This place has the best fries. And pie, and coffee, and basically everything I've tried so far." I'm rambling and I know it, but I can't tear my eyes off Jordie's mouth. Their lips wrapped around the cream-covered fry. It's impossible to stop musing about how it would feel to kiss them. "But you know, I've been wondering, who's Randy?"

"Definitely Jacob." Jordie winks, another shake-laden fry halfway to their lips. "But Celeste swears she met the actual Randy at a ballroom event a couple of her high school friends invited her to attend at Boston GLASS. She says Randy is a local chapter house father in the ballroom scene. She says he owns the diner along with his sister and her wife."

"Oh, cool. So he's a dancer?" I ask, still distracted by the sight of Jordie licking the dripping milkshake from their fry.

"Something like that." Jordie gives me a lopsided grin. "Ballroom as in the origins of drag, not like stuffy straight dance competitions, just to be clear. And Boston GLASS is a queer community center for Black and Latinx youth. So, if Celeste's right, Randy is all about creating safe spaces for the queer community to flourish."

"That fits the vibe." I nod. Then I cram more fries into my

mouth to keep from blurting out an ill-advised corny pick up line. Some nonsense about vibes and how watching them eat has got me envious of a pile of fries.

I shouldn't let my hopeless crush distract me from my goals. I've long since given up on ever living up to my older siblings' academic examples. It seems like they've always known who they are and what they want while I floundered through school. At least I finally settled on a career path, even if counseling troubled teens isn't quite as fancy and well paid as their prestigious careers: doctor, lawyer, and engineer.

Northeastern is as far as I've let myself dream. A place far from home, where I can figure out who I am before I have to figure out how to tell my folks I was never their precious little girl. I know that's not the only thing my family loves about me, but internalizing that it's the best way I stand out from my brothers is a factor in my fear of coming out to my family. If I do well here, it might soften the blow of telling them I'm a boy.

While I'm dwelling on my family, Jordie finishes the last few fries. I'm too busy stress eating all the other fried deliciousness to worry about that. My stomach is roiling with nerves over the test, and how much pressure I'm putting on myself to get good grades this year to make up for not being the girl my folks expect me to be.

"So, do you want to read the first question?" Jordie nudges me, and my acute awareness of how close we're sitting has my mind straying right back to horny thoughts about them.

I have no business wondering about how Jordie likes to fuck.

Even if they offered to take me to an adult store to find a packer when I mentioned feeling weird with the loose drape of my new boxer briefs. And how the men's pants they helped me shop for fit me funny in the front. For now, I've still got a rolled up sock safety pinned to the front of my underwear to help with the fit issue, but that lack still makes me self-conscious.

"Hey, are you listening?" Jordie interrupts me before I can get too far down the rabbit hole of how awkward a visit to the sex shop with my crush would be.

"Sorry. No. I got distracted." I flush and squirm at the idea of browsing sex toys with them.

Jordie rolls their eyes at me, but they repeat the study question. We alternate asking and answering the rest of the questions on the study guide as we demolish the sampler platter. In the end, there's only a few sad crumbs and soggy nachos left when Kal comes to clear away our plates.

We work our way through Jordie's flashcards for the next hour. They weren't joking when they said they knew this stuff. I have to go through the deck a few times before the stack of cards that have me stumped dwindles to almost nothing. Jordie explains the more difficult concepts with an eternal patience that makes it easy to see why they're planning to take on injustice and tilt at windmills as an attorney. I can picture that same dogged conviction serving them well in fighting for minority rights.

Their constant upbeat encouragement settles my nerves about the exam. It isn't doing a damn thing to help with my hopeless crush though. It feels good to have someone believe in me so unreservedly and give me this much time and attention.

My folks have always doted on me, but with four kids to cart between activities and busy careers, there wasn't always time. This much one-on-one focus on my studies was a rarity with me being the unplanned baby of the family.

"Atta boy, you've totally got this!" Jordie wraps an arm around me when I get through all the cards without missing one.

They ruffle my hair and pull me into a side hug that has me hyperaware of their chest's yielding softness pressed against me when I hug them back. I'm not sure which makes my heart pound faster, the affirming praise or the physical affection. Both have me walking on cloud nine and totally convinced that I can tackle the world and ace this first big test. Prove to myself that I made the right call coming here, plans or not. The more time I spend with Jordie, the more sure I am that this is exactly where I need to be.

Chapter Eleven

Jordie

"Jords!" Jacob slings his arm around my shoulders as I am locking up after myself. I wasn't expecting all of my friends to be waiting outside my apartment to ambush me tonight. I'm supposed to be meeting Ray for one final last minute cram session before our psych exam and my French midterm. It looks like my friends have other ideas though, since they're all here.

"Uh, hi?" I shrug out from under Jacob's arm and lock the door, then turn to face the entire crew. "What's up?"

"Did you forget you're coming to my sex toy party?" Jacob demands.

That does ring a bell now that he mentions it. It also explains why Celeste and Pixel weren't home after class. They must have met right up with the others. Jacob tugs me toward where the rest of our friends are waiting near the building lobby.

"Oh, am I?" I lift a brow at him, but I fall into step with him as we join the others.

I exchange greetings with everyone as we amble outside and

toward the student center. It's the same direction as I need to go to meet up with Ray, anyway.

Abe and Celeste are engrossed in discussing whatever advanced math class they had earlier. Those two are the biggest nerds in our group. Abe got a scholarship for solving some famous math riddle theorem thing. The pair of them are forever competing over their grades.

"Wait, Jacob's what now?" Lio repeats, scowling between Jacob and Sheila and planting their feet. "You neglected to mention that little detail. I was told this is a fundraiser."

"It *is* a fundraiser. I just left out some minor details because you'd have gotten in your head and made up excuses not to come." Sheila winks so exaggeratedly it's impossible to miss the double entendre is intentional, even before she adds, "And you deserve to come your brains out, Lio. No pressure though."

"Ugh, I can't believe you." Lio pouts, but their eyes are sparkling with good humor. "I guess if you're going to twist my arm, I have no other choice."

"Yay!" Sheila grabs Lio by both shoulders and rocks them from side to side. "It's fun as hell, you had a late lab for the last one, but this time is going to rock! Is it going to be Jen from Self Serve again? She was great! And she's queer as fuck too, so you don't need to be self-conscious about it."

Jacob laughs. "Yeah, it's Jen running the show. And we are raising funds for the Boston Alliance of LGBTQ+ Youth, so part of every purchase goes to help at-risk queer youth. I told all of you about this fundraiser ages ago. It's in one of the event rooms at the student center. A bunch of us spent the afternoon setting up. I know you were on the text chain, and I put up flyers, and posted on the community bulletin."

"Guess me and Jords missed the memo." Lio shrugs. "But I'm down for supporting BAGLY."

Jacob tsks. "I swear it's like herding cats to keep you all organized. Good thing I caught you in time. I'm expecting decent turnout, but the more the merrier and it's for a good cause."

"Uh huh, this has nothing to do with you wanting to pull from the newbies to the LGBT+ club," Celeste teases Jacob.

"Excuse you, I'm just doing my part. Anything to help the queer youth." Jacob turns to walk backward, making a show of affronted dignity that only makes Celeste snort and roll her eyes.

"And helping *this* queer youth to get his rocks off," Keith interjects with a gleeful smirk. "Self Serve has the best lube!"

"And cock rings." Jacob winks.

"Ugh, I'm surrounded by pervs," Lio whines, throwing their hands in the air. But they're smiling, so I'm pretty sure they aren't actually upset about it.

"It's fine. I'll buy you something nice to make it up to you." Sheila slings an arm around her bestie. Lio leans into the hug with a contented sigh before separating to keep pace with the rest of us.

"So, you're coming, right Jordie?" Jacob asks.

I shrug apologetically. "Sorry, I already made plans."

"With Ray? Invite him too. He might see something he likes." Jacob flexes, as if he's the something Ray might enjoy seeing. Which has me scrounging for excuses not to bring Ray to his sex toy party.

I want to keep my sunshine to myself, but that's probably selfish. Ray could use more friends. I noticed that from the first time I met him. The yearning way he drank in my appearance in class that first day we met. How he watched my every move in class for weeks while we got to know each other.

He readily took to me claiming him as someone to mentor and guide and definitely not to date. Our solo study sessions and shopping trips notwithstanding.

"Oooh!" Sheila, Keith, and Pixel chorus, their ears perked for gossip. Lio leans in closer. Even Abe and Celeste's conversation trails off, their interest piqued.

I roll my eyes at the lot of them. "Yeah, I'm meeting Ray. To study—nothing else."

"Oh, the cutie from Pix's show, who you haven't shut up about all semester?" Celeste taps her manicured nails against her sharp chin and gives me a knowing smile. "I approve of you keeping him."

"I mean, he's my friend, not a puppy I'm considering adopting." I hunch my shoulders against my friend's gentle teasing. It's too on the nose and I've had horrendous luck dating since I started presenting as femme as I like.

Ray might be my age, but he's new to embracing the full extent of his queerness. He's new to university and the country and basically everything. He hates getting teased about his baby face, but he's so innocent about so many things. I'd feel bad taking advantage of his puppy love crush on me as the first viable dating option he's met here.

Jacob smirks. "Just admit you like him."

Celeste wraps a comforting arm around me. "You don't have to invite him, but he might enjoy being included."

"Ugh. Yeah. Probably. They have, like, gender affirming products too, right?" It occurs to me that we still haven't gotten around to shopping for a packer for him. Tonight could be good for that. Not that I need to be involved in what goes on in his pants. For all I know, he ordered something online already.

"Yep!" Sheila grins. "Falsies and packers and anything else you might need."

"Got a steal on some cutlets from them." Keith chirrups, enthusiastically pretending to adjust a chest he only wears to perform his drag act.

Pixel slaps at his hands and I hunch into my bra at the reminder that the falsies filling the cups are cheap knockoffs.

Maybe I should stop putting off that appointment Pix has been bugging me to make at the student health clinic about getting on hormones. I'm just not sure they're right for me. Mostly because I enjoy using my dick and growing my own boobs might not be worth possibly trading in the ability to fuck the way I'm used to. The way too many of my past partners seem to expect.

I sigh. That is a huge part of the reason I know better than to mess around with baby queers who have less experience with queer sex. Nell always joked that dating me was the best of both worlds, in a way that made me uncomfortable without being able to put my finger on why.

Would Ray be like that? He's new to being out as trans, but he's not new to queer spaces. What would it feel like to have him snuggle into my actual flesh and blood bosom when I hug him? The way he felt pressed against my chest the other day when we hugged on his birthday was so nice. I noticed him checking me out, so it's not outside the realm of possibility that he'd want to take things further. I try to remind myself that I know better, but Ray makes it easy to forget.

"Pretty sure Ray needs the other side of things, right?" Jacob arches a brow at me.

I nod reluctantly. With this group, there's pretty much no such thing as TMI, but I'm still a little uncomfortable talking about Ray behind his back.

"Yeah. We talked about where to get him a packer, but I'm not sure he'd be into checking out the options with an audience. He's kind of guarded and private."

"What's a little sharing of privates among friends?" Jacob slings his arm around me again. He braces his other hand on my shoulder. This time his forearm goes across my chest, mashing my bra into me. I shudder at the way it feels for my boobs to be all disarranged and moving in ways they shouldn't. It forces me to confront the ways my body doesn't quite fit, the dysphoria surging through me in a nauseating wave.

"Quit it!" I shove Jacob off and aggressively fix my flowery blouse.

He holds up his hands like I'm overreacting. "Sorry, geez. Sensitive much?"

"Knock it off," I snap at him. "I'm not in the mood. Anyway, I promised Ray I'd help him study for a test tonight. So I can't just ditch him because you decided to throw a party at the last minute and forgot to invite people."

Jacob sighs, acting all aggrieved. "I knew you weren't listening! I invited you last week. And again last night when you were doodling hearts all over your notes at dinner and pining because Ray had an evening class and skipped out on joining us."

I grind my teeth, because he's not wrong. Now that I've introduced Ray to my other friends, I've been inviting him around more often. And now I do recall Jacob mentioning it last week and agreeing to hang out tonight.

I just didn't catch the details about the fundraiser party, so I figured it wouldn't be a big deal to bail in favor of another study date with Ray.

"Call your guy and invite him to have his horizons expanded," Sheila suggests.

"Or we can expand other parts of him." Jacob waggles his eyebrows suggestively. Pixel jabs an elbow into his ribs before I can, and most of the rest of us side eye him. "What? All in good fun," Jacob says defensively.

"Jacob's being a pig, but it really will be fun. Ray seemed really chill the other night," Sheila says, turning her back toward Jacob.

"Yeah, we all want to get to know any guy who can turn your

head, Jords," Celeste says.

I wince at the implication there. It's not like I've never had a crush. I've just been focused on other priorities than dating. I'm still focused on those other priorities, but Ray is sweet. And he's got that swoony accent, and soulful eyes like gazing into the ocean, and he's not a puppy I can take home, damn it. I pull out my phone to call him, anyway.

Ray picks up on the second ring, all flustered and breathless sounding. "Sorry! Are you waiting for me? I'm running late. Class ran long, but I'm coming."

I bite my lip. Those words in his breathy voice from jogging across campus have me all kinds of turned on. Bad Jordie.

"It's fine. I'm just calling to see if you'd want to come hang out with the gang first. Jacob is having a fundraiser party thing, and they all want you to join us. We can still head to the diner afterward to study."

"Oh, cool. Your friends really want me to come?" He sounds so eager.

"Yeah. Don't you all want Ray to come tonight?" I hold the phone out to my friends, hitting speaker mode. And immediately regret my phrasing at the lascivious wink Jacob gives me. Most of my friends call out variants on *yes, join us* and *the more the merrier.*

"Oh, well, I guess we can—" Ray starts to agree to the change of plans and remorse for putting him on the spot floods my veins. I should take him off speaker, right? Before I can, Jacob pipes in again. Damn the man.

"Excellent. We'd love nothing more than for you to *come*," Jacob drawls. "That's half the point of a sex toy party."

"Geez, Jacob, you're such a horny twat tonight." Celeste swats at his shoulder.

"Not cool." Pixel scowls.

"Dude!" Keith scolds Jacob.

"Behave, man," Abe admonishes with a shake of his head.

"A *what* now?" Ray squeaks.

I toggle off speaker mode and mash the phone back to my ear, mortified. "I'm sorry. Yeah. It is a sex toy party. But it's not like we're going to be actually using the products. It's more like, you know those boring MLM parties where a company representative suckers someone into inviting all their friends to push tupperware? Or like, pitching makeup and vitamins and kitchen gear, to them? It's like that. Except instead of crap no one needs, it's things to enhance your bedroom time."

"Or anywhere else where the fancy strikes." Jacob winks at me.

"Damn. You are extra thirsty today, Jacob. Where's Kale?" Celeste makes a show of looking for him, even though he isn't with us. "He'd gladly help you work out all that brimming libido if you gave him a second glance. Fuck only knows why."

"I didn't invite Kale. He's been getting clingy," Jacob says, shrugging it off like it's nothing. I can see past that facade.

I don't have the energy or inclination to worry about what exactly I missed between the two of them. They've been on and off fuck buddies as long as I've known them both. I'm much more invested in Ray's response to my invite than analyzing Jacob's boundary pushing tonight.

I get he's stressed over arranging the fundraiser. If he and Kale had a falling out, that explains why his fuckboy ways seem more pronounced lately. His flirting always nudges up against the line of acceptable behavior when he's upset or struggling with life. It's like he needs us to reel him in and show him someone cares. Blah. Not my job. But I can't quite bring myself to turn my back on the guy completely either.

"Oh. Um. I've never, uh, heard of something like that. Is it, uh, going to be super, um, like gendered?" Ray asks.

"No. Jacob's making it weird, but we did one last year and it was really fun." I shoot Jacob a warning look. He rolls his eyes at me.

"Okay. If you want to go and you're sure I won't be intruding, I'll be there," Ray says. The trust he's putting in me wraps around my heart and won't let go.

"Great!" I don't try to hide my enthusiasm. I'm excited to see him, no sense hiding that. "Meet us at the student center as soon as you're ready. I'll text you the room number."

"Um. Can I just come from class? I have to walk by there on my way back to the dorms anyway, and unless I need to change, I might as well save myself the extra walk."

"Sure, whatever you're wearing is fine. See you soon, sunshine."

"See you soon, Jordie."

I shiver at my name in his softly accented purr and then I

hang up. I tuck my phone away and notice my friends giving me questioning looks.

"Well?" Celeste asks.

"He's meeting us there." I grin as Celeste and Pixel offer me fist bumps.

"Nice!" Sheila's already bouncy stride gets more animated.

"You all better be cool to him." I jab an accusatory finger at Jacob. If he needs guardrails, then I can give him something.

"Scout's honor," Jacob vows, hand held in front of his chest, thumb to his pinkie with three fingers raised in a scouting salute.

"What honor?" Celeste ribs him. Jacob sticks out his tongue at her.

"Whatever, I can behave." He pouts.

"Prove it," I taunt as we approach the student center. I'm only half-joking. I really want Ray to have a good time. Jacob, even at his worst, probably won't scare Ray away, but that's only part of the point. "You know the party will raise more money if you aren't so over-the-top that you make people uncomfortable, right?"

"Yeah. Got it. Thanks." Jacob snaps. Then he sighs and rubs at his temples. "Sorry. It's been a rough week. I'll tone it down."

"Good," I bump his shoulder. Jacob forces a pained smile.

"We're going to raise a ton for the youth," Sheila declares, nudging him from the other side. "So quit stressing out and let's make sure everyone has a pleasant time, yeah?"

I know she's concerned about making the evening feel safe

for Lio to step out of their comfort zone because I have the same protective instincts about Ray. I want tonight to go well. So Ray will continue spending more time with my other friends.

"Yeah," Jacob agrees. "I want it to be fun for everyone."

"It will be. Jen is the best!" Shiela says with a skip in her step as she scurries to catch up with Lio and loops their arms together at the elbow again.

Jacob watches her with a bemused little smile. One of his rare genuine expressions, maybe he really will give the outrageous flirting a rest for the evening. I can always hope.

The more comfortable Ray is around the entire crew, the more we can hang out as a group. And maybe I'll be less tempted to cross any lines when we aren't alone together. As if that stopped me from lusting after him the other night at the club. Inviting him tonight is either Celeste's best idea ever, or her worst.

Chapter Twelve

Ray

The dingy little conference room in the student union's basement is easy to find. Jacob and Celeste's loud laughing voices carry halfway down the hall, letting me know I'm in the correct place. I slow my pace as I approach the room number Jordie texted to me.

I'm equal parts excited and nervous about the party. Jordie's friends are so loud and dramatic and just fun to be around. The few times I've seen them since Bella Donna and Pixel's show have mostly been in passing. Other than a handful of shared meals in the dining hall, and they're a little more subdued there.

If throwing fries at each other and making lewd jokes can be considered subdued. I love how vibrant they all are. So bold and unashamed and all the things I want to be. I've just never had the courage to step out of line. It's not me.

I get too wrapped up in my head and worry about the possible consequences. But Jordie's friends make it feel safe to just be myself. Next to them, even my most flamboyantly boyish wardrobe choices seem muted and dull. There's a comforting safety in that.

A sign on the door lists the name of the company doing the party: Self Service. The note says that the room is reserved for a fundraising party to benefit BAGLY, Inc. for the next hour. In case I needed more confirmation I'm in the right place.

This is it. My palms are sweaty as I try to psych myself up to enter the room. Jordie is in there. Along with a bunch of sex toys. Gulp.

When I step inside, there's a bigger crowd than I expected from what Jordie said. The room isn't as large as some of my lecture halls, but it feels like Jacob dragged most of the queer people on campus to this party. I guess that's good for the charity that he's raising funds to help.

Not so great for my nerves about browsing toy dicks in front of people who I want to make a good impression with. I can't help staring at the trestle table covered in neon dicks of all shapes and sizes in the center of the room.

Fuck. I swallow hard. Do people really enjoy having something roughly the girth and length of my entire forearm shoved inside of them? Where would that even fit? Nope, on second thought, I don't want to go there.

I'm getting twinges of sympathy pain just considering it. And maybe a tingle of warmth too. It's not like I'm a virgin; I've fooled around with girls and guys. Toys have never been my favorite for solo play. My ex girlfriend was a toppy fucker, so seeing her all lit up with sexual confidence more than made up for the unyielding hardness of her favorite dildo.

The products on the table all look bigger than that one. If they sell this stuff in so many larger variations, then it must have more going for it? Ugh. Is one of those massively girthy dicks what Jordie wants from a lover? The thought is like a bucket of cold water over my tentative interest in the array of toys.

If good sex requires a gigantic cock like the ones on display... I'm screwed. Or very not screwed. I mean, I know it doesn't, but the array of toys makes me dysphoric as hell.

"Oh! Hey, you made it!" Sheila is the first to notice me. She is standing in front of the guests next to the company representative and facing the rest of the room. She turns more fully toward me, a huge lime green cock flopping comically in front of her from the harness she's trying on over her pants.

The harness sparks something back to life in my chest. Maybe there is still hope for me if Jordie wants to get railed.

What was it Jordie said when they were helping me get dressed the other day? Oh yeah. They handed me that balled up sock with a safety pin through it to fill out my pants and said *If you can't grow it yourself, store-bought is fine.*

Then they winked and adjusted the breast forms in their bra and yeah. Store-bought might work for sex too. And Jordie brought the store to me. Or at least, one of them. Which is good, because the sock thing worked in a pinch to get my new underwear to stop bunching, but it's really not cutting it to help with the sense of something missing in my pants. I have every intention of leaving this party with a new packer.

That quote about store-bought came up again over dinner

when Pixel mentioned she needed a refill on her HRT. I mentioned wanting to go on testosterone, but that I wouldn't know where to start the process here in the States. Pixel told me she goes to the student health clinic on campus and has had no issues getting her HRT through them.

I've been debating whether to make an appointment ever since. The biggest thing holding me back is that once I go on meds, I'll only have so long to tell my family before they notice the changes in my appearance. Most places I've looked at say it takes a few months to get noticeable changes, but still, it feels like I'd be starting a countdown I'm not quite ready for. But I might never feel ready to tell them and I don't want to put off hormones for too much longer.

Pixel says student health does informed consent. So I can probably leave the appointment with a prescription instead of jumping through hoops. No need for documenting years of therapy to prove I'm really trans like she had to deal with back in her home state. I've been dreaming about this for years, but the idea of actually taking the plunge has eels writhing in my belly, an electric buzz of trepidation and excitement.

I really want to ask Jordie to come with me for moral support, but it feels super intimate to invite a friend to something medical like that.

"We saved you a seat!" Sheila points toward the empty chair. Next to Jordie, who looks amazing, as always. They must have changed after our psych lecture. Earlier, they had on a tight graphic tee with a cartoon kitten and the slogan 'be gay, do crimes' all striped in bi pride colors. Now they're wearing a ruffle-neck floral blouse that lends to a more femme silhouette. They look amazing and my pulse races at the idea they might have dressed up for our study date. For me.

"Thanks?" I squeak, waving nervously and shuffling toward the row of familiar faces near the front of the room. It's awkward walking past all the strangers, like I can feel their eyes on me.

"Hey sunshine!" Jordie turns and beams at me. My heart skips a beat at how delighted they seem at the sight of me. As if they value our time together as much as I do.

My cheeks ache from the size of my answering grin as I wave back. That bright smile makes me believe that if I scrounge up the courage to invite them along to the clinic for moral support, they'd be glad to stand beside me.

I should make the appointment and stop procrastinating. Throw caution to the wind and tell them how much I like them. My palms are sweaty and my mouth is dry at the prospect. The words don't quite reach my lips and I stand awkwardly at the end of the row of folding chairs Jordie's friends are occupying.

"Come join us; we're about to start. Sheila just got a little impatient." Celeste waves me over to sit in the empty chair between her and Jordie.

I shuffle past Pixel and Celeste to get to the free chair, but it's worth a tiny bit of awkwardness to feel Jordie's thigh bump against mine as I sit. Their warm hand on my shoulder sends heat pooling low in my belly. Apparently, I should consider if there's anything from the selection of toys here tonight to help curb my libido around my crush.

"Glad you made it." Jordie smiles at me. The sweet private smile I love that makes me feel like I'm not wildly grasping at straws to hope there could be something more growing between us. "I checked and they have packers and stuff. Thought you might be in the market for one."

"Oh, cool." I shuffle on the edge of my seat, awkward nerves thrumming through me at the tacit mention of what isn't in my pants. It makes my belly squirm, and I don't want to think about it.

Jordie's right, I came here with buying my first real packer in mind. It's just stepping way outside of my comfort zone to shop for my store-bought dick in front of my crush. Especially since there are a lot more people here than just Jordie's friends.

"Figured it might be less intimidating to shop among friends than at a store?" Jordie turns it into a question. "But if not, we can always still go to the place I was telling you about without these clowns. Or order online. Jen has coupon codes for the Self Serve website."

"Hey! I am a classy jester, not a mere clown, shank you very much!" Pixel leans across Celeste to interject.

"Of course you are, dear." Celeste pats her girlfriend's long blonde hair and nudges her back into her seat. "And the party is about to start, so let's all just sit back and let Jen do her thing, shall we?"

"Fine." Pixel huffs and crosses her arms over her chest, emphasizing her modest curves. I shiver.

It's weird to think that other people want the flesh lumps I'm desperate to bind into non-existence. People like Jordie beside me, with their flowy blouse draped to emphasize their subtle curves. I try not to think about how uncomfortable my binder is after wearing it all day. How sweaty I am under my shirt.

Nope. Not thinking about bodies at all as Jen finishes helping Sheila get the right fit for her harness. She is grinning as she takes it off and stows it in her school bag.

Except I can't help thinking about how much I like the way Jordie looks in their blouse with the padded bra. They showed me the inserts when I was feeling weird about packing. They always look good, but they look extra confident and happy with their curves on display. I can't help glancing at them over and over again.

Jen starts the party. It's surreal to sit among my new friends listening to a sales pitch for sex toys, but they don't make it weird. Even Jacob is on his best behavior. I get over the initial awkwardness the more Jen talks about the various items on display as casually as if they really were tupperware.

When Jen breaks out the strap-ons, I'm torn between the weirdness of her flopping around giant dildos while I'm sitting next to my crush and being fascinated by the various options. One of the dicks doubles as a stand-to-pee packer. Store-bought is fine, right? I swallow hard and try not to think too much about exactly who I want to try that particular item out with.

***

"Do you have this in pink?" Sheila runs her fingers over the selection of magnetic packing pouches Jen is showing us. That gives me the courage to reach for the cool cactus print one I really want.

The party wasn't as weird or uncomfortable as I'd worried it might be. Now that it's over, it seems like everyone is busily filling out their order slips from the little product magazine Jen passed out toward the end of her presentation. That gives me the courage to order a few things to try. When I ask, Jen has a basic model of a floppy packer that I can stick in my pants with her in the limited stock on hand. I'm ordering one that lets you stand up to pee too.

I'm still not quite brave enough to ask about the pack and play models in her product catalog that claim to go seamlessly from daily wear to sexy fun times. I ordered a harness like the one Sheila was trying on when I got here though. And a dildo with a vibe in the base to go with it. That was more than far enough out of my comfort zone.

I might not have gotten anything at all if Celeste and Pixel hadn't been distracting Jordie while I browsed. They're still standing with their roommates, poring over the order catalog on the other side of the room. Ordering sex toys right in front of the person I've got a hopeless crush on would have been a bridge too far. That doesn't stop my hornier thoughts from desperately wanting to try my new cock out with Jordie. Both of us tangled in my sheets, sweaty and naked.

I can't banish the image of Jordie's face caught in the throes of passion and lit by the colorful fairy lights decorating my cozy dorm room. I want to hear them calling me their sunshine as they gaze up at me with that bright, cheerful smile from earlier. Or have them straddle me on my rainbow bed sheets while they ride my new cock; their chest and curls bouncing with the effort of fucking themself to orgasm. I *really* want to make them come.

Once she finishes with Sheila, Jen scans my order sheet. She bags up the couple of items she has with her and passes me an invoice for the things that she needs to ship. By the time I finish paying, Jordie has their order form filled out and is standing supportively nearby. Close enough to help if I needed it, but far enough for a veil of privacy over the whole affair.

I step back from the trestle table to make space for them, not considering that means that Jen has to hand Jordie my bag of goodies to pass to me. My face flames at the knowledge that my crush is handing me my new dick. Fuck. That might be the only way they handle my junk if I can't work up the courage to declare my feelings. Part of me takes a guilty pleasure in the thought of it, another part desperately wants to say something suave and flirty. My mouth is too dry to find the right words though.

"Study time?" Jordie asks as we file out of the party.

"Study time!" I agree. That's much safer ground. Easier to

let my guard down without worrying that I'll give away my less than platonic feelings about Jordie and mess up our friendship.

"Sweet! Are we getting Randy?" Keith asks, bouncing between us and slinging an arm around each of our necks, hauling us down. Jordie shrugs him off.

"Control your boyfriend, Abe," they joke.

Keith messes with my hair, giving me a noogie that reminds me nostalgically of my brothers back home before he lets me go and saunters closer to his boyfriend.

"Don't be a pest, Keith," Abe tucks his diminutive boyfriend under his arm and Keith sighs contentedly.

"I'm in!" Pixel fist pumps. "Always down for a Randy's run."

"Sure, why not? I could use a coffee if I'm going to be up all night." Celeste stretches and drops an arm around her girl-friend's shoulders.

Pixel cackles. "Well, I'd prefer to be the one keeping you up all night. I suppose your econ prof is sort of hot in that uptight, older librarian way."

"Mhm, I often fantasize about her shaking her hair out of that bun, all silvery cascades of silk..." Celeste teases.

"Am I invited too?" Pixel pouts.

Celeste chuckles. "I mean, it's not happening, but sure, why not?"

"I am so down for the occasional third. I mean, to help your grade and all." Pixel winks.

"Hey, stop setting feminism back a decade you pervs!" Sheila turns to admonish them.

"Stop icking our fantasy, Sheila. We wouldn't actually do anything with a professor."

"And I don't need the help on my grades, unlike *some* people. Are you studying tonight?" Celeste asks pointedly.

Sheila pouts. "There's no point. I already know I'm going to have to retake the class."

Celeste rolls her eyes. "This is the first test. You can't fail the entire class based on one bad pop quiz. You're studying with me tonight. Go grab your notes and meet us at the diner."

"But research has shown that cramming isn't conducive to long-term data retention," Sheila says.

Celeste shrugs. "Maybe not, but it's a bit late to start a slow and thorough approach now."

"But studying is so boring..." Sheila sighs heavily and casts a pleading glance at Lio.

Lio throws up their hands in front of them, placating. "Celeste knows her shit, Sheils. It can't hurt to at least try to study."

"You can't prove that!" Sheila sighs. "I'd rather try out my new toys and just wing the test."

"And I'd rather try out the toys when you aren't using me as a distraction. The benefits go both ways." Lio crosses their arms and scowls at Sheila.

"Ha! Just like you," Sheila jokes.

Lio gives her an implacable stare, arms crossed over their chest like a disapproving parent.

"Ugh, fine. Tomorrow night then? We can celebrate Cel making me not fail." Sheila sticks out her tongue at Celeste.

Celeste claps a fist to her heart. "I solemnly swear to make you not fail Sheila."

"Yay! I have my notes in my bag. Just. Ugh. Math." Sheila drags her feet until Lio loops their elbows together. The contact perks her right back up. I'm still not sure if those two are super close friends or dating, but I'm not going to make it weird by asking.

"You mean yay, math!" Celeste and Abe both correct her, like it's a common refrain with them.

It's cute. I like the way they all tease and support each other. I wish I had friends like this.

No wonder Jordie is so confident just being themself when they know these people will always have their back. Maybe I can have that too. They seem to like me well enough. Or else they are tolerating me for Jordie's sake. All the more reason to bury my crush down as deep as I can stuff it.

I really like Jordie, but I need friends a lot more than I need a sex life. Heck, I don't even really know who I am or what I truly want yet.

We make our way from campus to the diner as a group. It's busy on a Thursday night. Much more so than when I was here with Jordie mid-afternoon on a Monday.

I notice Zo across the room. Their hair and outfit are both bubblegum pink tonight. I can't quite make out the name and pronouns pinned to their apron today from here. Jordie says they usually default back to Zo and they/them between their various experiments, so that seems safe enough.

It's a little weird to realize I recognize the guy manning the grill behind the counter. And the eccentric guy beside the register who spent a solid ten minutes last week telling us about his dirigible while we were waiting to pay our tab. Jordie called him Archie and told me he's harmless. The dirigible probably isn't real, since he's been talking about it being almost ready for his world tour for as long as they've been coming here.

"Hey!" Archie greets our group as we scan for an open table large enough for all of us. "Have I told you youngsters? We got a new compressor valve! Plans are moving apace for a spring liftoff."

"Awesome, man." Jacob offers the older man a high five.

Archie nods happily. "Abigail is overjoyed. It won't be long now."

"Better enjoy Kit's outstanding pies while you're still around to get them, then." Keith winks.

"Mm, excellent point." Archie smiles beneficently at us, then turns back to his plate of dessert, still mumbling to himself about his plans.

"How many?" Henry asks as he turns from bussing a table. He arches an elegant brow at us, a bin of dishes propped on one hip like it weighs nothing. I'm not sure how he can work in heels and keep his killer manicure so pristine, but he manages somehow.

"Nine." Celeste holds up her fingers, since it's loud in here.

Henry nods. "It will just be a minute. I can put a couple of tables together for you folks."

"Hey, babe," Henry sing-songs as he brushes past Cesar, who almost drops a pitcher of soda with how fast he whirls around to face Henry. "I need help with a nine-top when you have a second," he winks, Cesar flushes.

We all shuffle off to the side to get out of the way for a couple who came in after us. They make their way over to the counter and take the open seats next to Archie. I take in the bright neon and chrome that is becoming a familiar comfort.

At Randy's, I don't worry as much about how people see me. Even with all the gawky awkwardness of trying to find myself as a guy, there's something indefinable about being around other openly queer people. It's comforting to know I have a place where I belong. Jordie's arm slung around my shoulders fills me with a warm glow of belonging that might just ignite me. It certainly makes it harder to keep my thoughts about Jordie platonic.

Luckily, it's not long before we're sitting and there's a rare lull in Jordie's friend's banter as they peruse the daily specials. That doesn't last long, since most of them are familiar with the menu and the specials are the only thing that seems to change. My laminated menu is missing the paper insert with the specials, so Jordie leans in close to share theirs with me.

"Hey, folks, Henry and I are sharing you tonight," Cesar greets us once we're settled into the plush vinyl seats.

"You lucky dogs," Henry interjects with a saucy wink as he swings past with a pot of coffee for another table. "Be nice to Cesar."

Their banter makes Jordie snort, our knees bumping togeth-er as they suppress a belly laugh. It's so hard to hide how much I'm into them when their face is right there in kissing range.

"I'm always nice to pretty boys," Jacob winks, eyeing Henry hungrily. He flirts as naturally as breathing, and I wish I could capture one hundredth of his confident swagger.

It's a weird combination of comforting and affirming of my masculinity to see him vamping with the staff after the handful of flirty overtures he's made toward me so far. It makes his overdone advances seem less targeted at me and more like a smokescreen to protect himself from anything more serious.

Cesar seems flustered as he continues. "Fun fact, for any number multiplied by nine, the sum of the digits equals to nine."

"Even really big numbers?" Sheila asks, leaning over the table.

Celeste and Abe nod. "Yeah, you just have to keep adding the results for larger numbers."

"Even 7456?" Lio challenges, eyes narrowing skeptically.

"Sure, that's 67104, which gives you 18 which gives you nine," Abe rattles off the answer while Celeste nods along.

Cesar looks startled that our group took his fun fact and ran with it. I'm reminded viscerally of how much I miss my broth-ers. Abe and Celeste are the same sort of nerdy as Adam and Darren, acting like math is a fun game instead of a hair-pulling tribulation. Ugh. I might be doomed to fail my math class.

"Weird." Sheila shakes her head, looking bemused. I guess if I have to retake the course, I might be in the same section as Sheila since she seems to be flailing too.

"What about 6,578,123?" Lio arches a brow.

"I'm not your human calculator," Abe retorts.

"Nope, he's my human calculator," Keith leans in to kiss Abe's cheek. "You all wish you had a man this good at math."

Sheila, Lio, and I groan.

"I sincerely do not," Celeste says

"I don't need any man," Pixel tosses her hair, "But yes please to math cuties."

"I can do my own math. It's the French I need all the help I can get with." Jordie winks at me and I might swoon at even a veiled implication that I'm potential dating material. At least enough to joke about.

Sheila snorts. "I'll stick to conning my friends into meeting my math needs, thanks."

"Uh, do you all need a minute, or can I put in your drink orders?" Cesar asks with an arched brow.

Everyone looks chagrined at getting sidetracked as we go around the table with our orders. As soon as Cesar leaves, Jordie's friends pick up where their banter left off. It's boisterous and fun.

When our food arrives there's a lull in the chatter, I take out my notes to study for the psych test.

When Sheila notices, she scoffs into her pancakes. "Overachiever nerd, no wonder you and Jords get along so well. You're going to make Celeste think it's cool to grill me before I finish my pancakes."

"Good point, we might as well get started on the basics." Celeste points her fork at Shiela. "What is ROI?"

Sheila groans. "The ROI on these pancakes goes down exponentially if they get cold before I finish, cut me a break, Cel."

Pixel cackles at that. "Come on Cel, you have to admit that was a pretty good comeback."

It feels good to be drawn in and included, even if I'm a little flustered at being compared to my crush.

Part of me wishes it was just me and Jordie here again. Not the whole noisy crowd. But another part is relieved. This chaos doesn't feel like a date. Even if Jordie made a point of sitting next to me. And we're crammed in so close to squeeze everyone around the two tables that I can feel their body heat. I keep brushing up against Jacob on my other side too, but that's not nearly so thrilling. We review the entire study guide between bites.

When we get to the end Jordie grins and hip checks me gently. I could bask in the warmth of their approval forever, it's like sunshine on my face on a perfect spring day.

"See? Piece of cake, you're twenty for twenty. You've got this test in the bag, my dude!" Jordie offers me a fist and I bump it, beaming at the praise.

"You think?" I can't help leaning into them, digging for more of their kind words.

"I know it." They reach over and ruffle my short hair and my eyes flutter closed in sheer bliss at how affirming their touch is. I manage to swallow down my little moan of contentment—barely.

When I open my eyes, Jordie is watching me so intently that for a wild moment I'm tempted to lean in and kiss them. They're so beautiful, and something about the heat in their gaze gives me an inkling it wouldn't be unwelcome. I lick my lips, drifting closer, until Jacob claps a hand on my back and asks if I want some of his fries, breaking the spell.

"Huh?" I startle at Jacob's touch. "Um, no thanks."

"You sure? I might've ordered too many apps. There are extra wings too." Jacob waves one in front of me.

"I'll take a wing." Sheila reaches across the table for one.

"Help yourself." Jacob leans across the table to pass his food around. I turn back toward Jordie, but the moment between us is long gone.

Jordie digs their French flashcards out of their bag. Probably just as well that I didn't kiss them in front of all their friends. That might have been awkward. Especially if my attraction is one-sided. They aren't meeting my eyes, so I might have misjudged the moment.

"Ready to correct my pronunciation, mon petit chien?" Jordie holds up the stack of note cards with a self-deprecating grin.

"Oui." I chuckle. "Did you mean mon petit chou?"

I promised to help them with their language class. It's easy to ignore everything else in the world when I get to express myself in the language I'm used to using for all things school and social.

My family are Francophones, but home was the main place

we consistently spoke English growing up. My parents wanted us to have a strong foundation in both languages to improve our job prospects as adults. So there's something jarringly intimate about using English for everything since I moved here. And something comforting and wonderful about slipping into French with Jordie.

Of course, their class is taught using Parisian French, so their clumsy American accent is even more off to my ears and some of the vocab is a little different. But I'm used to that. It's still nice to hear the familiar language.

Nice, and at the same time it makes me homesick. That reminds me of the first time we came here and I heard a familiar accent from home after the drag show. It felt so good to hear a little piece of home in all the post-show buzz and the nerves that threatened to overwhelm me over meeting Jordie's friends.

I haven't seen Claude again since the night we bonded over a shared heritage and enjoyment of Keith and Pixel's the drag show. But as I'm sitting at the diner, I notice them across the room, fiddling with their phone. I wave, tentatively when I catch their eye, they wave back distractedly. I consider going over to say hi, but then their phone rings and they answer it, leaving a tip on their table as they head for the door. The missed connection is just as well, I need to focus on my tutoring duties, anyway. Jordie is stumbling over their conjugations and I'm not sure how to correct them without misgendering them.

So rather than just correcting them I have to focus on explaining making sure the gender of their adjectives and nouns match. We go off on a tangent, discussing iel and gender neutral conjugations. And how the language police back home—yes, that's an actual thing—aren't keen on the gender neutral language that best fits my friend. The language to describe who they are only exists in queer spaces because the linguistic authorities don't acknowledge it. So we end up settling on femme leaning descriptors for them if there isn't a neutral option.

We pause to annotate their flashcards with the unofficial neutral forms of the adjectives on their vocab list alongside the masculine and feminine forms. I hate having to dampen their delight at finding new words that fit them with the caveat that their professor may or may not be accepting of the changes. Grassroots changes to make the language more gender neutral are controversial.

People have weirdly strong opinions about language that doesn't affect them in any way and only serves to hold space for people like Jordie. It's the same in English with they/them pronouns, I suppose. And I guess not wanting to make room for people like us might be part of the point for those who object.

At least my brothers are cool with iel and they/them. For a long time, I thought that might mean they would accept me too, but I wasn't sure enough to gamble my future on that.

The diner is rowdy, and only getting busier as the night progresses. It's loud and full of distractions. I watch a couple of kids from the club wearing elaborate outfits chattering animatedly about something I can't catch. I overhear a distinct French accent that reminds me of home from the taller one of the pair in the thigh-high boots and lacy skirt.

There aren't any free tables, but they join a guy tapping away on his computer at the back of the diner. I feel a little bad for taking up a table when I'm too stuffed to eat another bite. And it's hard to hear Jordie over all the noise.

"Hey, um, it's kind of loud; want to come back to my place to go over the rest of these and maybe review the psych study guide one last time?"

"Oh." Jordie glances around. "It's busy tonight, huh? Yeah. We can study back on campus. You've got a single, right?"

"I do."

"Cool. I have a feeling Cel and Pixel will be trying out their new purchases loudly at my place when they get home. So no roommates to distract us sounds perfect."

"Perfect." I squeak, swallowing hard. My hands are clammy from the realization I just invited my crush back to my place. They're going to be in my room, maybe sitting on my unmade bed, where I totally left my binder hanging from the frame to dry.

"Let's go." Jordie smiles at me and my mouth feels like a desert, my heart racing. Gulp. I can be chill about this. It's not like anything other than studying is going to happen, right? Of course right.

Chapter Thirteen

Ray

Jordie takes one look around my dorm room and settles in at my desk. I join them, perching on the edge of my mattress nearest to them. We pull out our study materials in a sort of awkward silence. At first, it's just like every other time we've gotten together to study.

Except this time, I'm hyperaware of the fact that Jordie is in my personal space and we just spent over an hour looking at sex toys together. They literally passed me the dick Jen sold to me after the party. Which, in a real sense, means they held my dick in their elegant fingers.

I keep glancing over at them, trying not to stare, but wanting to drink in the sight of them right there. Their blouse seems to have more loose buttons down the front compared to earlier. A silky pink bra peeks tantalizingly over the lapels every time they move too much. It doesn't help that we're practicing French and they keep giving me flirty eye contact. Jordie keeps touching their face and neck. They fidget with their freshly touched up dyed hair as they try to recall their vocab words.

They gnaw on their lip as they flip through their flashcards and I can't stop thinking about how easy it is to get lost in their soulful gaze.

"Oh. So, wait a second. If I say 'je suis un avocate'... veux-tu me manger?" They startle a laugh out of me.

"Either way, it's un avocat, no hard 'a' at the end," I correct them. Their words make my cheeks burn because the phrase 'eat me' brings me right back to just how much I want to put my mouth on them. And wondering if maybe that wouldn't be unwelcome.

Jordie's eyes are smoldering as they lock onto mine and their tongue darts out to moisten their lips. And ok, yes, I desperately want to taste them.

I'm not sure what about the corny joke pickup line gives me the nudge to make a move. One minute we're laughing together about their dorky French mis*pun*ounciations, and the next I realize that I'm sitting too close. Our knees touch, their breath smells minty sweet from the candies they crunched all the way back here. I lean forward, closing the distance until the soft brush of their lips meeting mine brings reality crashing around me and I freeze.

Jordie deepens the kiss, sighing against my lips, opening to grant my tongue access. I tangle my fingers in the soft curls I've been dying to touch. Our kiss turns into soft moans and gentle nips.

Jordie might need to work on their French, but their French kissing is spot on. I don't want this moment to ever end. The way they respond to me is intoxicating. I can't help tugging a little harder on their curls when they moan into my mouth.

"Yeah, pull it harder," Jordie pants, then their tongue is in my mouth and their hands are on my face, holding me close. "How do I say it in French?"

"Tire-moi les cheveux," I say, tugging again to pull their lips back onto mine.

Jordie moans and scrabbles into my lap. They melt into me, kissing me desperate and needy, their hard bulge presses against my lower belly. I could kiss them like this forever. My world is reduced to their lips and tongue and teeth. Their hands cradle my face, their nose angled perfectly next to mine, their hair so soft under my fingers. Jordie fills my senses.

Fuck, I'm so turned on right now that it's unbelievable. They pull back, lips glistening and so fucking delicious I want to lick back into their mouth to taste them again. Their eyes sparkle and their mouth curves into the shape of my name and it's... there's nothing like it. I'm soaring on the euphoria of being kissed by someone who sees all of me and likes me. It's beyond intoxicating.

"Ray?"

"Huh?" I'm grinning so big my cheeks ache with it.

"You good?" They ask me, a concerned little furrow in their brow that I want to kiss away.

"So good." I can't stop grinning, and Jordie smiles back at me.

Then the smile dims into a slight frown and they wriggle on

my lap, sending tingles to my core. "So. Um. Should we talk about this?"

"What's there to talk about?" I ask. Wary apprehension overtakes my joy, dampening the giddy buzz of having just kissed the person I've been crushing on for months.

"This?" Jordie gestures between our chests. "Us."

"I, uh, sorry for kissing you without asking?" I try, hunching my shoulders and hoping I didn't terribly misread this entire situation.

Jordie snorts. "I think we were both pretty clearly into it. I mean, is that all you want?"

"No. I don't usually go around kissing people I'm not dating."

"So, do you want to date me?"

"Is that an option?" I ask. I sort of figured it was, from the way they kissed me back, like they were as needy and starving for it as me. It's hard to think with them in my lap and my lips still tingling from their kisses.

Jordie blows out a breath, easing out of my lap to sit beside me on the narrow dorm mattress. They run a hand through their messy curls, clearly having a hard time opening up to me. "I can't be your experiment, Ray."

"Um, why would you think that's what this is to me?" I ask. I get why that would be a problem, just not where they got the idea that it's something I would do.

"Because all of this is new to you and you haven't told your family about yourself and I would never pressure you to come out before you're ready, but..."

I press a finger to their lips to cut them off, chuckling a little over how worked up they are. "My family knows I'm bi. I never made that any sort of secret. My youngest brother gives me shit about picking a side whenever I bring someone home because he's a jerk like that, but it's mostly joking."

"Oh. But I thought..."

"They just don't know that I'm not a girl. I'm still not sure how to tell them that, but if you'd be cool with them knowing we're together, I have zero problem telling them I'm dating you. Or that you're genderqueer. I honestly don't think they're transphobic." And considering how well they've accepted my middle brother Darren's new partner, Ed, being non-binary, I know it for a fact now. I just don't know for sure that their acceptance of trans people extends to embracing me when I tell them who I am.

"So why haven't you told them about yourself?" Jordie asks, and there's no judgment in their tone, just genuine curiosity.

I shrug and can't meet their gaze. "I grew up as the only girl born on my dad's side of the family in two generations. It was a whole thing. And now that my brothers and cousins are having kids, I'm still the only 'girl' so... it just comes with a lot of expectations, you know?"

"I suppose that makes sense? But you still deserve to be happy and to have your family love you for who you are. Instead of living up to some weird notion of like, breaking the family curse."

I chortle. "Cursebreaker, that's clearly my dragon name."

"Maybe add it to your drag name too?" Jordie teases.

"So, is me not telling them I'm trans a deal-breaker?" I ask, nerves clawing at my belly.

"No. Not at all. It might make me sad to have to pretend around them, or misgender and deadname you, assuming meeting the parents comes up before you're ready for them to know. But I can handle that to keep you safe. And my family will love you."

"Yeah? You're not just saying that?"

"No. They'll like you, if only because being with you makes me happy. I've had so much fun hanging out and studying with you and normally that is *so* not my thing. Seriously, my mom will be thrilled that I finally met one of those mythical 'good influences' she's always on about. Jacob and the gang are always convincing me to skive off from class to hang out with them. They're all about making the most of our university experience, but it's been cool to have you challenging me to do my best academically."

"Yeah? So, you like that I'm a giant nerd?" I tease, leaning back and twisting to face them better.

"Love it." Jordie agrees. They scoot to angle themself more fully toward me.

"So, we're dating?" I ask, nerves prickling along my skin at just how badly I want them to say yes. I smooth my hands over my lap, missing their warm weight on top of me.

"Mhm, we are." Jordie captures my hand and squeezes. "For

starters, I'm taking you to Frisky's for dancing and drinks and then to Randy's for dessert after we get through midterms."

"Yeah? You're my date? Joyfriend? What term do you like?"

"Date, partner, or joyfriend all work. And that makes you my boyfriend, right?" Jordie cocks their head, giving me the chance to correct them.

That pause to confirm makes my chest swell with a sense of being truly seen. Jordie has a knack for giving me the room to be a guy and a boyfriend, but also holding space for the parts of me that aren't defined by my gender. That in-between liminal space inside me I haven't had a chance to fully explore while struggling with a dysphoria that I've had to keep bottled up for so long. I nod. Boyfriend isn't entirely right, but it's not wrong either. And I want to hear Jordie call me theirs.

"Alright then, boyfriend."

Wow, the rush of heat that word from them sparks inside me, electric with possibility. For the first time, I'm someone's boyfriend. It's incredible to be seen and accepted for the real me. There's still a niggling bit of doubt, not that I'm *not* a boy and a boyfriend, just that maybe it isn't as simple as that for me? A something I still can't put into words. Jordie's bold embrace of themself gives me hope I can explore myself too, but for now boyfriend feels right. Euphoric even, a bubbly joy in my heart. It's just that partner also feels right. "Partner works too."

"Perfect. We're official." Jordie grins at me.

"Yeah, we are." I grin so big it makes my cheeks ache.

Boyfriend or partner, both terms suit what I want to be to

Jordie, and with them. They give me the support I need to explore what that means. Later, because just then Jordie leans in and kisses my neck and I forget all about talking in favor of making out with my new joyfriend.

Chapter Fourteen

Jordie

Oh fuck. Ray just kissed me. And I liked it. I more than liked it. It's a damn good thing I'm not tucking today; I am so freaking hard that would be miserable. Bad enough that I'm straining against the extra padded front of my gaffing panties as Ray scrambles onto my lap, straddling me so we can continue to kiss. His hands in my hair send little tingles of pleasure-pain right to my balls and I'm moaning like I've never made out before. It's so good. And I told myself I wouldn't go here, but we both want it and I can't seem to help myself in the face of our mutual desire.

I think back to what Celeste said. About how it's not like I really have power over Ray. Sure, he's still new to being out as trans, but that's not the same thing as being new to his sexuality. He might not be ready to tell the world he's my *boy*friend instead of my girlfriend, but I believe his promise that he's proud to hold my hand in public. I've been building up this idea of a power imbalance in my head, but I'm putty in his hands as he grinds into my erection, tongue fucking into my mouth.

There's nothing tentative or unsure about his movements on top of me. I like that.

I enjoy being taken and used and I want to feel more of him, have him take me just like this. Except when one hand leaves my hair to fish my cock out, I'm struck with the realization that there is definitely more to discuss before anyone gets naked.

When I stiffen under him, no longer bucking up to meet each roll of his hips, lips parted as he pants for breath, Ray searches my face with concern.

"Sorry, too much? Should I get up?" He moves as if to climb off my lap and I wrap my arms around him and shake my head, keeping him in place.

"No, I like you on top of me. I want to keep going. Just. Need to know a few things first."

"I'm negative. Got tested back when I was dealing with all my visa papers, to be on the safe side. I haven't been with anyone new since," Ray says. And I'm glad he worded it like that instead of implying that I'm dirty because of the diagnosis I need to disclose to him now.

Hoping he'll take this well, I force a smile and dive in. "So, yeah. I get tested every few months. I've got herpes though. For a few years now. It's uh, anal HSV-2, so there are things we can do to reduce risk, but it is still possible to transmit it. I take antivirals so that helps reduce outbreaks and viral shedding between outbreaks and I always use condoms for anal and dental dams for rimming. So that should minimize our transmission risk. I also avoid hooking up when I'm having an outbreak. I like to bottom, but rimming I can live without if that's a concern."

"Oh." Ray looks at me, all wide-eyed, and I can't read his reaction.

"Is that a deal-breaker?" I force myself to meet his gaze and try to brace not to hold it against him if it is. It wouldn't be the first time. Far from it. Stigma sucks.

"No." He licks his lips, but there's no hesitation or doubt on his face. That's a relief. Tension drains from my muscles and I let myself believe this can be real. "Are you, um, having an outbreak now?"

"No. And I will tell you if I am."

"Okay." Ray nods and reaches for my nape to pull me into another devouring kiss. "I guess not having a bio dick to fuck you with lowers the risk too? Or you topping?"

"Sure, it's still best to use condoms for anal, even with a store-bought cock. We should probably use condoms regardless of who is fucking whom. I don't want kids." I glance at his lap and lick my lips, totally loving the idea of being inside of him.

Ray blanches. "Fuck. No. I don't either. I have an IUD. Haven't had to think about that in years. But can't hurt to use a condom if you're the one doing the fucking. Is that what you want?"

"Among other things." I shrug. This is why I prefer fucking other genderqueer folks. So many fewer assumptions and it feels less like stepping into quicksand to bring up my preferences. Ray arches a brow at me. He seems unsurprised at the idea I'd want to fuck him, and the way he licks his lips and keeps darting glances at my lap says he's into the idea. Still, better to ask than assume. "Are you cool with that?"

"I just like to feel good. Doesn't matter too much how it happens. I haven't really done the fucking, but I had a girlfriend who was a total top. Usually default to the front hole since it's less of a hassle and it feels better, but either way works. And I ordered that harness thingy earlier, so I'd be down to top your sweet ass. Or whatever you want to call it, your bussy?"

I snort. "My ass is fine. Or pussy is nice sometimes." I dart out my tongue to wet my lips. "And um, dick and clit are both good for my junk; I like to mix it up."

"Sure. I mostly default to generic terms, like hole or junk."

"Not dick?" I tentatively cup my hand over his groin. Ray grinds into it.

"Mm, maybe if I go on T and it grows enough to feel like a dick? It just doesn't yet." He sighs, shoulders hunching, as if thinking too hard about his body is taking him out of the mood. That isn't what I want, so I try to reframe.

"Maybe click for now? I've known some guys who use that to describe it. Not a clit, but not quite a dick either?" I rub the bulge through his pants and grin. "Whatever you call it, I want to make it feel incredible."

"I like that. Click." Ray perks up. "Oh, and my packer sort of feels like the real deal, so if you want to suck that dick, I think that would be hot."

"Is that your super subtle way of asking me to suck your dick, sunshine?" I tease, rubbing him more insistently through his pants.

"God, I love it when you call me that." His eyes roll back and his lashes flutter shut. He looks delicious, turned on, and needy for me.

"Sunshine?" I ask, rubbing his packer a smidge harder than I would a natal dick. Ray grinds into my touch, seeking more friction.

"Yeah." He nods.

"Let me suck you off, sunshine." I flash him a seductive smile.

"Do I get to go down on you too?" he asks. His fingers nudge at my waistband, brushing the bare skin of my hips and trying to ease my clingy leggings lower.

"After," I kiss him, lingering when his tongue darts into my mouth, savoring the taste of him and how well we fit together. "I want to focus on you this first time, if that's good?"

"Totally." Ray stands up, leaving my lap empty and my dick wilting a little at the sudden absence of his warm weight. He reaches for his side table, fishing out lube and pausing over a foil packet. "Um, are you good with using condoms for oral?"

"Yeah, that's fine. I'm sure it will feel good, regardless. You want me to use a dental dam on you?"

Ray shrugs and gives me a self-deprecating chuckle. "Up to you. I might last longer that way, but we'd have to cut up a condom and I don't have scissors, so I'm okay risking it if you are."

I get up and grab a couple of dental dams that I keep in my school bag for those in need and toss them onto his bed. "I've got you covered. Keeping supplies for baby queers is sort of my thing. Don't usually provide a full on demonstration of how they work though."

"Not my first time. I'm new to being out as a guy, but I've been with other guys and girls. So, like no need for kid gloves."

I pull my shirt over my head, leaving the bra on since it's holding my cutlets in place, and I want to feel sexy and curvy for this. "Yeah? You're that excited to have my mouth on your junk, sunshine?"

Ray's face glows with embarrassed heat as he nods. "I might've fantasized about this a few times."

"Oh? What did I do in your fantasies?" I stalk closer to him, reaching to unfasten his pants.

"First, you kissed me."

I close the distance between us, caress his cheek and tip up his face so I can kiss him. As our eyes lock, I move in slowly, holding the eye contact so I can savor the desire in his lust-drunk gaze. I give him a rougher kiss this time, nipping at his lower lip as we part.

"Like that?" I ask. Ray is gazing at me with a besotted look that matches my own feelings for him.

"Mhm, and then all down my neck. With your hands on me."

"Show me how to touch you." I kiss his neck and rest my palms on his hips. He presses his hands over mine, guiding them into his pants to cup his ass, squeezing and parting his cheeks. I moan as I suck a lovebite into his neck. His skin is clean and salty and I want to taste so much more of him. Lap his fluids from his folds, tease him until he's soaking wet and begging me to fuck him. I nudge my thigh between his legs, encouraging him to grind against me, his body doing the begging.

I brush over his pucker, then pull my hands free of his pants so I can get them off of his body. I want to see all of him. Touch him all over and make him come until he doesn't have another orgasm left in him.

"Mmhm, like that. Want you so bad, Jordie." Ray fumbles with my stretchy pants. I step back, just out of reach.

"Get naked, sunshine." I slide my legging and the clingy gaffing panties down my legs as I watch him do the same.

Ray strips down to his binder, fingers fiddling with the hem reluctantly.

"You can leave it on if you want," I suggest.

"I sometimes like nipple stuff, but sometimes..." he shifts his weight, like he feels bad about having a boundary.

"You don't have to negotiate with me about your dysphoria, sunshine. If playing with your chest is uncomfortable, then it's off limits until and unless you tell me otherwise."

"Yeah, that would be good."

"Good. I don't want to hurt you." I brush his cheek with my knuckles.

"I mean, I kind of like when it hurts a little. Like, rough sex." Ray's eyes dart all around the room, landing everywhere but on me as he talks. As if he's not quite comfortable discussing his preferences. Well, I can do my part to make it easier to open up. I reach out and cup his cheek, caressing along his jaw.

"Well, that's hot as hell, but it's not the same as offering to do things you don't enjoy to please me. Turns out, making you uncomfortable in ways you don't want isn't a turn on for me, okay?"

"Yeah. Okay." Ray swallows hard. "Yeah. I don't want you to play with my chest."

I nod. "Binder is off limits, got it. You can play with my boobs. I like the idea of having more curves and having you touch them while you plow me. Now, get comfy at the edge of the bed so you can fuck my face and leave me dripping in your cum."

Ray gives me a dazed look. His eyes dart to my chest and he licks his lips like he's thinking about how much he wants to touch me. He swallows hard, throat moving under my fingertips. "Fuck, you're hot."

He cups my boobs in his hands, getting enough of my chest underneath the falsies that I can almost imagine they're entirely made of flesh. I close my eyes and savor the way he squeezes me, with such tender care. It's too intensely sweet to take for more than a few seconds without the bittersweet ache of wondering how it would feel if I went on estrogen, so I shift the focus.

"So are you. Now let me see the goods, babe. Can't wait to have my mouth on you."

Ray perches on the edge of his bed, takes a deep steadying breath, then arranges himself on the mattress with his legs spread wide and his junk on full display.

I take off my pants and step between Ray's thighs, leaning

over him so that he has to look up at me. He looks so vulnerable and delicious as I take his lips in another bruising kiss. I place my hands on his thighs and work teasingly toward my goal. Just brushing his inner thighs, stroking him until he whimpers into my mouth and shifts, attempting to get me to explore more sensitive regions.

"Impatient boy," I tease, resting my forehead against his and smirking against his lips as they curve into a grin at the affirmation.

Ray huffs out a frustrated breath. "I want you to touch me."

"I *am* touching you." I tap his thighs in emphasis. "*Where* do you want me to touch you?"

"I want your fingers inside me and your mouth on my click."

"Mhm, that's better, much more specific. You want me to feel how wet I make you?"

"Ungh, you're a giant tease." Ray squirms as I inch my fingers closer to where he wants them.

I hold him open with two fingers and slip two on my other hand inside of him. Ray gasps. He said he likes rough, so I spread and twist my fingers as I pump into him, relishing the way he clenches around me. He rides my fingers, needy and eager and wet for me. I kiss away his desperate moaning.

"Your hungry little hole wants to be filled up, huh? Dripping for it, aren't you?"

"Yeah, oh, yes. Right there. Harder, Jordie, need…" he trails off as I sink to my knees and breathe onto his slick folds. I sink a third finger into him and reach for the dental dam.

"Open this and I'll give you exactly what you need, sunshine." I press the packet into Ray's hand and watch as his fingers tremble when I keep thrusting my fingers inside of him. I search along his inner wall for the spot that makes him arch and gasp. There. Ray drops the foil packet on my face, and I laugh as I rub him more insistently. "Good?"

"Esti! Qu-c'est bon! Good, calice. So good. More." He pants and squirms on my fingers. And I just discovered a new kink. Making my boyfriend babble at me in another language is next level intoxicating. His accent is always music to my ears, but he's beyond adorable when he's losing himself in pleasure.

"Damn, that's sexy." I don't stop what I'm doing. Ray, coming undone from just my fingers inside him, has my dick hard as a rock. I want to hear more of his desperate pleading. "Dis-moi ce que tu veux, Ray."

"Plus fort. Baise-moi à mort," he gasps out the request, breathy and sweet. And I might not know that exact phrase from class, but I get the gist of things even before he adds. "Damn, Jordie, you're fucking my brains out. Can't think straight."

"Well, considering how straight you aren't, that's fine; still need for you to open the dental dam if you want my mouth, though."

"Oh, yeah." He fumbles for the packet, and shakily opens it, lifting the sheet of latex toward me. "Here."

"Hold it over yourself." I instruct since my fingers are still busy and smearing his juices all over the barrier would sort of defeat at least part of the purpose of using it. "This is much more fun than just handing them out to the baby queers in need."

"Mhm, nothing like hands-on learning." Ray presses the latex over his click.

I glance up at him through my lashes as I lap along his folds to the swollen nub peeking out of its hood. He's clearly as aroused as I am. I flick my tongue over the tip and he bucks and whines.

"More?" I taunt.

"Fuck, yes," Ray demands. "No fair keeping my hands busy."

"You want to pull my hair, sunshine?"

"Yes. I want you all disheveled."

"Yeah?"

"I want to fuck that pretty mouth of yours until I come down your throat."

"Mhmm." I lower my mouth to his click again, sucking on him even as I trace patterns with my tongue.

Part of me wishes I could taste the tang of his body instead of the chemical latex flavor of the dental dam, but I also want him to last a while. I want to take him apart slowly. Linger over learning his body and his every shuddering response to my fingers and tongue.

I suck him more fully into my mouth, tongue mapping what he likes and inventorying his responses. How he shudders and moans, seeking more with every lick and thrust. He whimpers and bucks to meet me when I spear him with a fourth finger. I bet he'd happily take my entire fist. I hum around his click, and he trembles, clenching around my fingers, so slick and needy. It's beyond hot to know he's this wet for me, eager to take me.

"Fuck, Jordie. Plus fort. Need more."

I lift my mouth to grin at him. "More what?"

"No, don't stop!" Ray whines. "Ungh. You. Everything."

I lap over his click, teasing him. "You want my mouth here?"

"Yes!" He keens.

I continue my pattern of licking and sucking until his juices are dripping down my wrist and continue finger-fucking his hole until he's a whimpering, horny mess. The babble spilling from his lips is a polyglot mixture of nonsense and need. I could listen to the music of his pleasure all night. His responses have my dick aching, so I drop my free hand to stroke myself as I continue to pleasure him.

"Mm, you are so sexy, sunshine. Going to get off just watching you come apart."

"Uh huh?" he flushes at the praise.

"Yeah." I dip down to lick and kiss his click between words and he bucks up to meet me. "Love fucking my sexy boyfriend." I fuck my fingers into him harder in emphasis.

His eyes flutter, rolling back in his head. He doesn't even try to hide his arousal, and it's beautiful to behold. "Make me come, babe."

"I will. When I'm ready." I tease him, fluttering my tongue over him. I'm in no hurry to take Ray over the brink. Whenever he seems too close to coming, I back off subtly. I edge the fuck out of my new boyfriend, making our first time last and last until Ray loses all semblance of coherence. He lets go of the dental dam so he can tangle his fingers in my hair and hold my mouth tight to his click.

I reach between us with my free hand to hold it in place so I don't choke on the damn thing. I can already taste the musky tang of his arousal fluids, so I guess so much for good intentions. I lift away to remove the latex, balling it up to throw out later, and get my mouth back on him.

Ray gasps at having my tongue on his bare click, and I love being able to taste him. We'll have to practice keeping it in place better before he gets his mouth anywhere near my ass, but that's a worry for later. For now, I savor this moment of connection.

"Don't stop. Suce-moi la bite juste comme ça. Oh, so good, Jordie." He moans. In combination with his hands holding me in place, his French needs no interpretation as his fingers run along my scalp soothingly. He wants me to keep giving it to him just like this. And I'm going to nut any second anyway, too keyed up to last much longer.

"Oh, fuck. Je vais jouir! Gonna come."

As if I couldn't tell. I've got a front-row seat to just how gloriously close he is to his orgasm, and I want to draw it out now more than ever.

I keep sucking him, doubling down on his pleasure as his little dick jerks hard against my tongue. His fingers tighten more, tugging at my scalp. His hole clenches rhythmically around my fingers, leaving no doubt that he's coming.

I reach down and jerk myself to the same rhythm, imagining

his body clenching around me. Or his newly acquired strap-on cock pumping into me. I want to try both scenarios. I want to explore all the ways we can make each other feel this good. Pleasure coils tight in the pit of my belly and rolls over me. The sharp prick of pain as he tugs on my hair is what tips me over the edge. I love being wanted this intensely.

I don't stop until Ray goes slack under me. I gently let his spent click slip from between my lips, lapping once more over him before finding the balled up spit-slicked dental dam and tossing it in the trash. Ray gazed up at me through hooded eyes.

"Good?" I ask, suddenly feeling tentative and unsure. As though he might toss me out now that the heat of the moment has passed.

"So good. Do I get a turn to make you come now?" Ray reaches toward me and I let him pull me toward him. Up off the floor so I can park my ass on the bed next to him, mindful of my sticky hands.

I lean down to brush a reassuring kiss to his brow. "You already did, sunshine. You think I can be inside you like that and hold myself back?"

He flushes. "Yeah? You came from sucking me off?"

"Yeah. You're as hot as the sun, sunshine," I wink at him. "Next time I'd love to have your new dick inside me though."

"Yeah? You really want me to fuck you?" His eyes dart away, unable to meet mine. Adorable shy boy. I pat his thigh.

"Of course. If you're into that? I won't assume the harness you bought means anything about what you want to do with me. And there are other ways you can fuck me."

"You can assume a little. I want to fuck your pretty ass, Jords." He trails his fingers lazily down my back toward said ass. He just brushes the top of my crack and it's nice, but not enough to have me revved up for round two yet. "Tell me about these other ways?"

"Muffing. You know about tucking?" I scoot to create some space. Not ready to bare too much more of my soul to him tonight.

"Keith and Pixel might've mentioned that a time or two. Is that why I never see your bulge when you wear skirts?" Ray asks, leaning up on his elbow to watch me better.

"Yeah. I tuck sometimes. But part of the process is pushing your balls up into your body. And it can feel amazing if you fingerfuck up into the inguinal canals where the balls go when I do that. So you could fuck me that way sometime."

"That sounds super hot. Getting to be inside you, your body tight all around me." Ray crunches up off the bed and loops an arm around my nape to pull me in for a kiss on my lips. "We should definitely try it soon. But for now, do you want to cuddle for a bit before we put clothes back on?"

"Sure. You can whisper more filthy French into my ears."

Ray flushes. "Fuck, did I slip?"

"Yeah, but it was hot as hell making you lose track of yourself like that." I grin at him and his expression softens. He brushes a flop of curls back off my face tenderly, making me feel cherished, my insides all warm and fuzzy that he's being sweet with me after the orgasms.

"I'm just used to dating Francophones." Ray sticks his tongue out at me. "Context, ya know?"

"Sure. I'll just have to fuck you better so you associate sex with me and English." I wink at him. He laughs and tugs me closer for another kiss. I overbalance and we sprawl in his bed together, kissing sweetly until my phone ringing rouses us both from our drowsy naked snuggling. I groan, but reluctantly untangle myself from my lover because my family rarely calls this late for no reason, and I know it's Liam from the ringtone.

"Sorry, it's my brother. I should get that." I give Ray an apologetic look as I scan the floor for my clothes.

"It's okay." He gets up too, pulling on an oversized tee-shirt. The bottom reaches his mid-thigh and covers him up just enough to give me a tantalizing glimpse of his ass when he bends to hand over my shirt. I pass his discarded socks to him. "I should go over the study guide again before bed anyway."

"Yeah, let me just see what's going on." I snag my twirly skirt—extra fun because yay pockets!—from near his desk to fish my phone out, answering right before the voicemail picks up.

"Hey, what's up?" I cradle the phone between my ear and shoulder as I answer.

"Hey, Jordie, sorry it's late. You know that history essay I asked you to help me with?" My brother sounds stressed. And I feel very weird talking to him with no pants on, so I wriggle back into my clothes while we talk.

"Yeah, bud?"

"It's due tomorrow, not next Friday, like I thought. Oops."
My brother gives a nervous titter of a laugh. Mom will not be
happy about the mixup. But Liam can be forgetful about stuff
he doesn't care about, and he's supposed to have an education
plan to help him stay on track with due dates.

"It wasn't in the schedule?" I rub at my temples and look
around for my socks. I mouth an apology to Ray, because I
know where this is going. It's shaping up to be a long night
working on this essay with my brother and studying for my
exams.

"It was, but I've been going to taekwondo every night this
week to get ready for our next competition. I forgot to check the
school schedule because I thought I had more time. And—"

"It's okay, take a breath. The important thing is that you
noticed and we are going to get the assignment done in time,
okay?"

"Yeah," Liam takes a deep breath. "Okay."

"I am going to head back to my place and call you back, email
me the assignment and get your books organized, alright?"

"Yeah. Thanks, Jordie. I'll send it to you." He sounds so
relieved that I can't hold the inconvenience of the last minute
call against the kid.

"No problem. Talk to you soon, Liam." I hang up and slip my
phone into my pocket. I turn toward Ray with an apologetic
grimace because I'm really not ready to go, but I know I have
to. "It's my brother, sorry, Ray. He's having a minor homework

crisis. I hate to come and then go, but he needs me."

"I get it. Family comes first." Ray forces a smile. "Call me later? I'll be up late studying."

"I'll text first. This has nothing to do with what we just did, okay?" I reach out and rub my palms down his arms, wishing I could stay and continue learning every plane of his body.

"Yeah. I know. We should do it again soon." Ray gives me a wobbly smile.

"I had a great time, and I'd love to stay longer." I pull him into a hug, pressing a kiss to his temple and hoping I'm not messing up our budding relationship already.

"Next time you can stay longer." Ray rests his head on my shoulder, hugging me close. I hold on, rocking him from side to side and savoring the affection.

"Next time." I agree, then I tip his face up for a proper goodnight kiss. I take my time tasting him. Our tongues tangle in a sensual dance that has my cock perking up for another round. That won't be happening tonight unless it's with my hand while I'm reliving what we just did.

I sigh and we part reluctantly. I gather up my school stuff, taking my time to linger in Ray's presence and stealing glances at him.

"Go help your brother with his homework." Ray nudges me toward the door.

"Goodnight, sunshine."

"Night, Jordie." Ray stands in his doorway, watching as I walk down the hall to the stairs. I wink at him and blow a kiss that he pretends to catch with a goofy lovestruck grin before I push through the doors and out of sight. Damn, I have the cutest boyfriend ever. That can't be wrong. Even if he is new to figuring out his identity and part of me is still concerned about him growing away from me once he no longer needs a mentor to guide him through the first steps of his transition.

It wouldn't be the first time I guided a baby queer right out of my life. But I still want to go on that journey with him. Explore every part of him as he gets ever more comfortable with himself. I want to see him bloom and stay by his side.

I can't shake the sense Nell ingrained in me that Ray is going to outgrow his uses for me. But when he does, from where I'm standing now, the pain of that parting will still be worth the joy of the precious moments we've been sharing along the way. I just need to protect my heart against that inevitable end, even as I savor my first real taste of Ray's lingering sweetness on my tongue.

Chapter Fifteen

Jordie

I flush as I turn in my French midterm to the TA. I drew a blank halfway through the last section where I was supposed to write sentences in various verb tenses. Turns out, practicing for my exam with my boyfriend was simultaneously among my best and worst ideas. Best because he has a way of making the words and concepts from class stick in my head. And it was a perfect excuse to spend extra time with him, so points for snagging the adorable little twinky all for myself.

The problem is that I can't quite seem to stop associating the near future conjugations he helped me work on with the breathy way his voice broke last night. While he was moaning that he was about to come. Not that I mind the reminder of being with him for the first time.

Fuck, he was so hot coming with my fingers knuckle-deep inside him. I called him after we got Liam's essay finished, and we might've gotten a bit carried away. I jerked myself off listening to Ray finger himself as he described all the filthy things he wants to do with me.

The boy is not shy about sex. Even if he is new to presenting as a guy and he stumbled a little over how badly he wants to fuck me with his big fat cock. If things continue to go this well between us, I want to taste his salty-sweet release. I love listening to that adorable accent of his thickening when he gets turned on and his words slip between languages.

For the exam, I came up with some ridiculous sentence about going to pick apples because Ray mentioned that he usually does that with his family this time of year. So I think I did alright on my midterm, even distracted with thoughts of my sexy new boyfriend and the breathy way the French dripped from his tongue last night. I can't wipe the grin off my lips or keep the pep out of my step just thinking about him. Giddy delight thrums through my veins.

I text Ray as I'm leaving the building.

Jordie: Nailed it. Thanks to my sexy boyfriend whispering French in my ear last night ;)

Ray: I'll nail you :P But srsly, happy to be of service.

Jordie: :P or just happy to service me? ;)

Ray: Both.

He follows that up with the *Road to El Dorado* 'why not both' GIF.

Jordie: Typical bisexual :P

Ray: You're one to talk. Have time for a last minute cram session before the psych exam?

Jordie: You're going to do fine, but yeah, we can meet up. Want to grab lunch at Randy's with me?

Ray: Sure. Meet you there after my English lecture. Probably for the best to study in public since *someone* is too randy to focus if we met in my dorm.

Jordie: I can't help that my partner is a sexy beast ;) Cya there <3 *kissy face*

Ray: Horn dog. À bientôt.

Now that we're official, I don't skimp on the flirty emojis. I want Ray to know how much I like him. There's no sense playing my emotions close to the vest at this point. I should probably at least try not to be a bad influence.

Jordie: And quit texting in class :P

Ray: You can't make me. It's boooooooring. Ugh. Can't wait to see my sweet delicious coffee...

Jordie: Hey! What about your sweet delicious joyfriend?

Ray: Hmm, might have to taste them again to be sure if they're really that sweet and delicious XP

Jordie: *pouty face*

Ray: Aw, my joyfriend is a needy bottom. And, yes, I can't wait to taste your mouth again. And maybe other parts of you ;)

Jordie: Hmm, I dunno, maybe I'll make you earn it...

Ray: Thought I helped you pass your test? ;P

Jordie: Touchee. Pay attention to the rest of your class, then come and claim your kiss, sunshine.

He doesn't reply right away to correct my poor grammar, possibly because he's given up on me ever keeping my accent marks straight. I have to dodge through a crowd of students playing frisbee on the green as I cut across to my apartment. I tuck my phone away and hurry to grab my study stuff so I can meet Ray for lunch at Randy's.

It's just past the noon rush when I arrive at the diner so I can claim an open table with a good view of the door for when Ray arrives. It's slow enough that there's a guy with his gaming rig set up at a booth playing an online game. I vaguely recognize the images on the screen from watching Keith, Abe, and Celeste playing it like the nerds they are at heart.

I spot a familiar face, Arlene, standing at the counter and sidle up to chat while I wait for Ray.

"Hey, Arlene, right? We met a few weeks ago, through Claude." I chatted with her while Ray gabbed away in French with Claude and another regular at the diner, Avery, who overheard them.

"Oh, yes. Jordie, wasn't it?" she asks.

"Yep, you got it. How've you been?" I smile at her.

"Keeping busy. I've made more cupcakes than I could hope to eat lately. So, just grabbing a quick lunch to go," she gestures toward the kitchen, looking flustered.

"That bad, huh?" I scrunch my face up in sympathy.

"Yeah. I'll be fine once I get caught up again." She waves away my concern and I don't push.

The bell over the door jingles and I glance over in time to see Ray walk in, chatting with Claude in French. Ray hit it off with them right away, bonding over their shared connections to Quebec. I could tell how happy it made Ray to have that little auditory taste of home to go with his poutine the first time they met. So I'm glad they've remained friendly.

The two of them spot us right away. Claude's eyes light up at the sight of Arlene as much as I'm sure mine do when I see Ray. Interesting, but not my business. I wave the two of them over to join us, then say my goodbyes to Arlene at the first break in conversation.

I tug Ray over to a nearby free table and drag him down to sit next to me so I can greet him with an enthusiastic kiss. Henry, one of the more flamboyant servers, wolf whistles playfully from across the room. I smirk against Ray's lips.

Ray smiles dazedly up at me. "Guess you're happy to see me?" he jokes.

"Very." I lean in so I can whisper the rest into the shell of his ear. "If we didn't have an exam in an hour, I'd totally drag you back to my place to ravage me properly."

Ray flushes, swallowing hard, eyes darting to the rest of the dining area before he hides behind his menu and murmurs an invitation. "Come over tonight? No roommates to worry about at my place."

I nod. "It's a date."

Claude, still standing close by, clears their throat, an amused twinkle in their eyes. "Well, I'm grabbing pie to go. I'll see you two around!"

They shuffle closer to the counter to stand next to Arlene so they can order their dessert. Henry returns from bringing the gamer guy in the corner a soda and steps up to the register. He flirts outrageously with Claude as they place their to-go order. I watch the interaction out of the corner of my eye until Ray draws my attention by setting aside his menu.

"You know," Ray drawls, "my dad always said it's not a date if you aren't going someplace public."

I arch a brow at him. "You want to fuck me in front of an audience, sunshine?"

Ray chokes on his spit. "I think he meant that sex doesn't count as a date."

"And is that also how you feel?" I cock my head and devour him with my eyes. He seemed super into fucking last night. I don't get the impression he's shy about sharing his body, even if he has some no-go areas.

"Not necessarily. I'm not wording it well. I want to fuck you like nobody's business." Ray licks his lips. "But I also want to take you out for dinner or to a movie or dancing at a club. I want more than sex and study dates."

Understanding lights me up, followed by a flood of relief. He's proud to be seen with me. Isn't that what I've been afraid of? Being relegated to his dirty little secret sexcapade? This is a good sign that I'm not an unwitting experiment like I was for Nell. She at least dated me openly. Unlike some folks with one foot still firmly planted in the closet who I hooked up with before I learned my lesson and established my no dating baby queers rule.

"I am all for that. Name the time and place. I usually have family dinner at my folks' place at least one day each weekend, but otherwise my schedule is flexible."

"Cool. It's not really a date, but I, uh, made an appointment to start hormones. At the student health center. Next Friday."

"Oh! Really?" I squash down the surge of jealousy that he's ready for that step while I'm still on the fence. Under the surge of intense want is the irrational fear that Ray taking another step into himself is one step further on his path away from me. I need to let go of that fear. He isn't like the other newly out gays I've loved and lost when I was too queer for them and they didn't need an experiment anymore.

"Yeah. Come with me?" he asks, all shy, sweet innocence.

He wants me to be his guide in this again. I can't say no to him, even though supporting him scares me. I want to be there for him, despite the sick certainty brewing inside me—he's going to outgrow me like a teenage musical phase.

"Yeah. Of course I'd be honored to hold your hand, sunshine."

"Yeah?" He beams at me and I find a more genuine smile for him.

"Yes." I nod and grab his hand to give him a squeeze. "I'll always want to support you."

"Yay! I'm kind of scared because it means I'll have to tell my family sooner than later. But I want it so bad, you know?"

"I know. I can hold your hand for that too," I promise before I can let the old fears creep up on me again. Ray won't lead me on and hurt me the way Nell did. That sort of malicious intent isn't who he is. If he outgrows me, then so be it, but I'm going to grab onto every sweet moment I can with him by both hands.

"That would be amazing!" He smiles at me like I hung the moon and I fall for him even more. This boy is hazardous to my heart.

"Maybe I can make an appointment too. To ask about estrogen," I suggest, then immediately wonder if it's overstepping or somehow stealing his moment. His grin just gets even bigger, and he grips my hand harder, waving our clasped hands around as he talks.

"That would be so cool! We can have the same HRT anniversary! And you're sure about being there to tell my family? You don't have to. I want to do it in person, you know? And it's a long drive. Or flight?" He pulls a sour face and some of the light goes out of his smile.

"What's wrong?"

"Nothing." He worries his lip between his teeth and I resist the urge to thumb it away, waiting him out as he decides how much to share. "It's just tickets are pricier than I hoped, so it's probably not worth going home for the November break since my family won't have time off from work, anyway."

"Oh, right. I guess it's not a holiday there?"

"Nope." Ray sighs.

"Well, if you're feeling homesick, I'm down for a road trip with you. I've even got my passport from my high school graduation vacation with the fam. So long as you're ready for me to meet your family." I wink at him with false bravado. "And if you're comfortable meeting my fam, you wouldn't be the first boyfriend I've brought home. Liam is dying to meet you now that he called and caught me in the afterglow. It would be awesome to bring you to family dinner, but we can go on some just us dates that aren't for studying first. No pressure."

Ray hesitates. "You want me to meet your family?"

"Yeah." I shrug. "It's like what your dad said. If you're worried about messing around with someone who isn't proud to be seen with you, then I want you to know I'm serious about us. And if you hadn't noticed, I'm close to my family. So I want you to meet them. They'll love you. But only when you're ready."

"Yeah. Uh, okay. If we're doing the family thing, you should come to my aunts' place next weekend. We're doing a pie party and maybe another Frisky's night. I can't skip since I flaked on their invite to hang out last weekend in favor of studying and they're so going to report back to the rents that I'm stressed if I skip again."

I know Ray has a standing lunch arrangement with his aunts, but inviting me to join him feels huge.

"And are you?" I ask, because I've noticed that he doesn't really talk about other friends on campus and he's got to be lonely and maybe a little homesick. At least he's been hanging out with my friends more and more. Eating dinner with them even on the days when I have an evening recitation so I can't join the group.

"Yeah. I'm getting used to things. It's similar enough that sometimes I forget it's a whole other country and other times I miss home. But that hasn't been as much of an issue now that

I've been hanging out with your friends."

"Our friends." I correct him.

"You think so? They aren't just tolerating me for your sake?" He gnaws his lip. This time, I indulge the urge to brush a finger against his mouth to get him to stop. He flashes me a grin at the touch.

"Nah, you think Celeste would keep her opinion to herself if she didn't like you? Or Jacob?" I arch a brow at him, because that's a ridiculous notion. And that's not even getting into Pixel and Keith's inability to keep a good roasting to themselves.

"Maybe?" Ray squirms in his seat.

"Nope. They like you for yourself, not just because I brought you around. And they'll like you more the more they get to know you. Trust me on that."

Ray opens his mouth, but then he just licks his lips. Before he can formulate a reply, Henry sashays our way to take our orders. We break out the study guides for one last down and dirty review before the test. And I keep having to shove aside thoughts of all the filthy things I want to do when I have Ray alone again.

Chapter Sixteen

Ray

"Sorry, this is probably a terrible date idea," I apologize after we sit in the waiting room. Up to the moment we spoke to the receptionist to register, this felt like an exciting life event to share. The sterile neutral colors of everything from the walls to the decor and the antiseptic odor of the clinic waiting room bring it home that this is a medical office. The outdated magazines on the table beside have well-worn edges from handling.

I'm antsy sitting there, but I try to play it cool in front of Jordie. Our dating relationship is new enough that I'm still self-conscious around them and eager to prove I can be a good boyfriend. A *boy*friend—even thinking the word makes me grin. They notice and smile at me.

We've both been so busy with classes and other obligations that not a ton has changed between us so far. Other than now that we're together, I get to hold their hand around campus and kiss them. We've made out a lot over the past week too.

That's great and all. I just want to spend all my time with

them, and not just in a big group setting, though that's nice too. Sitting here, I kind of wish I'd planned a better date than this already. Maybe we can go dancing and grab dinner at Randy's, just the two of us, to celebrate this weekend.

"It's not a bad date. This is going to be great for us both." Jordie gives me a tight smile and reaches for my hand.

My palm is all sweaty. Everything I've read says we should both leave here today with everything we need to start our respective hormones. Despite that, I can't stop the anxiety roiling in my gut that something is going to go wrong. Some unexpected roadblock derailing my transition goals before I can really reach for them.

Jordie squeezes my palm. Their hand is as clammy as mine. Knowing they're also nervous is reassuring. I make a silly face. "I mean, usually if you invite a date out for shots, it's at a bar."

"You're the one who's here for shots; I just have to take a couple of pills." Jordie winks at me. It's not really a joke, but it makes me laugh anyway.

"True. I'm glad you're here with me." I give them a sappy smile.

"Me too. I've been waffling about whether to do this for ages, you know?" Jordie says. They bounce our joined hands on their thigh, the silky material of their skirt cool and soothing.

"What held you back?" I ask. They usually lean more fem in their presentation, so I'm not surprised that they've been considering estrogen, just curious about why they haven't taken the leap yet. They've always struck me as being supremely confident in themself.

Jordie glances between me and the bored receptionist, then leans in to murmur near my ear, "I like using my clit to fuck. Hormones can, uh, interfere with that." They hold up their hand and make a gesture, evoking a limp dick, one finger wilting toward their fist.

"Oh." I flush at the mental image of them fucking me in my bed. So far, we've only made out and gone down on each other a handful of times, but I want to try more with them. Everything.

"Yeah. But I think we can work around that, right?" They push their curls self-consciously behind their ear. Damn, they're so cute. I love tangling my fingers in that hair while they suck me. How much better is that going to feel when I've got bottom growth from the meds I'm here today to start? I shiver in delicious anticipation. There is so much I want to do with them.

"Definitely." I nod, licking my lips. "We'll make it work. There are plenty of other ways to enjoy each other."

Jordie grins, eyeing me as salaciously as I'm watching them. "Yeah, we will."

The door to the back opens, and the nurse calls my name. I jump up and glance between Jordie and the nurse, reluctant to drop their hand. I take a deep breath to steady myself. Jordie gives my palm one last squeeze, then releases me.

"Good luck, sunshine," they say.

"You too! Meet you here after we're both done?" I check, hesitating now that the moment is here.

"Yep!" Jordie grins. I pause again at the threshold, glancing back over my shoulder at them for one more hit of courage. They flash me two thumbs up while making a goofy face to make me laugh as I follow the nurse into the back, my heart thundering in my chest. This is it. A turning point.

The nurse measures me and asks me about my medical history and why I'm here. I answer by rote. Then I get shepherded into an exam room where I stare awkwardly at the wall diagrams of various organ systems and medical jargon until the doctor comes in. She rubs on hand sanitizer as she introduces herself and confirms my name.

She briskly asks the same questions, then delivers a spiel about HRT that she reads off a computer monitor. We talk until she seems satisfied that I understand what I'm getting into and that some changes are irreversible. She prints the document on her screen and asks me to sign the informed consent form. Then she hands me a prescription and tells me to wait again because the nurse needs to draw my blood for baseline monitoring and teach me how to inject myself.

I'm dazed, staring at the little square of paper that's going to change my life. I drum my heels against the legs of the exam room chair. My phone buzzes in my pocket.

Jordie: How's it going?

Ray: Good. Got it!

I snap a selfie, holding up the prescription with my tongue out because I feel kind of silly doing it. Jordie sends back a heart GIF followed by a selfie of themself with their fingers crossed beside their face in an exam room almost identical to mine.

Jordie: Ah! Congrats! I'm waiting for the doctor. Wish me luck.

I send a lucky charms GIF with psychedelic marshmallows flashing on a spoon to them.

Ray: All the luck. It was just like Pix said, lots of talking threatening me with a good time, and then sign the paper and get the prescription.

Jordie sends me a laughing GIF.

Jordie: I mean, that's fair for you two. You both wanted all the effects. I'm a little nervous about some changes. *nervous face emoji*

Ray: Yeah. It will be okay. You can always stop if it's not what you're expecting.

Jordie: True. That's what Lio did.

Ray: Oh?

Jordie: Yeah. They got the prescription and then decided they didn't actually want to transition medically.

Ray: Cool. So long as they're happy, good for them.

Jordie: Mhm. You done already?

Ray: No, waiting for them to take all my blood for testing and show me how to do the shots.

Jordie: Cool. How do you feel about injecting yourself?

Ray: Squirmy?

Jordie: Well, I'm game to learn how if you need help.

Ray: Might take you up on that.

There's a perfunctory rap on my door and I fumble out one last quick message before shoving my phone away.

Ray: TTYL

The nurse gives me a weary smile and confirms my legal name and birthday. It's jarring to hear my full name after months of everyone outside my family using Ray to address me. Even my professors have been good about using my chosen name in the handful of smaller lectures where I actually interact with them much.

I need to look into getting my ID documents officially changed. Which means telling my family. Ugh. Now that I'm starting meds, it's only a matter of time before they know, one way or another.

The nurse draws my blood with brisk efficiency and hands me a brochure on how to inject myself. She briefly explains the process, but I can't really get past the idea of having to stab myself to pay attention to the details.

"Um, I'm not sure I'll be able to figure out how to do this on my own."

"You can ask at the pharmacy if you need more instructions. Or bring your supplies here once you have them and book a nursing care appointment for one of us to give you the medication. There are good videos online too."

"Yeah. Okay. Thanks." I shove the brochure and prescription into my pocket. A brief flash of delight at how well they fit in the spacious pockets of my new wardrobe is enough to overshadow my nerves. It's been months and I'm still delighted at what a difference Jordie's simple style change suggestions can make.

"No problem, dear. If you want us to help you with the first shot, book an appointment on your way out. You'll also need to get another round of monitoring labs in about three months. Tiff at reception will get you set up. Have a nice day."

"Okay, thanks. You too."

Even with the daunting prospect of learning how to self-inject and tell my parents hanging over my head, I'm still on cloud nine. I float down the hall back to the waiting area. I'm grinning as I make my followup appointments with Tiff. I can't help pulling out the prescription to stare at it in awe when I plunk back down in the hard plastic seats to wait for Jordie's appointment to be over.

I scroll on my phone, perusing my group chat notifications from our friends. It's still weird to think of them as *ours* instead of Jordie's, but Jordie wasn't wrong when they said the others like me for my own sake. It still hits me like a sugar rush whenever I'm hanging out with them; I'm making friends who know all of me for the first time.

I'm forming my own friendships with the entire gang. Jacob pops into my DMs with borderline flirty memes. Lio and Pixel have been sending me trans shit-posting jokes and hanging out with me between classes while Jordie is busy. I've even gone for coffee with Celeste and drinks with Abe and Keith.

I can only hope my brothers will be equally supportive when I tell them the big secret that's felt like a massive invisible wall between us. It's been a weight on my mind for so long; I've forgotten what it's like not to have an unspoken barrier holding me back from being fully present with the people I love. Words on the tip of my tongue that I keep swallowing down out of fear of how they will react.

I get caught up on our friends' plans for a drag brunch on Sunday and pull up my private messages with Jordie. I text that I'm done. Then stare at the screen, waiting for a reply.

When it comes, it's a beaming picture of Jordie with their prescriptions held up beside their face. They look so happy. I want to kiss them and celebrate this milestone together.

Ray: Amazing! Next stop, the pharmacy ;)

Jordie: Hell yes! See you soon.

They send me a GIF of a vampire, so I figure that means they're getting their blood drawn too.

Ray: I'll be here when you're done.

I don't get an immediate response, so I figure it won't be much longer. While I wait, I poke around on my social media. Darren changed his profile pic to one of him with the cutie he's been seeing and his relationship status to officially dating Ed. I congratulate him, then scroll through the positive responses from my extended family.

The entire thread of messages fills me with hope. If they can publicly embrace Darren dating a trans person, that maybe they'll accept who I am too. Even if I'm not entirely sure how to describe my gender beyond not a girl, while also not as uncomplicated as just being a boy. From what I know about Ed, zir gender isn't straightforward either.

Darren's new profile pic has him and Ed gazing adoringly at each other as they embrace in front of the botanical garden's gorgeous rose trellises. I can practically smell their sweet perfume and it makes me miss home in a way I haven't since falling in with Jordie and my new friends. Crisp fall afternoons wandering through the gardens have always been a highlight of the season. I thumb the like button and close the app.

Perfect timing, because that's when the door to the exam rooms swings open and Jordie strides through with a triumphant smile for me. I stand and go to hug them, and they feel so right in my arms. Soon, they'll be the one with the soft curves pressed against the squashed smooth planes of my chest, and that will be even better. I squeeze them tight, ignoring the way my binder digs into my skin and constricts every breath.

"Can't believe we did it, huh?" I ask, all breathy enthusiasm.

"I know!" Jordie bounces us both in a circle.

I'll need to message Darren later to give him a more personal congratulations. And to grill him about Ed. It's tempting to come out to him too, but I don't want to steal focus from his relationship going official, besides this is in person news. I want to be in the room with him when I tell him.

I still need to work out the details. Because being Ray here has shown me that there's more nuance to how I feel than just a binary choice between girl and boy. I've known for ages that woman will never fit me, but it turns out that something about man chafes too. It can't fully capture all of me, but it's closer and I can't wait to see how the hormones impact things.

A part of me wonders if looking the part might help to embrace it more fully. But a part of me still relates to certain parts of the femininity I was raised to aspire to. Holding the prescription that can unlock a world of possibilities for me, I might be ready to tell everyone soon. But until I am, I have Jordie in my corner at least.

"You ready to go get these filled?" They ask me, and there's just enough of a suggestive lilt to their tone that I can't help thinking of other things I want to fill. I'm going to be in trouble if the meds increase my horny thoughts about them because, damn, just being around Jordie already has my libido in high gear.

"Yeah." I lick my lips, then lean in to murmur in their ear, "And that's not the only thing I want to fill."

Jordie snorts delicately as they loop our elbows together. "Well, what are we waiting for? The sooner we run our errands, the sooner we can celebrate." They wink, drawing out that last word in a way that makes it drip with innuendo that I can't wait to act on.

Chapter Seventeen

Jordie

"You brought him!" Liam opens the door as soon as Ray and I reach the front steps of our family's tidy brownstone. It blends in with the matching turreted homes on either side. The living room's bay windows let in plenty of afternoon sunlight for my brother's plant collection and the family cats to nap. Liam has clearly been watching for our arrival. We aren't late for dinner, but we could have been here sooner.

I feel a little bad for making out with Ray back at his dorm instead of heading over here right away after classes. We didn't actually fuck and show up late, though, and my boyfriend is a snack, so I can't really be blamed for needing a taste of him. He's been so horny lately; it's a shame my meds have the opposite effect to his, but I've still been enjoying helping him get off every chance we get.

Most of our study dates have been in one of our rooms lately, so I can reward him for a good session with coming. And even if I'm not always interested in getting off too, I'm always into the way he touches me. Ugh, even E isn't enough to fully blunt my response to the mental image of Ray coming for me, and the stirring in my groin is uncomfortable. I shove those thoughts aside and focus on introducing Ray to my family. My brother standing in front of us helps me set my libido aside.

"I did! Ray, this is my little brother, Liam." I pull Ray in front of me and nudge him toward my brother. "Liam, this is my boyfriend, Ray."

I love the warm thrill of getting to claim Ray in front of my family. Liam steps back and eyes Ray over. "You're nice to Jordie?"

"Of course." Ray nods, glancing over his shoulder at me with a smile.

"Good." Liam gives Ray a slightly manic grin. "Keep it that way."

"I've heard so much about you. It's nice to meet you, Liam." Ray waves.

"Mhm. Come meet our cats." He grabs Ray's hand and hauls him through to the living room where Tigger is almost definitely sunning himself on the windowsill. The three-legged orange tom is a cuddler, so I have no doubt he'll be perfectly happy with Ray. Spleen, Kara's diabetic tortoiseshell rescue kitten, is still coming out of her shell around people though, so that's the real test.

I trail after Ray and Liam, only for Kara to come pounding down the stairs of my folk's old brownstone to pounce on my back.

"Jordie's here!" Kara shrieks to our parents, mouth inches

from my ear. Ouch.

"Hey, rascal!" I grab my sister's knees to support her as she wraps her spindly arms across my chest and giggles as I spin us in a circle. Her legs seem more gangly than I remember and I have to be careful not to bang her feet into the wall. She's always been a happy kid, but I love making her laugh like this.

"Welcome home, Jordie. We're in the kitchen," Mom calls.

"Just in time. Come test the popover filling before we pop them in the oven," Dad adds. Fruit-filled popovers are his go-to dessert. His flavor pairings, on the other hand, are very hit or miss lately. Kara and I groan in tandem, then laugh.

"Not it," she mutters under her breath.

"Sure, be right there, Pop!" I call back to him. "How's school going?" I ask Kara as I carry her piggyback down the hallway. She has to have grown several inches since the fall.

Kara shrugs, squeezing me tighter with the motion. "Boring. I've got another chess tournament on Sunday."

"Nice! Going to win again?"

"Obviously. Destiny is going down," Kara boasts. Well, it's not really boasting if it's true, I guess. But it's cute how competitive she gets with her bestie.

Liam jokes that it's a crush, and from how furiously she blushes at the teasing, I suspect there's at least a kernel of truth to it. But it's too strange to think of the baby whose diapers I changed growing up into an actual adult, so I'm not touching that at all.

"Nice. Let me know how it goes. I'm cheering for you."

Her kitten darts out from under the coffee table, mewing and twining around my ankles, almost tripping me.

"Ah, you're going to knock me down, Spleen. Here, get down now, kiddo." I deposit Kara on the couch and turn to smile at her. It's weird to see that the baby-faced grade-schooler I adore is truly turning into a lanky adolescent. "Who gave you permission to shoot up like a weed?" I demand, ruffling her hair.

She scowls, playfully batting my hand away. "I'm, like, the shortest in my class. So someone better give me permission to grow more soon."

"Yeah? Weren't you the tallest a few years ago?" I ask, reaching down to scritch Spleen's chin. The kitten rears up to rest her forepaws on my knee and lets me rub behind her ears.

Kara sighs wearily. "Yeah. Want to lend me a few inches?"

"Wish I could, squirt." I pick up Spleen and pet her as she purrs.

"Aww, she remembers you gave her that catnip mouse last time," Kara says.

"Bribery works." I wink and pass her kitten to her. Spleen bumps her forehead into Kara's face, looking for affection. "Be nice to Ray, and I'll bring more donuts next week."

Kara salutes. "Sure, we'll just give him the shovel talk before dinner. I want the strawberry ones from Holes. And Jordie?"

"Yeah?"

"He seems nicer than Nell already." Kara juts her chin toward Liam and Ray. They're both standing by the turret windows. Ray is petting Tigger while Liam waxes poetic about the shelves overflowing with his plants.

"Oh?" I arch a brow at her. I still haven't shared all the hurtful details of mine and Nell's breakup with my family, but that was almost four years ago. So Kara's been holding her dislike close to her chest for a long while. Kid can hold a grudge like a champ.

Kara nods toward Liam. He can talk about his plants all day to anyone who will listen. Ray does just that, giving every sign of rapt attention. "Yeah, he's actually treating Liam like a person."

That hits right in the center of my chest. Yeah, I don't have the best track record with dating, but Liam never said anything about Nell, or any of my exes, mistreating him. If he had, I'd have dumped them at word one, which in retrospect might be why he kept his silence. But also, my last few exes haven't really been all that interested in meeting the family or spending time with my little siblings. I'd have ended things much sooner if I'd noticed them outright being rude to either of my siblings.

Kara notes my stormy expression and rushes to add, "Oh, she was always nice when you were around; it was just little comments when you were out of the room that I picked up on. You deserve someone nice, Jords. Not all the excuses to avoid meeting us, or the weird faces behind your back when Liam talks about his plants."

"You're right. Thanks, rascal. Next time tell me if someone seems off?"

When I glance over again, Liam is gesturing excitedly at one of his pitcher plants and Ray is nodding along. He catches my eye and grins. That's a stark contrast to Keith mouthing a plea for help, eyes glazed over at all the species names my brother rattles off like most people can recite their favorite actors or sports stars. When Liam gets going about his plants, it's hard to get a word in edge-wise. Keith was totally out of his depth, trying to follow the conversation the last time I had a few friends over for family dinner. He wasn't rude about it, just overwhelmed, trying to keep up with Liam's plant knowledge.

"Obviously. I'm not a baby anymore. I've got your back." Kara stands and hip checks me.

"Thanks." I offer her a fist bump and Kara returns it. "I should go see what Pops is planning to subject us to for dessert, right?"

She pulls a face. "Good luck with that. He found a curry glazed carrot recipe the other day and now he thinks he can just add curry powder to everything to make it fancy. Spoilers, curry blueberry turnovers are about as good as they sound." She makes a gagging sound and I laugh as I turn toward the kitchen.

"I'll see if I can salvage something. Maybe if he's got some peaches?"

"Mhm, good luck with that. I'm going to grill your boyfriend while you're gone," Kara singsongs.

"Be nice to him." I wag an admonishing finger at her.

"Uh, huh. I make no promises," she taunts.

"Donuts," I remind her.

"A full dozen?" Kara bargains. I scowl, she cackles. "Relax, Jordie, I'll be nice unless he gives me reasons not to be. No bribes needed."

Spleen's ears prick up, gaze intent on the hallway, then she jumps down from Kara's arms and dashes out of the room. My sister laughs at her cat. "There she goes, chasing invisible mice again." She brushes cat fur off her lap and saunters toward the window.

"Hey, Ray, right?" Kara taps Ray's shoulder, then holds out a hand to shake. "I'm Kara. I'm sure Jordie told you all about me. They haven't stopped talking about their adorable new baby trans friend all semester."

"Oh?" Ray looks startled, then a slow grin stretches his pretty lips. "Nice to meet you, Kara. What else has Jordie told you about me?"

"Well, for starters, you think their weird puns are funny. Honestly, if you laugh at their tragic jokes they should probably never let you go," she teases with the dryly cutting humor that's been far beyond her years for ages. The brat.

Ray bites his lip to suppress a laugh. "Ouch, I can't tell if you're making fun of Jordie's jokes or me for laughing. You're brutal, kid."

Kara shrugs. "I'm the baby of the family. They have to love me. And as long as you're nice to my sib, you won't have to find out how brutal I can be, alright?"

"Deal." Ray bites his cheek, like he thinks she's bluffing, but he offers her a handshake that she makes a show of accepting.

"Careful," Liam interjects as he reaches for another of his plants hanging from the curtain rod to show off the massive purple pitchers on one of his favorite hybrids. "Kara hid J's high school girlfriend's car keys in the litter box. She had to have the car rekeyed before we found them, and little sis still blames Mittens, our late cat, for doing the deed."

"Mittens was always a curious cat," Kara says, pretending to examine her fuchsia painted nails. "And I was seven. You can't prove anything."

"Uh, huh. Nell was not happy." Liam observes, still focused on checking out his plants.

"She got off light. Liam talked me out of the laxative brownies that I wanted to make her in my Easy Bake oven." Kara smiles sweetly, her cherubic expression at odds with her threats. Ray snorts.

Even though I should go talk to my folks, I wander closer to see how the meeting goes. For all I'm struggling to accept that I might be enough for Ray to stay with me, I desperately want Ray and my siblings to get along.

"Makes sense. I'm protective of my older siblings too. I have three older brothers, Adam, Darren, and Luke."

"Ugh." Kara rolls her eyes. "So three times as overprotective as two overbearing big sibs, huh?"

"Exactly, you get it!" Ray offers her a fist bump which Kara reciprocates. "Still, they're all giant nerds who need someone to look out for them, you know? Like one of Adam's ex-girlfriends was awful to me whenever Adam wasn't around. She was queerphobic toward Darren and Luke too, but never in front of Adam. So eventually I got sick of it, borrowed Adam's phone, and texted her. I made it seem as if he accidentally sent her a text meant for another girl he was setting up a date with."

"No!" Kara smothers a scandalized giggle. "And?"

"She was so pissed thinking he was cheating on her," Ray cracks a small smile.

I glance between my siblings to gauge their reactions. On some level, I trust their judgment more than my own, considering how easily Nell toyed with my heart. I don't think Ray is like her, but when I gave Nell my heart, I didn't think she was like that either.

Liam seems too caught up in noting humidity reading on the dials next to his more finicky plants to be more than indifferent to the story. The fact he isn't bothering to mask his disinterest and that he's still hanging out instead of retreating up to his room is a good sign. Kara is hanging on Ray's every word.

"What happened?" Kara leans conspiratorially closer to my boyfriend. Her eyes are alight with a delighted sort of kinship that settles something inside of me. My sister likes Ray. More than that, I think he just won her over entirely with that shared little sibling proclivity for getting up to good mischief in the name of protecting family.

"They broke up and he didn't forgive me for months. Until he found out that she'd been dating another of their friends behind his back most of the time they were together. Another time, Darren was seeing a guy who treated him like crap. So my youngest brother and I left dirty laundry all over Darren's room and hid old tuna cans in his vents when we knew the jerk was coming over."

"Teach me your ways," Kara claps in glee. "The best prank I pulled was on our annual road trip to visit Gran. I sprinkled ghost pepper seasoning into Liam and Jordie's bugles bag when I was eight. They like making weird little ice creams out of them and that cheese with the creepy red cow on it? And I couldn't have any because I would throw up if I had dairy while we drove. So I got my vengeance." Kara cackles. I groan, and Liam makes a yuck face, like he can still feel the burn. She loves telling that story.

Listening to Ray and Kara compare notes about their best pranks is weird. For one, I might be in trouble if I let those two collaborate on any kind of surprise with their plotting, but that only makes me grin. It's weird because it feels like I'm watching two people I care about forming a bond independent of their connections to me. It makes this budding relationship seem more tangible, like something that could actually take root and grow.

"Wow, that's cold." Ray whistles, low and impressed. "I just ate my older brothers' favorite snacks before they got to them when I was peeved with them as a kid. Or, like, pretend sneezed on them."

"Road trip snacks are sacrosanct." Liam complains. "I still can't eat bugles from an open package without feeling the burn. You're the reason I have trust issues." He winks though. I'm pretty sure he's mostly joking since Kara rarely pulls mean pranks. She's gotten better at using her judgment on how far to take things over the years.

"Ugh. See? She's already diabolical enough, sunshine. Don't contribute to the delinquency of a minor," I protest.

"You're not a lawyer yet, Jords! Tell me everything, sunshine." Kara wheedles. And Ray flushes at my nickname for him coming from her, but he smiles and seems comfortable comparing pranks with my little sister.

"I'm with Jordie on this one; little sis comes up with enough pranks on her own. Check out my *Nepenthes rajah*, Ray." Liam holds up the jewel of his collection of carnivorous plants. Dark purple pitchers as big as his head trail down from the end of its oblong leaves. "They're endangered in the wild. This one was ethically cultivated; I grew it from a tiny seedling, so no worries there. They can get up to four feet tall and they've adapted to catch shrew poop as fertilizer. How cool is that? Mom says I can't get a shrew to feed it though." Liam makes a face at that. I try not to laugh at the way his thought processes send my brother on weird tangents. Only Liam would get a pet shrew for his favorite plant.

"Wow, how does that work?" Ray asks, leaning in to study the massive pitcher with genuine interest. Liam's face lights up at having an avid audience to tell about his special interest, and something settles in my chest. Ray is going to be fine with my siblings.

Kara smiles at me, and sidles close enough to murmur out of the corner of her mouth. "Your new boyfriend is a nerd. I like him."

"Me too," I smile at her, and then raise my voice a little to break into Liam's lecture about his favorite topic so I can address Ray. "You good with these two while I say hi to my folks?" I ask, giving his shoulders a squeeze. If he's not comfortable, then I'll just stay, or bring him into the kitchen with me.

"Yeah, I'm trapped anyway." Ray gestures to where Tigger has draped himself over his lap.

"Cat trapped." Liam and Kara both echo, then fist bump.

"Go say hi to the rents." Kara waves me away dismissively. "We'll entertain your boyfriend for you."

Ray seems totally fine with that, and my heart is all wibbly wobbly over how seamlessly he fits with my family. Like he really could be in this for the long term. That's an overwhelming thought that makes my breath catch in a good way. I want that so much, it's hard to even admit it to myself. I shove that glowing ember of hope down, letting it simmer where it can't burn itself out prematurely. Instead of gushing my emotions everywhere, I fall back on familiar teasing.

"Fine, you better be nice to him." I wag my finger at my siblings.

Kara pretends to bite at it, flashing pearly teeth in a feral grin. "I make no promises, but he seems cool." She winks at Ray, who smiles back.

Liam shrugs off my concerns, undeterred from sharing more fun facts about his favorite topic; his plants. "Oh! How's this for nice? Did you know what's cool about Nepenthes? They're dioecious, which is rare in flowering plants, neat right? The only way to tell if an individual plant produces ova or pollen is to let them flower." He grimaces. "Which is a pain, because I'd rather have them spending that energy on more pitchers than a flower spike."

I've heard his flower spike talk before. Liam brought it up when I told him about being genderqueer. He told me how plants don't care about gender norms, and neither does he. Then he launched into more weird plant facts and how vegetative cloning is a more efficient way to reproduce anyway. If he's sharing his favorite plant facts, Ray is already on his good side.

I give Ray's shoulder one last reassuring squeeze and go to the kitchen. My folks greet me with hugs and I'm relieved to find Dad isn't putting weird experimental things into my favorite peach and ginger popovers.

We exchange the usual small talk and Mom asks where Ray is, smiling when I tell her my sibs are unsubtly grilling him in the living room.

"And you aren't worried about that?" Dad arches a brow at me. "You usually hover when you bring home a date."

"Nah, Ray can handle Liam and Kara," I say. It goes without saying that my siblings can hold their own with him. "I trust him."

It hits me with the force of a mack truck that's true on a level it hasn't been with most of my exes. I trust Ray to be kind to my siblings and answer their questions honestly and to their satisfaction, with no ulterior motives to hide or reveal.

"Good, let's get everything on the table. I want to meet this boy." Mom smiles as she picks up the large casserole dish and tips her chin toward the stack of clean plates. "Come set the table and tell me how your law school applications are going. Have you heard back from any of your top choices yet?"

I grimace at the reminder that my future is rushing toward me fast. It's got so much more than the adorable twink in the other room in store for me. I only have one semester and change left of the life I know, the routines I've settled into and the friends I adore. So little time to really get to know Ray. I'm not ready to close this chapter, but that's not an option.

Law school with more years of grueling classes looms ahead. I don't feel ready for it, but at least it will mean having a direction once I get my degree in May. A direction that is all too likely to lead me away from Ray. If he's even still interested in me by the spring. I've gone down this road before with overeager, newly out potential friends who seemed to want more than a sounding board for figuring themselves out. Until they found the confidence to leave me behind, just like Nell did.

Ray doesn't seem like them, but that's another reason I've avoided anything approaching a serious relationship since Nell. She dripped her honeyed lies into my ears until I was no longer useful. Not that I suspect Ray of anything so nefarious. I just can't banish the lingering phantom pain from the scars Nell left behind. There's no point getting too emotionally invested when I don't know where I'll be in a year. I can't shape that choice around someone I only met a few months ago.

No matter how much that sweet sunshine smile of his makes me want to bend all my rules to the breaking point. The plan hasn't changed. I'm going to bask in his attention for as long as I have it, and not expect more than that.

"Jordie?" Mom breaks me out of my melancholy doom spiral. Right. She asked about law school. As if she and Dad wouldn't be the first to know my news if it wasn't way too soon for that.

"Um, I haven't heard from anyone yet. It's still too early. I applied to every law school in Boston and I'm looking at a few others in New England, in case none of the local schools work out."

"Good, I'm proud of you, Jordie." Mom sets the casserole in the center of the table and gives me a hug. She asks more questions about my applications and my classes, but I have nothing new to tell her. Classes are good and law school is equal parts exciting dream and scary unknown, and that won't change until I'm in the thick of it.

Dad brings in two bowls with salad and corn to set them beside the main dish and the loaves of bakery fresh bread sitting on the cutting board already. I help my folks finish setting the table with butter, condiments, and pitchers of water, juice, and lemonade.

Dad goes to put his popovers in the oven. I trail Mom back into the living room where Ray is still snuggling with Tigger. Liam has moved on to explaining the genetics of his favorite pitcher plants and his rare plant wishlist so he can try his hand at breeding new hybrids with bigger, bolder pitchers.

Tigger stretches languidly, then lowers himself from Ray's

lap to greet Mom with a chirping mew. He's a mama's boy.

Ray stands awkwardly and brushes Tigger's fur from his lap. I go to him, looping an arm around his shoulders in solidarity as I introduce him to Mom. "Hey, sunshine, ready to meet my mom?" I murmur in his ear.

Ray flashes me a tight smile and nods.

"Mom, this is Ray, my partner. Ray, my mom." I gesture between them.

"Lovely to meet you," Ray steps toward her, offering a handshake.

Mom pulls him into a hug. "A pleasure to meet you. Anyone Jordie cares about is welcome here."

"Thanks." Ray smiles awkwardly. Mom notices his discomfort and turns toward my siblings.

"Well, dinner's ready. Why don't we all head to the dining room?" Mom claps her hands together to get Liam's attention. Liam sets the plant he was holding back in its spot on a rack over a tray of water and fiddles with the humidity sensor beside it. He checks the temperature controls next to his favorite highland plants that are more sensitive to the climate.

"The plants are fine, Liam, wash up for supper," Mom says, gentle but firm.

"Mhm," Liam hums distractedly as he pours more distilled water into the tray and mists the plants sitting on top of it. Mom purses her lips and watches to be sure he actually finishes up his fussing. She gives him a minute to change gears and reassure himself that his plant gadgets are all in working order to maintain the humidity and light each plant requires.

Kara nudges a few of the pots back into alignment and then both of my siblings head for the table. I keep my arm around Ray's waist as we make our way to the table. He settles right in when we all take our seats. He's more guarded with my parents than with my siblings, but he still smiles and participates in the conversation.

It's a good night, but I notice Ray's smile fraying in unguarded moments. Like when my siblings tease each other with running jokes and my mom breaks out the embarrassing kid stories. My family doesn't pick up on his cues, but I can't ignore the melancholy way he draws into himself.

I gnaw my lips, wondering if he's uncomfortable with my family or missing his own. Is he wondering and worrying whether he'll get to hear the affection in his own mother's voice as she recounts the early signs of his transness, the way mine does? Proudly.

I was not subtle about borrowing her clothes and playing with her makeup to put on little princess plays. Nominally, I did it to entertain Liam when he was a mostly nonverbal toddler. Liam's autism wasn't the only reason our sperm donor didn't stick around, but that's the reason I can't forgive him for. Mom tried to shield us from his rejection of who we both are.

She always indulged my love of swishy skirts and bright colors. When it turned out to be more about expressing who I was rather than just enjoying the sensory experience, she loved me through that process of self-discovery. Even when she didn't always understand and it made life more difficult for all of us.

Ray tries to hide his melancholy when Mom packs up left-overs and hugs him at the end of the evening. He tells me he's just homesick, but I think there might be more to it. The way he glanced so longingly between me and my folks when they gendered me correctly and talked about my future plans in glowing terms. How he went quiet when they asked if he's visiting home for the upcoming holiday break.

They said we're welcome to spend the extra long weekend with them, driving to visit my gran like always, and I promised to think about it. In truth, there's something I've been mulling over ever since he mentioned not being able to afford tickets home.

There's definitely something worrying Ray, something bigger than just being overwhelmed with new people. I long to share the plans that have been forming in the back of my mind, but I don't want to get his hopes up in case it falls through. I still need to wedge a few more pieces into place.

After food, Liam insists on finishing his plant tour and Kara challenges Ray to a game of chess, which she loses by the narrowest of margins. When I catch Kara's eye afterward, she winks at me. The fact she let him win tells me he's won her over, clear as words. And Liam wanting to share his favorite plants is all the acceptance I need to know my family likes my new boyfriend. And I like him too. So much.

Chapter Eighteen

Jordie

When we get back to campus, I take Ray's hand and follow him back to his dorm room. I can't fix whatever unspoken worry is bothering him, but I can take his mind off his mood.

"How was it?" I ask him, wanting a verbal reassurance that he liked my family as much as they liked him.

"Great. Your siblings are a hoot." Ray smiles at me. "It kind of made me homesick for my big brothers seeing you three together."

"Yeah? I got that impression. What do you miss the most?"

"I don't even know. It's weird going from being the baby and always being surrounded by built-in-buddies to just, alone? I mean, it's been better now that I've been meeting people and have friends to do stuff with. Seeing you with your siblings just reminded me of how much I've been missing home, I guess. And maybe what it could be like if I'd had the courage to tell them who I am sooner."

"You can still tell them now. It's never too late."

"Yeah. I want to. Soon. I miss all the noise and chaos and always knowing they have my back."

"Yeah?"

He shrugs. "Yeah. I've missed them more than I thought I would. Distract me?" Ray crowds into my personal space, leaving little doubt as to how he wants me to accomplish that.

"Hm, however could I possibly take your mind off it?" I tease, pressing in close and kissing his cheek.

Ray's lips curve into a grin, and he grinds his packer into my groin. He turns to catch my mouth in a quick kiss. "It's a mystery." He drops one hand to my ass and grinds us together more insistently, moaning against my lips.

I kiss him deeper, gazing into his gorgeous blue eyes and losing myself in him. He usually tangles his fingers in my hair about now, and I shiver in anticipation of the sharp prickling tug of that, except it doesn't happen. Instead, Ray gently disentangles from me, holding up his little tupperware of leftovers from Mom with a rueful grin. "Let me just put this away."

"Oh, yeah. Do that." I step back and try to collect myself, adjusting my shirt and primping with my hair.

I wore a blouse and the soft material of my bra is irritating against the newly tender breasts budding from the estrogen. I haven't really noticed much growth there yet, but my nipples are more sensitive when Ray plays with them while we make out lately. At first, it was too much, but now it feels good when he takes me in his mouth while he's grinding his erection against my thigh. And I've read that the soreness could be a sign things might develop more soon, so I'm hopeful it's a good sign of amazing things to come.

Ray turns and opens his mini fridge to shove the food containers inside. I admire the delectable curve of his ass as he bends to balance the leftovers near the back. My libido has taken a hit from the E, but I can still appreciate how sexy he looks. My dick doesn't immediately plump up, but it's not uninterested either.

I lick my lips as Ray turns, nudging the fridge shut with his foot and strips off his shirt and pants. He plays with the hem of his binder before sliding that off too. He's getting more comfortable putting on and removing the constricting garment. I try not to stare at his chest, but I appreciate his trust in baring it to me.

"Um, still off limits, but I've had it on all day and it's chafing," he explains apologetically as he rubs at his chest to ease the ache.

I can empathize with the soreness. That sparks a wave of euphoria in my heart, my pulse racing in an exaltation I can't put into words. I want to kiss him. I want Ray to grab handfuls of my boobs and motorboat them. Let me savor his stubble scraping over the smooth skin of my chest. I want him to sink into me and fuck me until I'm screaming his name. Or maybe not screaming, since the dorm walls are thin, but definitely coming with him inside me.

"That's fine. Same, kind of." We exchange knowing smiles. "Want to take off my bra for me?"

I bat my lashes at him and pat his mattress in invitation. Ray grins, losing any lingering self-consciousness to stalk closer and straddle my lap. Our lips meet in a needy clash of tongues. He slides his hands up my blouse to work the clasp. It shouldn't surprise me he has the thing unfastened in seconds. He arches a questioning brow at me as he lifts my shirt to expose my chest, silently asking permission to strip me.

I nod and he tosses my shirt and bra alike into a pile with his discarded binder. The man knows his way around a bra. He's learning his way over every inch of my body. Finding all the spots that make my knees weak and my clit throb for release. He angles one tender nipple toward his lips and kisses it, thumbing over the wet nub as he suckles gently on the other one. Ray coaxes and teases me until both nipples stand erect from my chest. He fondles me gently as he kisses my collarbones, then up my neck to just behind my ears. Want pools low in my belly, welling up like water behind a dam.

"Want to fuck you," Ray murmurs into my ear, hands cupping my chest to continue massaging the nascent buds of my breasts. His thumbs keep circling the sensitive nipples, keeping them hard—twin peaks. I shudder at the raw passion in his voice.

"Mhm. Want to take you so bad, Ray. Wish I could let you fuck my wet pussy. Make you come inside me."

"Damn, yes." Ray trails his fingers over my belly and into my pants and rubs at my clit. He pays extra attention to the slick tip, like it really is a natal clit and he knows just how to make it feel good.

He circles the tip with firm pressure as he grips my jaw with the other hand, claiming my mouth in a demanding kiss. His tongue delving into me in an assertive claiming, just how I want him to handle me when I finally get him inside me. I could weep from the desire coursing through me. It's strangely different from what I'm used to, more of a diffuse warmth.

Instead of an arousal that just focuses on my cock and getting it inside him, my whole body sensitized to his every touch. Ray kisses down my throat, grinding against me. I lift to meet his thrusts, my pants getting in the way and chafing against both of us. Condom. I should probably... hmm, that might not work so well when I'm still semi-soft despite how turned on I am.

If my clit was an accurate representation of how much I want Ray right now, it would be stiff enough to hammer nails. This new response to arousal might take getting used to. Ray doesn't seem to mind though, riding me with lusty grunts of pleasure. If anything, he's as into me as ever.

"Damn, you're dripping for me, baby," he teases, dragging a thumb through the moisture at the tip of my clit. "Ta chatte est mouillée et prête à être baisée."

I rock along to his rhythm, enjoying his neediness. The soft press of his chest against mine when he wraps me in his arms and tumbles me down onto the bed is bliss. Ray kisses me breathless as we dry hump like there's no tomorrow.

"Gonna get off humping me?" I tease when I feel him tensing over me like he's about to come. After a month of making out with him, I'm getting used to his tells. Enough to spot them and I'm not ready for this to be over.

"Hn?" Ray gives me a dazed look, his hips stilling. "Want to be inside you, but I don't want to stop long enough to strap up." He circles his hips again, and I moan as my clit rubs into his click.

His new harness and strap-on dick arrived earlier in the week, but we haven't had a chance to take them for a test ride yet. Tonight's not looking like the night either. I don't want to wait for him to figure out the harness when we're both horny as hell and he's already feeling off kilter over missing his family.

"Me neither." I bite my lip, groaning as I lift my hips to rub against him. "Remember that thing I mentioned? Where you fuck your fingers into me?"

"Muffing?" Ray asks, already shifting enough to work a hand between us and into my panties to play idly with my sac. "You want me to push inside you? Here?" He circles his finger in the general vicinity. I let my eyes flutter shut as I reach down to guide him, already anticipating the illicit thrill of such a powerfully transgressive act. I know from experience that it's an erotically pleasant physical sensation, but I also love the mental stimulation of being penetrated in a way that feels feminine to me.

"Yeah. Like this." I massage my balls out of the way, years of tucking while I'm wearing skirts making the motion familiar. I guide Ray's fingers to the twin openings on either side of my dick. Gently, I swirl the tip of his finger around the opening, gathering enough loose skin from my sac to push inside of my body. It reminds me of parting pussy lips to fuck into a cunt.

"You just push the skin in, ah." I gasp and bite my lip as he eases inside of me, the dual penetration making my nerves sing. "Mm. Yeah, like that. Gently."

Ray works his way in deeper, penetrating me on both sides. Fucking me open and making me feel euphoric as he stakes his claim.

"You like this, babe?" he asks, delving in deeper on either side. Fingering just below my clit, like I really have a front hole for him to fuck.

"Want you inside my pussy," I agree.

"Yeah? You want me to fuck this tight little pussy, Jords?" He pants, thrusting a little more confidently as he asks the question, knowing the answer. "How much can you take?"

"More." I demand. "Want your mouth on me while you open me up. Please?" I remember my manners at the last second.

Ray chuckles. "Grab the condoms and a vibe from that drawer?"

He gestures to the dresser in arm's reach from my head and I arch off the bed to grab the supplies. And a tube of lube my fingers find next to the other stuff, just in case. I've played with myself this way enough to work up to three fingers on each side, so I'm confident I can take him.

Ray slips from the bed to kneel between my thighs and peels my leggings and the floral panties that match my bra down to my ankles. He shuffles to kneel on top of them, pinning me in place as he eases his fingers back into the inguinal canals like I showed him. My half-chubbed clit twitches at the sensation, making me self-conscious about it.

"Sorry, I'm really into this, just, uh, dick's been reacting differently lately." I wince at having to admit it out loud, even though I'm sure he's noticed by now.

"It's fine. We talked about HRT side effects. You have nothing to apologize for. You still want this?" He nudges his fingers inside of me and I bite back a moan.

"Oh, yeah. Still want you to suck me, if you don't mind it staying soft? Still feels good." I reach between my legs to stroke my clit and press my palm against where he's inside me. He wiggles his fingers.

"Yeah. Just one problem; I'm not sure how the condom is going to work with that. Maybe we could skip it?" he offers. "All our blood tests from the clinic came back negative again, so it's lower risk, right? We'll still use barriers for butt stuff."

I hesitate, but I trust him. I desperately want to believe that this isn't some experiment for either of us. Ray insists that I'm not his gay sex starter pack. He won't take me off like training wheels as soon as he doesn't feel like he needs me anymore, or if a better offer comes along. I have to believe that. And even if I don't trust my judgment about it after Nell, I trust how much my family liked him. How he made a genuine effort with them because he wants to have a future with me and he knows how important they are to me.

"Jordie?"

I meet his worried gaze. "Yeah, we can skip it for oral. I'm not having an outbreak or anything, but like you said, still better to use a dental dam for rimming. You're sure?"

"I'm sure." Ray smiles wickedly, then he mouths the head of my clit. He laps over the slit before slurping me between his lips and sucking me gently to the same rhythm he's fucking his fingers into me. My boyfriend is fucking me like I have a pussy. The combination is intense, not just physically, but on an emotional level. There's a vulnerability to sharing myself with him like this. No barriers, each of us trusting the other with our bodies in ways that have a deeper meaning than just getting off.

Ray sucks and fucks me until I'm almost incoherent with pleasure. Time loses all meaning. My world narrows to where he's touching me. The diffuse pleasure spreads through me like the languid relaxation of a warm soak in the bath. Like he can infuse all of me with sweet sensation.

"Want to fuck you like this, with my click, can I?" Ray asks. I'm not at all sure that's going to work, that his click can really penetrate me, but I love the idea of trying. Even if he just rubs against me, I'm more than happy to try it. I like the idea of it, having his cute little cock inside the nearest thing to a pussy I'm ever going to have short of surgeries I don't want.

"Yeah. Do it." I nod, arching toward him. And whining as his fingers slip free of my body.

"You sure? Don't think a condom will work for mine either and, uh, I'm pretty wet." He gestures vaguely at his crotch.

"Yeah. I'm sure. Want to feel how hot you are for me, sunshine. Come all over me. In me."

His eyes burn with lust—or maybe something more that I'm

not ready to put into words—as he scrambles to his feet. He yanks my ankles up to his shoulders and lines up our groins, teasing the engorged head of his cock against me. I reach for him, guiding the sensitive head to my opening, working two fingers in and spreading them so he can fuck between them. He doesn't really have enough bottom growth to get inside me yet. It still feels wonderful, and he groans and thrusts against me, enjoying the sensation of fucking into me as much as I want to be fucked.

"Mm, good?" he asks.

"Yeah, here, I've got something to make it even better." I slick the bullet vibe I grabbed from his drawer with lube and work it into the canal he was rutting against. Once it's in place, I turn it on and hold it steady with one hand. I cup the back of his neck and pull him into a kiss. Having his lips on mine is well worth being bent in half to give him access to fuck me. Ray rocks his cock against the base of the vibe inside me and moans.

"Oh, that's good." He fucks me harder. Ray's fingers work back inside of me on the other side and he thrusts into me with his whole body, fucking me in every sense. His tongue pushes into my mouth and tangles with mine as he makes love to me. This feels more intimate than anything else we've done. He's inside me and I can feel the slick of his arousal dripping onto me with every thrust.

Ray moans and fucks me harder, rutting into me like I'm the best thing he's ever felt. The vibe unleashes the pooled up pleasure that's been building since he crowded into my space to kiss me. I lean back. The effort of crunching up to meet his lips is too much when I'm teetering on the brink of an orgasm that feels so huge it might shake me apart.

"Ah, so close."

"Do it, come, gorgeous," Ray grunts, continuing to thrust into me, the vibe an unrelenting background buzz driving our shared pleasure to new heights. He adjusts his angle slightly and thrusts again.

"Oh, oooooh. Yes, Ray. More." I throw my head back and let pleasure wash over me in waves.

"C'est si beau de te voir jouir pour moi," Ray practically purrs, inches from my lips, as he caresses my cheek with the hand that isn't buried inside me. He trails his fingers down my chest to squeeze my boob. He thrusts in deep, fucking me with more force. "Come with my cock in your sloppy wet pussy, Jordie. Ride me so good."

I don't even try to stop the way the orgasm rises through my whole body in a wave of heat. Every nerve suffused with a warm glow of pleasure. It's a total body experience unlike anything I've felt before. Transcendent.

I moan his name over and over as he whimpers through his own orgasm, his thrusts stuttering into an erratic rhythm as he pulses against my opening. His release is a wet heat between our bodies. Fuck, is he squirting? That's so damn hot. I lift to meet the last few rocks of his hips into me. I want this to last forever, to be connected to him for as long as possible.

Far too soon, he pulls away, and the vibe goes from a perfect buzzing pleasure, to ebbing, to too much. I reach between my legs to ease it out and turn it off, then collapse back onto his bed, boneless and thoroughly fucked out.

"Sleepy?" Ray asks, brushing sweat-lank curls from my face.

"Yeah. You fucked me to death," I grin goofily up at him, throwing the literal translation of one of his idioms back at him.

He chuckles and reaches for the package of wet wipes we got to make cleaning up easier when it became clear that he's messy when he comes. "Sorry, I made a mess all over you."

"Mhm. Let you fuck me without a condom once and you jizz all over me." I wink at him. "Good thing you can't knock me up."

"We can certainly keep trying, just to be sure. For science." Ray winks, then he wipes me clean. He bites his lip. "And you weren't inside me when you came and I've got the IUD in, so I'm probably alright on that front too, right?"

"Yeah." I fumble for his hand to give him a reassuring squeeze. "But if it would make you feel better, we can grab some Plan B?"

Ray considers, then shakes his head. "Nah, it's okay. I don't think I'm at too much risk, but thanks for offering."

"Of course." I squirm at the cool wet touch interrupting my muzzy afterglow when he goes back to mopping up our mess.

"Hold still a second." Ray swabs me clean, then leans over me and gives me a perfunctory peck on the lips. "That was hands down the hottest fuck of my life, you liked it?" he asks as he curls up beside me.

"Yeah, same. That was intense. Funny how much of a difference it makes when your partner really knows you, huh?" I tease.

Ray sighs. "Yeah, that too. You let me be all of me, and I enjoy getting to know all of you."

"Doesn't hurt that you're a good lay, sunshine." I turn onto my side so I can pull him into a gentle kiss, framing his face with both palms, enjoying the fact I get to touch him. I give him a silly leer. "And just think how much better we'll get the more we practice."

"Mhm." Ray's fingers tangle in my hair and we lay naked in his bed exchanging languid kisses for a long time after that. His body is starting to feel so familiar pressed against mine. I want to explore it through all the changes we're both experiencing. And the scared part of me I've been holding back, guarding my heart, is starting to believe he wants the same. Not completely sold yet, but I can maybe see a future with him in it.

Chapter Nineteen

Jordie

I pull in front of Ray's dorm with my step-dad's rust-bucket of a sedan right on time to meet Ray and fire him a quick text. He steps outside the dorm lobby with his suitcase and scans the crowded sidewalk. I scramble out of the car to wave him over, since he isn't expecting me to be driving.

"Hey! Over here, Ray!" I wave both arms above my head to get his attention and a brilliant grin blooms on his gorgeous features when he catches sight of me.

The HRT is really starting to show in subtle ways for us both. I've got the first hint of swelling breasts and more curves in general. My hair and skin are looking amazing now that I've adjusted my skin care routine to account for being less oily. I don't have to shave or wax *quite* as often, not that I was ever super hairy. Poor Liam is going to have a hell of a time growing any facial hair with our genes.

As for Ray, from the pictures he's shown me of his dad and brothers, it might be a while before he can grow more than a peach fuzz mustache. His jawline is already looking a little more chiseled though. His voice is scratchy with the first signs of a drop in tone. His once unblemished skin boasts a sprinkling of acne and, most notably for me, his libido and sensitized click have him begging for attention several nights a week.

I've spent more nights in Ray's bed sucking his cute little click than sleeping on my own over the past few weeks. He's already got a bit of growth there. Enough that he seems more confident about it during sex. He even called it his dick when I sucked his brains out through it the other night and afterward he said it's starting to feel like a dick. So I've been following his lead on using both terms.

It's just as well he is cool with everyone knowing he's mine, because I doubt any of our friends would buy that I spend my nights with him to study. Most of the studying I do in his room these days is sexual, learning my lover's body. I'm confident that I'm acing the subject if his sated smiles are anything to go by.

Ray hefts his school bag onto his shoulder and drags his roller suitcase roughly down the concrete steps from the dorm. "Nice wheels. What's up? I thought we were going to grab an Uber to your folks' place?"

"Change of plans. I borrowed Dad's car, so I can take you to visit your family for the break. I know they don't have the holiday, but you seem like you need a taste of home. And Dad won't need the car until Monday, since they're taking the van to see Gran."

Ray's eyes are a little too bright as he nods. "I mean. Yeah. I miss them. And I really want to tell them about everything, but

I want it to be in person and..."

"Hey, breathe. I know." I rest a comforting hand on his shoulder. "So I figured we could rip the bandaid off together. Tell them you're Ray and see how it goes when you've got backup."

"And if I'm not ready?"

I shrug. "Then you can introduce your hot new joyfriend to your family. I won't out you to them no matter how much I want to correct them when they misgender you."

"Yeah?" His tentative smile is so heartbreakingly hopeful it makes my heart squeeze with emotion for him. I really like this guy.

"Yeah. I want to support you, whatever that looks like. And you seem like you need a little family time to recharge before finals."

"I *really* do. And I should tell them before it gets too obvious. But are you sure about missing time with your Gran?" He worries his lip and I nudge him to get him to stop.

"When and how to tell them is entirely your call, sunshine. I'll see Gran in a few weeks during winter break and we might video chat while my family is there, if that's cool? It's fine to miss this one visit. So, ready for our first big road trip?"

Ray giggles. "OMG. Relationship test right there. International road trip trial by fire."

I grab his suitcase as an excuse to lean into his personal space and steal a lingering kiss.

"Fire can't compare to how hot you burn, sunshine. This is

going to be epic."

"If you say so. I'm a little nervous. But thank you. No one's ever done something like this for me before."

"You good with it? We can always go visit with your aunts before meeting my family for the road trip to Gran's as planned, if you aren't feeling it."

"No." Ray shakes his head. He takes a deep, steadying breath. "No. I want to go. It's nice. Really nice. And I even have my passport, since I didn't want to risk leaving it on campus for the entire break."

"Perfect, and I've got mine. Playlist is popping, snacks are in the back, both our bags are packed, we are ready to roll!" I fist pump enthusiastically and he giggles, clearly happy with my surprise.

We exchange smiles as I load his things into the trunk, along with my suitcase. The backseat is loaded with a selection of snacks that Liam and Kara would approve for the road. I make sure we both have our passports in easy reach. We hit the road with a club mix Pixel helped curate blasting through the speakers.

I had to dig up an old laptop from my folks' basement to burn the music to a CD for the old car's archaic sound system since it isn't equipped with bluetooth. Totally worth it to watch out of the corner of my eye as Ray dances in his seat to the tunes. The music sounds slightly tinny over the ancient speakers as I navigate through downtown traffic toward I-93. Once we get on the highway and out of the city, it should be smooth sailing for a while.

Ray calls his folks to let them know about the last minute plans. From the side of the conversation I can hear, they seem excited to see him and meet me. I glance over expectantly when he hangs up, texts his aunts about the change of plans, and puts aside his phone.

"My folks are good to host us for the weekend. They have work until the weekend, but Mom says she's going to have all my brothers over Friday night to meet you. So I'll probably tell the sibs and their partners then? If telling Mom and Dad goes well, anyway." He blows out a nervous breath that turns into an uneasy titter and scrubs at his eyes. "Otherwise I guess we'll see?"

I flash him a sympathetic smile. "Nothing says you have to tell anyone anything you aren't ready for yet. You've got time before the HRT makes any major changes that you can't chalk up to time and distance. And I'll be there for you no matter what."

"Yeah." He leans across the console to kiss my cheek, making my heart swoop at the raw affection. It's nice to be there for him, to know I make him feel comfortable and supported. There's a wary, cynical part of me that can't help wondering if that support is why he's with me. What if all I am to him is a temporary crutch while he finds his feet living as a guy? I ruthlessly crush those doubts down deep. They're my insecurities to deal with, not his fault at all.

"I can't believe you're really driving me home." Ray shakes his head incredulously.

"Believe it, sunshine." I grin over at him and pat his thigh. "I want to be there to support you when you tell your folks. *If* you tell them."

"I'm going to do it!" Ray declares. "Before I chicken out. I want to get my name changed officially before I'm on hormones for too long. That way, all my documents match how I look, you know?"

"I know. Have you looked into the paperwork already?" I slip into the queer mentor role so naturally, but it's different with him. With Ray, I'm emotionally invested in his life. Way more than I usually allow myself to connect with the baby queers I've helped in the past. I've held a piece of my heart back from getting entangled since Nell. And that's always been a good bet. It feels beyond reckless to bend my rules for Ray.

"A little. Might not get it done this visit, but I want them to know the real me. Not the version of me that tries so hard to match who I think they want me to be, you know?"

"Sounds like it's been hard to keep it to yourself." I squeeze his thigh.

Ray drops a hand on top of mine, his thumb rubbing over my knuckles. "Yeah. It was hard to talk about it too, though. Until you made it easy."

If I wasn't weaving through traffic, I'd definitely kiss him for saying that. As it stands, I flip my hand to twine our fingers and give him a squeeze. "I didn't do anything, sunshine. You just needed a little boost of confidence that comes from talking to an accepting stranger. The stakes were lower with me."

"Yeah, well, you aren't low-stakes anymore. And I've been kind of thinking..." Ray plays with the rainbow enamel band on my finger. Spinning it around.

"What?"

"How did you figure out that they pronouns were the right fit for you?"

I shrug. I've sort of been expecting a conversation like this with him. "Trial and error. My bestie at the time had the patience of a saint with me early in my transition process. She never complained once when I was switching every other day for a month and going through every neopronoun. Not to mention all the permutations of combining different pronouns and names until I figured out that they fits me best. I settled on the one that makes me grin when other people use it. My mom, step-dad, and sibs helped pick out my name, and that fits too. I like that it's still from my family and it just works for me."

"Yeah. The family thing is why I chose Ray. My folks had it picked out for me before they found out my gender." Ray swallows hard, licks his lips and rushes out with. "Maybe I could try a mix of he and them?"

I glance over at him, flashing them with my best reassuring smile. "Absolutely, sunshine. Want to hear how it sounds?"

"Uh, kay?" Out of the corner of my eye, I watch as he shoves his hands under his thighs and bites his lip.

"This is my handsome boyfriend, Ray. They are studying to be a play therapist so they can help kids. He's from Montreal and has the sexiest accent ever. I can't wait until I have them alone where I can go down on his hot ass before they plow me like a field." I wink at Ray. "Like that? What do you think, babe?"

He shoves my shoulder and snorts a laugh. "I *think* you're horny. But I can't wait until tonight either. I get to fuck you in my home country."

"Mhm. And we'll have to be quiet so your folks don't hear us. Bet you'd like my hand covering your mouth while you moan for me."

He squirms in his seat. "You're a tease."

"Nah, just super into you, sunshine." I make quick eye contact and they look just as lusty as I feel. Ugh. Too bad we have almost five hours of driving ahead of us where I need to keep my hands on the wheel and my eyes on the road. Both would be much more fun to put on him—I should probably turn down the flirting a notch. "Anyway, how does using they feel?"

Ray shakes his head. "I don't think it's quite right for me? It's like when Jacob calls me *man*. Not wrong, but not quite right? And not nearly as wrong as girl or woman. But still, it's only mostly correct? Dude is a big yes. Guy, yes. But man is, like, too far?" His nose wrinkles adorably. "I'm probably overthinking it. Maybe it will fit better when I've had top surgery and been on hormones longer and I sound like a dude when I talk?"

I pat his knee. "Maybe. Or maybe you're nonbinary. Both are good."

"I'm definitely trans masculine. I read that book from the queer book club Pixel bullied me into joining and um, the character used the term demi-boy. And that's...yeah. It felt so right, like one of those PowerPoint slides slotting into the perfect alignment?" He makes a face. "Damn, that was a terrible analogy. This is why I am not an English major. But you get the point?"

"Yeah. It resonated with you. That's not nothing. Are you telling your folks that part?"

Ray chews on his lip and then shrugs. "Maybe? I might just start with telling them I'm not a girl and see how things go? I guess that helped make it tolerable to be misgendered for so long. Like, the only alternative I had the words for wasn't quite right either? I dunno. It's not a huge deal. I'm just happy to have people who understand to discuss this with now. So thanks. You're the best possible person who could have happened to me in Boston, and I'm really fucking glad I took a leap and met you."

"I'm glad you met me too," I tease. Then I lean across the console to brush a kiss to the side of his face because we're stopped at a red light and I can take advantage of the moment.

"Agh, you got my eye! Fais attention!" Ray shoves me away, laughing. "Eyes on the road, Jords."

"True. I've got precious cargo." I glance back and see the traffic light has changed as the driver behind me lays on their horn.

"You're a giant sap," Ray accuses me.

"You like it." I tease, poking at his ribs when we're stopped at the next light. He squirms away, laughing, and grins at me. I smile back when he ruffles my hair.

I want to rub his thigh again, but he beats me to it, putting his hand just above my knee. Traffic is crawling with holiday travelers. So it's not like there's a ton to distract me. At least not until we're free from all the congestion once we get on the highway and leave the city limits.

"Nah, not like. I think I might love you." Ray leans his head on my shoulder, and I don't get a good enough look at his face to be sure, but I think the admission embarrasses him.

"Oh? *Might* is it?" I tease him, fishing for him to say it again with more confidence. Partly to see if he will and partly with the same sort of morbid curiosity of probing at a cold sore with my tongue to see if it still hurts. Oddly, it doesn't.

Somehow, Ray saying he loves me doesn't scare me as much as I thought it would. Maybe precisely because he knows me well enough to soften the impact with that might shoved in front of it like a shield. I can tease him about it, because I've felt the truth of his declaration for a while now.

My ever present doubt that letting myself love him will end in heartbreak fades to the background, a vague future worry. I'm too pragmatic to trust that love will be enough to build a future together if our paths diverge too much after I graduate. But for now, it's enough to allay my fears that he'll prove as fickle as the exes who hurt me.

Ray buries his face against my shoulder with a groan. "Okay, you got me. There's no might about it. I love you, Jordie."

There it is with no frills or loopholes, music to my ears.

Ray loves me. Buoyant hope courses through me like a shot of adrenaline at the sound of those three little words. I want to shout it out from the rooftops, dance in my seat, pull him into a kiss and never let him go. But I'm driving, so saying it back to get a rise out of him will have to suffice.

"Well, then I *might* love you too." I drop a tender kiss on his temple without taking my eyes off the bumper of the car idling along in front of us. It sounds even better without the safety rails of think and might, but I can't resist making him sweat a little. Ray loves me, and I might just be able to take him at his word.

"Hey!" Ray splutters, shoving away from me. "Might?"

I laugh as I stick my tongue out at him. "I love you too, sunshine."

"Guess you must, since you're voluntarily driving me home to meet my entire nosy family." Ray grins and rests his face back on my shoulder and his palm on my thigh.

"Damn right." It feels good to tell him, and to feel secure that it's true for both of us. I wasn't sure I could feel this secure with a partner again, but Ray makes me believe anything is possible.

Traffic inches along toward the highway on-ramp. I press my cheek against his short hair and revel in the easy affection between us. The sweet moment only lasts a few heartbeats before the song on my road trip mix changes and Ray sits up, laughing incredulously.

I crank the volume as the opening bars to "Sunshine" play over the speakers and One Republic serenades us with a catchy pop beat. Ray cracks up laughing, his grin brighter than the sun.

"Seriously?" He chortles, his face lit up with little boy glee. I love making him smile like that, all unselfconscious, his expression hiding nothing.

"Oh yeah! I put this one on here just for you." And yeah, I can happily spend a lifetime falling deeper in love with this boy beside me. Ray offers me his most vulnerable parts with all the trust in the world. As if no one's ever hurt him. Sunshine is such an apt nickname for him. He's just so damn bright and full of life.

We haven't even left the city and I already feel closer to him. Like he's letting me into his innermost heart. When he smiles at me with his whole heart in his eyes, it banishes my insecurities about why he's with me to the murkiest recesses of my heart. It's probably fucked up that I can trust him so completely with my body as to have unprotected sex, and still brace for a rejection even as we exchange our first love declarations. But I know I've got scars around that.

I loved Nell too and look how that turned out. I grip the steering wheel so hard it creaks. Thoughts of my ex sour my mood until Ray shines his light on me again. He dances along to the songs I picked for him with abandon, just like I knew he would. I can't wait to take him dancing again. He's worth taking a risk on love again.

"You're a giant dork with all these sunshine songs, but I kind of love it. Also, this party needs snacks." Ray beams at me. Then he turns in his seat to rummage through the groceries I packed, turning back toward me with a bag of my favorite road trip tradition. "Want some bugles? Is there a cooler with cream cheese for them?"

"Behind my seat, I got Laughing Cow instead, because it's a shelf stable snack cheese. Thanks, babe."

"Sure. I'll feed them to you like your very own tiny ice cream minion," he teases.

"Sexy."

Ray snorts as he digs out the ingredients and starts scooping the corn chips into a wedge of soft, cheesy goodness. I savor the way his fingers feel against my lips as he feeds me the first tangy, crunchy bite. It's nice to have someone who thinks about me as much as I think about him. And yeah, he asked me to help him experiment with his pronouns. But he listens to me and remembers my dumb story about making mini-ice cream cones in the car with my siblings when my family road-tripped to see our grandparents. Ray cares about me as a person, not just his queer mentor.

As he bops in his seat to the music while feeding me more snack, I can already tell this is going to be the best road trip ever.

Chapter Twenty

Ray

B y the time we reach the border, my newly HRT sensitized
dick is throbbing with need for Jordie. I might have spent
the last several hours teasing us both with my hand on their
thigh. I let myself inch closer to their groin by the mile until I
bumped up against the outline of their clit through their jeans.

Then I spent most of the scenic drive through Vermont idly
tracing my joyfriend's cock, enjoying the way it plumped up the
more I played with it. And the growing damp patch of fabric
near the tip that's a match for how wet my boxers are feeling.

I had to stop when we filled up the tank before joining the
idling traffic waiting to cross into Canada. Now I'm sort of
regretting how keyed up I got us both. I press my thighs together to ward off the needy horny throbbing between my legs
that's been insatiable since I started dating Jords. The hormones
might also have something to do with it. All I know is that I
want to fuck my lover as soon as we're some place private. It's
not just the hornyness talking.

This trip is the sweetest gesture I can imagine. They want

me to feel comfortable coming out to my family. To support me and be there for me and they said they love me too. I can't imagine being closer to anyone than I feel to them today. I'm glad I packed the strap-on I haven't worked up to trying yet, just in case. Jordie is the first person I want the privilege of getting to be inside of as a guy.

I want physical and sexual closeness to mirror the new leap forward in my emotional closeness to them. Soon we're going to be under my parents' roof. It wouldn't be the first time I had a not so PG sleepover there, but I really want them now. Just a taste to take the edge off my thrumming nerves and horniness.

I keep squirming in my seat, and Jordie keeps shooting me knowing glances. Their eyes drag over me before they lick their lips like they're just as hungry for me before focusing back on the line of cars crawling closer to the border crossing ahead of us.

When we finally pull up to the crossing, Jordie hands over our passports and answers all the border agent's questions. We get waved through, and Jordie surprises me by pulling up to the information center in the tiny town on the other side.

"What are we doing here?" I ask as I unbuckle. A chance to stretch my legs sounds amazing.

"I promised the sibs shirts, figured we could get it out of the way here, if that's cool?" Jordie says.

I laugh, but nod. "Yeah, sure, let's be tourists. Have you been to Canada before?"

"Nope. The folks took us on a big Caribbean beach hopping

cruise by way of Mexico for my graduation, hence having a passport. So that was lucky."

"Nice. Well, welcome to the true north, I guess? It's not that different."

"Except I can practice my French here." They waggle their eyebrows at me and I laugh.

They're ridiculous and wonderful. I want to bask in their attention forever. I trail them into the store. Together, we browse the displays of moose, mounties, and maple syrup themed tchotchkes. I'm surprised the small town gift shop has a modest selection of red and white "I heart Canada" merch drowning in a sea of white and blue Québec fleur-de-lis designs.

"Regarde-moi!" Jordie grabs one of the shirts with a delighted squeal. They turn to arrange it under the edges of their light autumn-weight jacket. I'm only puzzled for a second before they spin to show off their efforts. "Que penses-tu?"

"Je pense que tu es une petite canaille." I shake my head at their ridiculous antics, trying to stifle my laughter when I read the slogan on their chest. With the C and half of the D strategically covered up, they have *I <3 ANAL* proudly blazoned across their body.

I resist the urge to cover it up as I feel myself flushing. A family with two young kids enters the aisle with us. I step into Jordie's personal space and tug them into a sweet kiss by the lapels of their jackets. I tell myself it's so the kids and their parents won't see why my joyfriend is grinning like a twelve-year-old at their dirty joke. Any excuse to kiss them.

"I don't know what that means, but I am assuming you think I'm adorable and you want me?" Jordie teases. Their breath is hot on my pulse point as they nuzzle into my neck.

"Close enough, brat. You aren't getting that for your baby siblings," I hiss into their ear.

"Fair. C'est vrai though." Jordie licks my ear and I squirm away, laughing. They wink at me. And yeah, I want to take them up on the shirt's crude invitation. Soon.

We take our time picking out souvenir shirts for their younger siblings and shot glasses and maple candies to surprise Celeste, Pixel, and our other friends. I find every excuse to touch Jordie. My fingers linger along their arm as I show them various trinkets, our shoulders bump as we walk. I even brush up against their back as we squeeze past a display that takes up too much of the aisle to walk easily side-by-side.

When we get to the cashier, Jordie happily greets the attendant with a cheerful bonjour and their face falls when he immediately switches to English on them. I stifle a snort. Their accent still needs work, but it's adorable to watch them doggedly keep trying. They stumble through a request to practice their French that has the worker smiling bemusedly at their efforts. They get through a chat about the local weather, border traffic, and whether we might see a real moose like on the tee-shirts.

I enjoy watching them try to fit into my home province, making an effort to be a part of my world. We get back on the highway and they crow about how well they held up their side of the conversation. My heart swells with affection for them all over again. They give me a questioning look when I point to the first provincial rest area we come to on the highway.

"Need you to come in with me," I mumble.

They park in front of the little building and follow me inside without complaint, flashing me a knowing grin as we cross an empty lobby to an unoccupied, accessible washroom. When I pull them inside the single occupancy room with me and turn the lock, their lips curl into a wicked smirk.

"Want to take the edge off before we show up at my folks' place?" I ask, voice all husky with lust and the effort not to be too loud.

"So classy, offering to blow me in a filthy rest area toilet," Jordie teases.

They crowd into my space and shove my jacket off my shoulders so they can kiss along my neck. The heat of their kisses takes any sting out of their words. I arch into them, stifling a soft moan. I don't even try to stop myself from rubbing on them. Jordie's erection presses against the bulge of my packer, lighting up my sensitive t-dick with pleasure that's almost too much to take. Fuck, these hormones are no joke.

"Crisse! That's good."

"Yeah?" Jordie smiles against my lips and presses the heel of the hand to my bulge, really grinding it against me and making my eyes roll back.

"Mm, need you so bad, Jords," I tangle my fingers in their curls, tugging them closer.

Their lips part, and I kiss them hard, grinding our bodies

together with a desperate longing to live in this moment. I need to block out what they're taking me home to do. I want to be ready to face my family, but I'm still scared that it won't go as planned.

This stolen moment of losing myself in pleasure with my partner lets me anchor myself in their love and acceptance. Jordie might be the one who calls me sunshine, but they've become my guiding light these past few months. The compass that leads me back to myself every time I feel lost in Boston and the new life I'm building there.

Whatever happens once we go home, I want to memorize what it's like to be filled with hope and love and joy. Just in case.

Jordie deepens the kiss and I tug on their hair, just enough to elicit a soft moan from them. They rub me harder through my pants and I want so much more than kisses and groping. Need to taste them and make them come undone. I want to be on my knees worshiping all the perfection that is my amazing joyfriend.

I pull back, and we both pant for breath, lust-filled eyes locking. "Want to suck you, please?"

"Tu veux leche mon chat?" Jordie bats long lashes at me, trying to distract me from the way they butcher the pronunciation and noun gender. The point is that they're trying to talk sexy for me and I adore everything about them, even their jarring American accent.

"Bien sur. Je veux te sentir te transformer en un désordre frémissant pour moi."

"Mm, love it when you get all French on me." They smile at

me, their eyes hooded and full of lust. I trace the outline of their clit through their skirt.

"Oh yeah? And do you love it when I turn you into a trembling mess for me too?" I press harder on their clit as I scratch along their scalp with the other hand.

"Yes." Jordie's eyes flutter shut and they take a shuddery breath that draws out the single syllable.

"Then lift your skirt and let me go down on you. Je vais te faire la mienne."

Jordie gives me a smoldering look, then gathers up the flowy material, hiking the skirt up past their knees. They make a sexy show of exposing their silky smooth thighs. So they shaved before our trip. That certainly has my cock taking notice, twitching against the soft fabric of my packing pouch. It's weird how much more natural the masculine words for my anatomy are feeling the more I feel like myself. I still like click. But dick and cock feel right too, especially when Jordie has their mouth on it.

I feast my eyes on the sight of them baring it all for me. Soft thighs, I want to run my fingers all over. The little V of lacy floral fabric that covers their half-hard clit so enticingly it makes my mouth water for a taste of them. I've gotten used to the changes in their physical response to sex. As long as Jordie says they're into it, that's what matters to me, not seeing them hard enough to pound rocks.

"Well? It's not gonna lick itself..." Jordie gestures when I stare too long and make them self-conscious.

"Tu est parfaite." I lock eyes with them, wishing I could beam into their mind just how much I'm into every single part of them.

Jordie licks their lips, but holds eye contact as I sink down onto my haunches to crouch in front of them. It feels coquettish and flirty to be gazing up at them through my lashes. A part of me wants to kneel there for them to use, but I don't want to kneel on the dubiously clean washroom floor.

Instead, I balance on the balls of my feet and cling to their thighs to steady myself, eye-to-crotch with the love of my life. Even if I was a bit too chicken to tell them just how head over heels I already am without a bit of prompting. I wasn't certain they would say it back. The fact they did is part of why I just have to show them how much I adore every bit of them in this tangible way. Connect with them on this level before we see my family and I face their uncertain reactions to my coming out. "Mon ange ravissant."

"Uh huh, get on with it, sunshine. Baise-moi s'il te plaît," Jordie winks, making it a gentle nudge instead of a demand, but they also tuck their chin to their chest. Their gaze fixes somewhere off to the side, like they're uncomfortable with the endearments. Duly noted.

"Montre-moi tes yeux pendant que tu t'effondres pour moi. Je veux voir ton âme trembler," I say. I keep one hand on their leg to steady myself as I ease the fingers of the other into their sexy panties and find their pussy. Ass play is out for a quickie without protection, but they love muffing. I gently swirl the loose skin of their sac around my fingertips as I press against the internal twin slits to either side of their cock. "Want me in your pussy, baby?"

"Fuck, Ray." Jordie practically whines as I gaze up at them and lick their bulge.

The synthetic lace is scratchy on my tongue, but I revel in the heat of them around my fingers as I work the tips inside of their pussy. Slowly fucking them open as I go down on them feels incredible. Everything with Jordie feels so effortlessly right and safe. They make me dream of a fully realized technicolor future full of possibilities that seemed like stick-figure fantasies before I met them.

The first few swipes of my tongue are too dry and a little awkward. Jordie holds my head in place, silently encouraging me to give them more, showing me what they like. They nudge me away from touches that aren't doing it for them. I want them to take all of me. But for now, I settle for lathing them in kisses and slurps until they're humping against my mouth as I finger them. Their clit plumps up under my attention, the salty-sweet tang of their skin joining with the dampness of my spit soaking their panties and filling my mouth.

"Mm, close," Jordie pants, one hand still pinning my face to their clit, guiding the swirling licks near their crown that they like best. Their other hand drops between us, pushing inside of their inguinal canal along with the finger I'm thrusting with.

Jordie quirks their fingers to hit just the right nerves that have them coming against my tongue within a few hard thrusts. I want to whine and pout about this being over too fast, but their moans of pleasure echo in the enclosed space.

Right, we probably shouldn't draw out a rest area bathroom quickie. And anyway, I love making them come, even if I want to keep them teetering on the brink longer next time. I'm giddy at the thought of having a lifetime to make them come. They love me. And I love them and together we can face anything.

"Mmm, so good. Fuck, yes, sunshine. Love you so fucking much," they babble. I'm really glad that's not the first time they're saying it, but fuck do I adore everything about them.

I don't stop fucking and licking them until their shuddering dribble of cum bursts, salty and sweet, across my tongue and their body quakes with the force of their orgasm. They produce less jizz since starting hormones, but I'm not complaining about less to swallow. I swipe my mouth dry on the back of my hand and get shakily to my feet, only realizing as I stand that my cock is still aching with arousal. I wet a paper towel to try tidying Jordie up. They wink at me as they slip their saliva sodden panties off and drop their skirt back into place before hugging me and stuffing the wadded up lacy fabric into my back pocket.

"Hold on to these for me?" They ask innocent as a lamb.

I nod woodenly, mouth dry and dick throbbing at the thought of them naked under their skirt. Ready for me to lift it up and just...

Jordie smirks at me, with an all too knowing glint of mischief in their eyes. It's totally a big sibling trolling look. "Did you need a hand with something, sunshine?"

"I'm fine."

"Mhm. Not dying to fuck me before you introduce me to your family?"

I'm not sure if my boner gets worse or better at the thought of my jizz dripping down their thighs while I introduce them to my parents. Hot, but also humiliating. Honestly, maybe it's just a different kind of horny? Is there such a thing as a humiliation boner? I might have one right now, so probably. Gah. Jordie is very good at helping me discover all kinds of new things about myself. I just stare at them and rub my thighs together for a bit of friction.

Jordie snorts. "You're so needy. Come here and let me take the edge off for you."

They grab a fistful of my hoodie to haul me closer. Before I can say a word, they've sunk to their knees, shoved my pants and boxers—along with my packer snug in its pouch—down to mid thigh. Then they wrap their lips around my cock and blow me like I'm their favorite fucking candy.

"Ah. Mm. Jords. Oh. Fuck. Jordie! Je vais jouir..."

"Mmmhmm." Jordie hums encouragement. Because that's obviously the point. They want me to come fast so we can get back on the road and get on with our trip.

So I don't hold back. I explode with embarrassing speed. Damn. I pant in the aftermath as they tuck me back into my pants and nonchalantly turn to fix their disheveled curls in the mirror. When they're set to rights, they casually flush and walk out. I'm still standing there, panting and dazed at how hard they made me come with so little effort. Even through my starry-eyed adoration for the gorgeous personage I'm following out of the accessible toilet, I notice the scowling mom with a crying toddler glaring at us for occupying the restroom.

Jordie sweeps open the door to the little toilet building and winks at me. They know the other adults we just passed know exactly what we were up to in there, and they don't care. And I can't quite make myself care either. No one was around when we went into the single occupancy room. Fuck, I love Jordie so much it makes my chest ache and I never want to stop feeling this giddy joy when our eyes meet.

We get in the car and buckle up and I hold their hand over the console as we rock out to their playlist all the way to my parent's place. It's like they sucked out all my nerves and borrowed worries along with that orgasm. Basking in the afterglow leaves me relaxed and primed to enjoy the rest of our first road trip as a couple.

Chapter Twenty-One

Ray

We pull up to my childhood home a little before supper-time and find street parking nearby. As soon as I step inside, my youngest brother gloms onto me, hugging me tight before I can fully cross the threshold. I'm buzzing with nerves over what I came here to do.

I need to come out. And no matter how certain I am that my family will love me regardless, I can't shake the lingering *what-ifs* that have kept me silent for years. What if they don't want another son? What if I have to watch them grieve a version of me that only ever existed in their heads?

I keep thinking of how open Jordie is with their parents. Remembering how deeply weird it was to sit at a family dinner knowing that Jordie's parents and siblings know something so personal about me that my own don't.

"Missed you, baby sister." Luke rocks me side to side, mashing my chest against his gym-honed pecs uncomfortably. I squirm away, my insides equally twisted up at the familiar wrongness of the nickname.

Jordie stands awkwardly behind me waiting for an introduction, but they notice my discomfort and place a supportive hand on my shoulder.

"Missed you too." I'm kicking myself for not wearing my binder. I debated whether to just rip off the bandaid by showing up flat-chested, but in the end opted for comfort during the hours of driving. So I took it off about an hour into the drive and just wore my baggy hoodie in the car.

Now I regret not putting it back on before walking through the door because the hug makes me hyperaware of the things I don't like about my body. I disentangle myself from Luke and drag Jordie between us. "This is my partner, Jordie."

"Hi." Jordie waves, artificially cheerful in a way I'm not used to seeing them. I don't love the painfully brittle fake smile, but their big grin deflects from my discomfort, so I appreciate it.

I texted to let the rents know we were close. Dad texted back that he's just getting on the bus home from work, so he'll be home soon. Mom is probably in the kitchen judging from the delicious aroma of dinner wafting down the hallway. This is the perfect time to tell Luke who I am and that I'd rather he not call me his sister. Except my tongue gets tangled on the words and he's smiling at my joyfriend. I don't want to spoil the moment.

"Ah, yes, the famous study buddy you kept being so dodgy about. How did you trick them into coming home with you?" Luke play-punches my arm. The big goofball might call me his sister at every opportunity, but he treats me like our older brothers treat him. This same rough and tumble act has made me feel included, even at my most dysphoric.

"Hey!" I pout theatrically.

"What? Iel est bandant." Luke fans himself playfully. And I can't express how much I appreciate him using neutral language to the extent possible. We've all been practicing for Ed, even before I told my brothers about my own nonbinary partner.

"Don't be rude; Jordie is still learning French." I elbow Luke and Jordie looks flustered.

"Aw, but they *are* learning? For you? That's sweet, sis. C'est adorable."

I flush. "No, not *for* me. And quit it. He's just saying you're cute." I turn toward Jordie, feeling weirdly protective of them.

The *sis* nickname rolls off my back harder than before I got used to being gendered correctly by my friends at university. I need to tell Luke that I'm trans on this visit because the nicknames are beyond old. They bother me more now, after being around people who use my chosen name and correct pronouns without question.

"I'm saying you're a hottie and sis needs to lock that down." Luke winks playfully at my partner. His charming dimples are on display. He's such a pest.

Jordie bites their lip and glances at me, like they're checking how to respond. Ah. Yeah. because there it is again. You'd think after twenty-one years of being my big brother, Luke, could come up with a better nickname for me. Ugh.

The need to just blurt it out and ask him to call me Ray, or even bro, wars with all my angsty what-ifs. Standing here, I still only have a vague grand plan about how to tell my family who I am. I subtly shake my head for them to leave the gender stuff alone for now. Jordie lifts one brow at me, wordlessly asking if I'm sure, but not pushing me before I'm ready. I grab their hand and squeeze, warmed to my toes at their willingness to stand up for me. And a little besotted with how nice it is to be so in sync with another person that we can communicate volumes with a glance.

"Okay, so I guess I need to practice my French some more. You guys talk fast," Jordie says with a self-deprecating chuckle.

"Hey, I don't try to scare off your dates, Luke." I pout at him. Technically true, even if both of our other brothers could argue that point.

"It's going to take more than your brother hitting on me to scare me off." Jordie winks at me.

"Perks of not dating anyone." Luke cackles.

I stick my tongue out at him and pointedly loop my elbow through Jordie's.

"Come on, Jords, let's go find Mom to say hi. We can talk slower if you want to practice your French more while you're here." I shove past my annoying brother, dragging my suitcase and my joyfriend behind me. Jordie grabs their bag and follows. The hall isn't really wide enough for us to maneuver our bags like that, so they untangle their arm from mine.

They give my hand a reassuring squeeze, reminding me that whatever happens when I decide to spill the boy beans, they will be here for me. I need that unfailing support more than

I thought I would. Before I get more than five steps toward the living room looking for Mom, an unearthly shrieking from around the corner startles me.

"What the heck is that?" I whirl toward Luke.

Luke laughs. "*That* is Socks. AKA destroyer of dude fingers. AKA defender of all feminine virtue. AKA hell-spawned man-hating demon from the abyss."

From Luke's description and the loud whistling that comes next, I'm half convinced Mom somehow got a sentient teapot or something.

Just then, the front door opens and Dad lets himself in, setting aside his work bag and removing his jacket and gloves. "Hey! You made it. Give your old man a hug."

Dad brushes past Luke and pulls me into a hug that reminds me of home more viscerally than walking through the front door did. This is what I've been missing at school. Knowing I will always have a safe place to land and unconditional love. This is what I'm scared shitless of losing when I tell my family my truth. I cling hard when Dad's grip loosens like he might step back. I'm not ready to let go. He takes my cue and hugs me harder.

"It's good to have you home, kiddo," Dad murmurs to me, patting my back. He holds me as I do my best to banish my doubts and fears that this might be the last time he hugs me before I upend my whole life. "Everything alright?"

He holds me at arm's length and scrutinizes me with a concerned expression. I can't make myself tell him.

"Yeah, tired from the drive. But I'm glad to be home." I give him a wan smile.

Dad nods his acceptance, even though I know he can tell something is up. He turns to Jordie, giving me space to come to him with whatever is on my mind when I'm ready. I want to be ready. I'm beyond ready to *be* out about my gender. It's just the actual words I'm not quite ready to say.

"This must be the famous Jordie? Welcome! It's a pleasure to meet you."

Dad hauls them into a bear hug as if they're already part of the family. Typical Dad, this is how he's greeted all my dates, regardless of gender, since I was a teenager.

"Nice to meet you," Jordie agrees. They tense at first, but then relax into Dad's hug. "I've heard so much about you all."

"Well, we'll get better acquainted over dinner. I put a roast in the slow cooker this morning. There should be plenty for everyone, no new food restrictions, right? Or any other big changes we should know about?"

"None," I say. It's on the tip of my tongue to protest that I'd have told them about any major changes but he's looking at my short hair, so I guess that was a subtle dig about not telling them I wanted a new style.

"Alright then. Your mom is probably in the den with her new baby if you want to say hello."

I pout. "But I thought I was the baby of the family forever."

"Yeah, well, so did I for three blissful years. That's the breaks, sis." Luke slugs my shoulder playfully, crowding closer to us.

"So, this Socks is my replacement?" I complain.

"Yep, empty nest," Luke jokes. "We keep telling her it's not meant to be literal, but you know how she gets." My brother ruffles my short hair. "This is still so weird. It's going to take some getting used to until you grow it back out."

I swallow down the retort that I have no intention of growing my hair back out and stick my tongue out at him again. Dad kisses my cheek and takes my suitcase from me. "I'll go put this up in your room. Go say hi to your mother and her new emotional support parrot."

"Pft, sure. As in, the parrot needs *her* for emotional support," Luke says.

"Your brother is not wrong." Dad rolls his eyes. "My new demon overlord seems to think that she has dibs on Alice, particularly her shoulders."

"Socks hates all men. So, *you're* in luck anyway. Bet she won't savage your poor fingers." Luke waggles several bandaid-wrapped fingers at me.

"I have failed you as a father if you don't realize that any self-respecting demon lord requires regular sacrifices," Dad says. He's such a dork. But Jordie is smiling, so I can't be too put out by my family's over-the-top ridiculousness.

"Yeah, blood sacrifices." Luke sulks. He folds his arms across his chest, presumably in a much belated attempt to protect his bandaged fingers.

"Here, I'll bring your bag upstairs too, Jordie. Are you kids bunking together? Alice made up the cot in your old room, but if you each want your own, we have plenty of space."

Jordie looks at me and arches a brow, like, is this a trick question? I smile. "Put everything in my room, please."

"Sure." Dad hesitates, takes in how close Jordie is standing to me, and adds. "Don't know if you need them, but there are condoms and lube by the sink, like always. It's a fresh box, no questions asked."

"Dad!" I groan. Luke cackles.

Jordie snorts. "Thanks, Mr. Gagnon."

"What? None of my business what you use them for. I hear they make excellent balloon animals." Dad winks.

Just then, Mom sweeps into the entryway, a lemon-yellow parrot perched on her shoulder, nestled into Mom's long hair like she's wearing it.

"*Dad!*" I repeat, more vociferously. As if that ever stopped him from delighting in inflicting maximal embarrassment.

"I mean, I'm clearly no expert considering there are four of you kids." Dad fires his parting shot. He hefts both mine and Jordie's bags up the stairs with a grunt of effort.

"I should have packed bricks. Just for that, I'm going to sacrifice *you* to the feathered overlord," I call after him.

"Don't be silly—Socks, sovereign of the seven hell, is perfect-ly happy with offerings of fruit and jewels to beak at. Come here, my darling girl. I've missed having another lady in the house. Socks is going to love you!" Mom says.

Mom opens her arms to hug me. I go to her, heedless of the sharp beak that apparently won't touch me and sharper words that hurt all the more because they make me feel invisible. Like a caricature of myself with these people I love.

It's as if I'm interacting with them behind a sheet of thick plastic and they can't see the real me at all. It hurts so much more now, after experiencing acceptance. Jordie and their friends gave me a taste of what it's like to exist without the stifling role I got cast in at birth and can't seem to stop playing.

I'm on the verge of tears at what should be a happy homecoming, because my family will always see me as a girl. And even a tiny bundle of feathers needs to rub in that inescapable reality. I feel foolish for even thinking I'd somehow discover the courage to say something—finally just tell them. My heart sinks and I wish my mom could hug away all my fears and make this okay the way she's always tried to make all my hurts better.

I want to lock away all these feelings that have gotten so much stronger since Jordie helped me find the strength to let them out. It hurts for the people I love most to be so confidently wrong about something so fundamental to who I am, but I don't know how to fix it. Hot tears sting my eyelids and I fight to hold them back.

"OW!" I jerk away from Mom. The sudden sharp sting feels like getting my ear pierced. A burning shock followed by angry flapping and squawking.

"No bites!" Socks squeaks in a high-pitched voice.

"Socks, what's gotten into you?" Mom pulls back, giving me a strange look as the startled pain melts into relieved hilarity.

I burst out in raucous laughter, even as I rub my ear, checking for blood. Luke wasn't joking about that beak hurting. All my fears and angst, and I'm going to let a tiny ball of feathers out me to my family.

Mom's parrot somehow sees me. Knows that I'm a boy. I can't help myself; I laugh until my stomach aches and Jordie is rubbing my back, a knowing smile on their face. Mom and Luke are looking at me like I've well and truly lost the plot.

"You okay?" Luke asks.

"Huh, she usually only bites men. I could have sworn the rescue was clear about that. They must have been mistaken." Mom is studying my face intently, tilting my chin to examine my ear. "You aren't bleeding."

"You know, I've never seen anyone enjoy her bites like that," Luke muses. "Keep your weird bird kinks to yourself, sis."

"Enough Lucas," Mom chides my brother, still fussing over me. "Are you alright, dear?"

"Yeah. I'm... Mom, they weren't wrong."

"Hm? About what?"

Luke's eyes widen in comprehension, and he covers his mouth. "Oh, shit!" His gaze flicks between me and Jordie, then he points between us. "Toi aussi? Tu est comme ellui?"

I wobble my hand in front of me in a so-so gesture. "I'm trans too, if that's what you mean."

"Oh." Mom stares at me. And I hold my breath, on the brink of shattering if she doesn't take it well. Rejection would hurt so much more than a bird bite. I don't want to watch the emotions playing out on my mother's face, but I do. Searching for the confusion, anger, betrayal, or hurt. The disappointment I was so sure she'd feel. She's just looking at me though.

"Um, dude, sorry if I made things weird with all the calling you sis." Luke fidgets. He taps his toe on the ground and rubs at his nape. It's like he's running our entire interaction back and cringing as much as I did the first time. "Guess I should have guessed." He runs a hand pointedly through his own short hair, then glances between me and Mom. "Um, are you going to say something, Mom?" He shuffles over to stand shoulder to shoulder with me, on the opposite side from Jordie.

And infuriating as my youngest brother is, I could hug him for asking the thing I'm desperate to hear and too fragile to ask. Mom shakes her head, and ice grips my heart.

"So, what do I call you now?" she asks.

"Um, your son?" I hunch my shoulders, bracing for a rejection that still doesn't come.

Mom laughs. "Oh, of course darling, that goes without saying I meant your name."

"Oh." I can breathe again. The ice around my heart melts and my mom still loves me. "Ray."

Mom gives me a funny look. "Is this why you asked me what we were going to call you if you were another boy? You've known that long, and you never said anything?"

"Maybe longer?" I shift from foot to foot, swaying into Jordie and taking strength from the contact. This is hard, exposing all my most vulnerable parts to my mom. Leftover adrenaline still claws at my insides. I'm somewhere between lightheaded, giddy relief and a creeping nausea for all the years of pointlessly lost time as her reaction sinks in.

I can't put into words how isolating it has been to feel like the people I love were looking straight through me. Only seeing my painstaking projection of who I thought they wanted me to be. How terrified I was that if I showed them the real me, they'd turn their backs on me. I love my mom, but this has been a barrier between us for so long and I was the only one who seemed to notice. My eyes sting. I want her to make those years of hiding okay the way she made all my childhood scrapes and bruises better, to hug away the ache of lost time and wasted fears.

"Oh, darling, come here!" Mom reaches for me, arms open for a hug I want to dive into. Let the invisible barriers fall and figure out how to be myself with her again. If I let go of my control, I'll fall apart knowing I have people to put my back together again. But there's more to discuss, so I hold myself back.

"Uh, I don't need Socks to re-pierce the other ear." I hesitate, warding Mom off with both hands. I glance at the cute little murder beak still perched on her shoulder. Humor always helps when things are too serious like this. I got that from Dad, so Mom is used to it and takes my protest in stride.

Mom lifts Socks onto a finger and holds the bird out to the side for a one-armed hug.

"Problem solved, now come here and let me love on my baby boy." Mom wiggles her fingers at me and I step into her. Relief flows through me. She still loves me. We can figure the rest out from there.

I melt into Mom's embrace, and it feels so good to have the truth out in the open. Relieved tears burn behind my eyes and when I pull away, I'm fighting them back. Jordie gives me a knowing smile.

"No fair, usurping my youngest status all over again," Luke teases, easing some of the tension as I flip him off.

"Hey, Ray, you know what this means?" Jordie nudges me playfully. Their touch grounds me, makes me feel less off kilter.

"What?" I sniffle.

"Now you're officially AMAB. Assigned Male At Bird," Jordie jokes.

Luke snorts. Mom shakes her head with a lost smile, like she doesn't quite get the joke. I laugh harder than it merits, swept up in the cathartic torrent of relief and joy. Socks preens Mom's ear, then ruffles her feathers out and beaks at her wings, grooming herself.

"Let's see what your gender reveal parrot thinks about me next!" Jordie jabs a finger at Socks.

"Don't tempt the fates," I groan, grabbing for their arm as Socks cocks her head. The parrot fluffs up her feathers and whistles before reaching out her beak to tap Jordie's shiny enamel pronoun ring. The tiny ball of feathers makes an adorable kissing sound. Apparently, she can be deceptively sweet when she cares to be.

"Rock on, little birdie." Jordie is grinning. "Hey, what's it mean when the sovereign of hell kisses your ring?"

"You are truly among her favored servants," Luke intones, playfully bending at the waist in a bow toward Jordie. They eat up the teasing.

"The gender bird has spoken; I'm woman enough to keep my skin intact," Jordie jokes. "Tremble before my majesty. So, Mrs. G, what do you say? Can I join you for the girl-bonding while Ray catches up with his brothers?"

"Oh, it's Ms. Tremblay, actually." Mom smiles at them. "But of course, dear. No sense letting a perfectly good day of pampering go to waste. I'm looking forward to getting to know you better. Ray, would you want to join us?"

"No, thanks." I wrinkle my nose and exchange a look with Luke. "You two can enjoy that without me."

Mom shakes her head fondly. "Four boys. Goodness. That might explain some things. Why didn't you say anything sooner?"

I shrug self-consciously. "It seems stupid now."

"Didn't I always say you could tell me anything?" Mom's eyes pinch at the corners, lips set in a trembling line, like she's trying to hide hurt feelings.

"You did. But I know how much you loved the idea of having a daughter." I shrug, hiding my own old hurts. They made it *so* clear my gender mattered to them, darn it. I was certain my folks would meet my news with disappointment, at the least.

"I did. But you know what I love more than that?" Mom lifts an elegant brow at me.

"What?" I arch a brow right back at her.

"You. And your brothers. I love you so much more than I could ever have imagined loving the idea of you."

"Yeah, but I didn't want to disappoint you guys." I hug myself, wishing again that I'd worn my binder when my arms mash into too-soft flesh that I'm no longer used to. "At least, not more than I already do. I'm not smart or athletic like my brothers and I didn't want to fail at the one way I stood out from them. See? Stupid."

"Oh, darling boy, you could never disappoint us." Mom cups my face in her hand, and then tips my chin up so I'll meet her eyes. "Unless you really are making sacrifices to other demons. Because we owe very strict fealty to Socks now."

I crack up laughing, all my tangled feelings about her reaction melting into hilarity. There's no sense wasting more time on bitter regret over borrowed fears that turned out to be utterly unfounded.

Mom hugs me again, jostling Socks into flight. The bird shrieks a protest as she wings her way over to perch on a framed family photo and shows her displeasure by shitting on it. Luke snorts. Mom sighs.

"I suppose we'll have to look at updating that now, won't we?"

"Really?" I ask, startled because there's acceptance and then there is showing she means it all the way.

"Yes. I want all my boys to always feel welcome coming home. I don't know too much, but when you and your brother told us your new partners are nonbinary, Dad and I did some research. The parent forums all said affirming photos are important."

"You don't have any photos of Jordie." I point out, deflecting from how her complete and unquestioning acceptance has me totally off kilter. Of all the ways I expected my family to react, this is beyond my wildest hopes. It doesn't feel real, like I'm floating on air or living through a dream that's too good to be true. Jordie squeezes their arm around my shoulders.

"Well, no." Mom smiles at me. "That's true, but I also don't have any photos of all my boys looking handsome in their suits. We'll plan something, maybe after Jackie has the baby?"

"Yeah, that would be nice." I smile. It would be nice to have updated family photos. Mom scheduling it for after my nephew is born makes it feel less like I'm the sole reason to drag my brothers into formal wear.

"Good. We can get it scheduled for your winter break. Now, you kids must be hungry after your trip. How was the drive? I have potatoes baking, and Dad's famous roast is in the slow cooker. Luke brought over a tarte au sucre for dessert. If you're hungry, I can make you two some radish sandwiches or some-thing to tide you over until supper," Mom offers an assortment of my favorite meal options.

Jordie's brow scrunches. "Sugar pie? Am I translating that right?"

Luke's eyes twinkle with mischief as he says, "Yep, it's exactly what it sounds like. Has Ray told you about the time sh—he, sorry—ate an entire tarte au sucre with his hands? It took dad half the night to scrub the filling out of his hair."

"I have the pictures," Mom volunteers.

Jordie rubs their hands together gleefully. "Oh? Do I get to see the embarrassing baby photos?"

"I was a toddler!" I protest. "And it's still the best pie. Sort of like pecan, but without the nuts."

"Makes sense that you'd like your sweets equally with and without nuts," Luke teases me relentlessly. He's such an infuriating pain in my ass, and I've missed the crap out of him.

"I do like my dates sweet as pie," I agree, winking at Jordie.

They make a silly face at me. "I'm not that sweet. And wait, did you say radish sandwiches?" They wrinkle their nose. "Is that a thing?"

"Mhm, a delicious thing. Come try some." I grab their hand and tug them toward the kitchen, pleased that they don't seem too overwhelmed by my family.

"What did I miss?" Dad asks as he rejoins us in the entry hall. "Why are we standing in the hall? Come inside and get comfortable."

Mom gives me a look. "Should I share Socks's revelations, or do you want to do the honors?"

It's easier to find my words now that I've broached the subject and Mom and Luke made their support clear. The tightness around my chest that wouldn't let me voice the words earlier is still there, but it's eased enough for me to speak.

I take a deep breath. Jordie puts a comforting hand on my shoulder. Mom nods her encouragement and even Luke shoots me a thumbs up.

I can do this. I swallow down my nerves. Years of putting on a smile over my dysphoria have taught me how to make a flippant joke when anxiety is like a bucket of eels wriggling in my belly.

"Oh, you didn't miss much, just me coming out," I say.

Dad's brow wrinkles in confusion. "But we already know you swing both ways, dear. Unless that's changed?" He glances between me and Jordie, as though unsure how their identity fits into the calculus of my sexuality. That's not awkward at all.

Luke literally face palms and I almost crack up laughing at his exasperated expression. That makes it easier to keep my cool and maintain my pretense of nonchalance. "I'm a guy. Like, as in transgender. And I'm going by Ray now."

"Oh." Dad shakes his head, face unreadable. He asks, "So I guess the short hair is here to stay?"

"Huh?" I'm not sure how to react to him fixating on something so trivial. Part of me is indignant that he isn't taking this seriously, but the more logical part of me knows humor is how Dad copes with even the most dire news. But this isn't bad news.

Dad rallies. "Because, you know, plenty of men are growing out their hair these days. Nothing says you *have* to keep it short to be a guy."

"Dad!" I groan. This is so typical of him, but he rarely sticks so doggedly to a bit. Still, it's classic Dad to use ridiculous humor to defuse a tense situation. That tells me more than any heartfelt declaration that my identity won't change how he treats me in the least.

"What? I've tried to convince your brothers to grow theirs out too," Dad protests. I have no doubt he has; he started balding when I was still a toddler, but I've seen the pictures from when he and Mom met. His hair was longer than hers. He used to spend hours helping me try out new styles, putting my long, thick tresses into elaborate braids to keep the tangles away. I realize with incredulity that he might actually be this disappointed about my hair for its own sake.

"No dice, Dad." I shake my head, then bite my lip, shuffling from foot to foot as residual anxiety courses through me. I need to hear him say he accepts me for who I am point blank before I can relax fully. "So, are we good?"

"You're my baby, Ray. Nothing is going to change how much I love you. Bring it in." Dad hugs me tight, thumping my back before releasing me. "Just means Mom and Socks will have to cheat even more outrageously when we play guys versus girls on board game night." He winks, rubbing his hands together in a parody of an evil villain monologuing.

Mom scowls and shoves playfully at Dad's shoulder. "Careful that you don't unleash the wrath of Socks, dear. Anyway, Jordie will be on my team, won't you, dear? Or do we need to have a separate enby team?"

"Technically, I'd be on that team with them," I say. The fact she knows enough to realize nonbinary people exist as something other than a category of woman light gives me the courage to share a little more of myself. My family takes it in stride.

Mom nods. "Good, that will even out the teams a little. And

Jackie will be on my team."

"And Darren's been seeing that genderfluid paralegal, so ze can be on your team too," Luke pipes in.

"First of all, Ed has a name, and ze makes your brother happy, so ze is always welcome at board game night. But also, rats. You realize this entirely ruins my diabolical plans for board game domination." Dad pouts. "So much for increasing my team's advantage by having three 2SLGBTQI+ sons. Fine, I suppose we can have a three-way."

"Dad!" Luke and I groan. I drop my face into my hands and peek between my fingers at Jordie to gauge their reaction. They have a hand pressed delicately to their mouth to suppress a laugh, eyes twinkling with glee. At least someone thinks Dad is funny. He really is trying if he's up to date on his government official acronyms for the queer community, at least. Even if it sounds a little weird to rattle off all the letters aloud.

"What? A three-way *competition*. What else would I mean?" His expression is so innocent I can almost buy that he doesn't realize the other connotation of what he said. The man thrives on embarrassing us kids. Still, it's nice in a way. Falling into familiar patterns of banter. Being treated the same as always and having Jordie folded into the family like they've always been a part of us.

"Nevermind that, dinner is almost ready. Come carve up your roast. I'm sure Jordie and Ray are hungry and tired after their drive. Step up, little demon lord." Mom lifts Socks onto her finger, making kissy noises near her beak. "I'm just going to get her settled in her cage with her evening sacrifice."

"All hail her unholy highness, Socks," Luke intones.

My family is as weird as ever, but Jordie is grinning, totally unphased by them. The fact they're all being their usual strange selves makes it easy to believe I won't have to sacrifice my relationships with my family to be myself. The rush of relief as that sinks in hits me like a wave and leaves me lightheaded.

The unrelenting weight of their unknown reaction isn't hanging over me anymore. For years, it's seemed like a massive Sword of Damocles hanging over me. Where any slip on my part risked severing my connection to the people who love me if they realized I wasn't the girl they thought I was. The big secret I've carried so close to my heart for so long is out in the open and everything is going to work out just fine. I still need to tell my two oldest brothers, but I'm not as worried about their reactions after how Luke and my folks responded.

I sway on my feet at the enormity of it all, and Jordie slings an arm around my shoulders to support me. The pride shining in their eyes melts my heart for them all over again. I lean in and kiss their cheek.

I can't wait to have them alone again so we can celebrate. Not that I need an excuse. I've been horny as hell since starting T, so that has only amplified all the new relationship honeymoon type feelings I have about Jordie.

I'm practically floating. I feel so light as we head down the hallway to eat dinner with my family. It's like I've shed the last vestiges of the old me and can truly embrace myself wholly as

Ray in all areas of my life.

There is nothing holding me back anymore, all because Jordie gave me the confidence to finally let the words past my lips. I want nothing more than to kiss every inch of them, and I can't keep the smile off my face as I watch them joke around with my family. They fit here with me.

I love how right it feels when Jordie holds my hand. They call me their boyfriend and no one bats an eye at the affection. This is the first night of a future I scarcely dared to believe I could have. My family and my truth, coexisting, both all mine.

Chapter Twenty-Two

Ray

"I'm so proud of you, babe!" Jordie kisses me as soon as we're behind closed doors. I kiss them up against the rose pink door of my childhood bedroom as I fumble the lock closed before cupping their ass and grinding against them. Jordie moans into our kiss, scraping their teeth over my lip.

"I can't believe I told them!" I grin, still giddy from the positive reaction and the fact that Jordie cares about me enough to plan this trip. They gave me the chance to tell my family before the holidays. Having them with me for this is something I'll always treasure.

"You did! And it went so well, didn't it?" They grin at me, hands roving over my back, pressing me close without demanding more.

"It did." I stroke their cheek, fuck, I adore them. "Thanks to you."

"All I did was drive. You were the one who had the courage to tell them." Jordie gives me a peck of a kiss. They won't quite meet my eyes, but it's been a long day of driving, so I could just be reading too much into being tired. "I'm so proud of you, sunshine."

"Seriously, thank you for being here to support me. I don't know if I could have done it without you." I try to hold their gaze, beam into their brain just how much I love and appreciate them.

"You could have. But I'm glad I was here for you."

"Me too." I nuzzle into their neck, taking comfort from the closeness. I suck a lovebite into the tender skin there.

"Mm. Love you, sunshine, but if you keep that up I'm going to be a horny mess," they caution me. Their saucy wink convinces me I was imagining things earlier. Everything is fine. Better than fine—amazing.

"So? We've got plenty of condoms. Dad bought a brand new box." I pull back to grin at them.

Jordie snorts a laugh and shakes their head. "Your dad is hilarious. You sure you're good with fucking me while your folks are down the hall?" Their breath is hot as they lean in closer to murmur into the shell of my ear, "Because I want your cock inside me, Ray."

I shiver in anticipation. My joyfriend wants me to fuck them. And I want that too. This won't be the first time I've gotten frisky with a partner in my childhood bedroom. Heck, I've had sex here on more than one occasion.

Ever since my brothers all moved out, the rooms next to mine are both empty. Mine is the smallest and farthest from our folks' room. It's also got the best window, looking out over our tiny backyard and getting full light in the evening.

"Yes. I want you. Get naked and prep yourself." I gesture to the ensuite washroom that Dad added in a remodel when I was a pre-teen as compensation for the size of my room. My brothers all had to share the hallway washroom, but considering how long my hair took to wash and dry, even they benefited from not having to share with me.

"Fancy." Jordie grins at me as they lean into the washroom to check it out. It's really not, just a narrow corner shower stall, toilet, and sink. The cellophane wrapped box of condoms and a tube of lube stand out on the vanity since I put away all my toiletries and makeup before I left for university. "Give me a minute to clean up?"

"Take as long as you need." I cross the room to close the curtains and dig my strap-on cock out of my suitcase while Jordie does whatever they need to do to prep in the washroom. I've been waiting for the right moment to use it and this seems like the perfect chance. My last girlfriend topped me with a dildo, but I was afraid to try it.

Afraid that it would feel too right to be the one fucking her. That doing it would betray how much of a fraud I felt like playing the role of girl. Or that it would be too hard to take the cock back off and go back to being seen as a girl afterward. It was too big and too emotional and too hard to put into words with someone I wasn't ready to share the most vulnerable parts of my heart with. Far easier to let her into my body than my heart and soul.

With Jordie, it's easier to do this. To trust them with all of me. I slip out of my jeans and shirt and replace my packer and underwear with the strap. When I glance down and see the erection jutting from between my thighs, the wave of euphoria threatens to overwhelm me.

Jordie comes up behind me, hugging me. "You good, sunshine?"

"Yeah." I squeeze my eyes shut and jerk the firm length of fleshy silicone. It feels just like jerking the cock I sometimes wish I'd been born with. I have to blink away tears at how right it feels. "I'm good. Want to fuck you so bad."

"Yeah? How bad? Want to slick that cock up?" Jordie kneels gracefully down in front of me. "Want to fuck my throat first? Fill up all my holes?"

They jerk me idly. I buck into their fist.

"Yes. Suce-moi la bite," I croon to them, fingers scratching over their scalp. Fuck, it feels good to say that, telling them to suck my cock. The harness holding it snug against my body and the heft of it between my thighs makes it feel like an extension of my t-dick.

Jordie moans as I tangle my fingers in their curls, pulling them closer. I stop just shy of thrusting past their parted lips to let them close the final distance. They stick out their tongue to lap at the blunt head.

"Mhm, love it when you pull my hair, sunshine. Make me take it." Jordie sticks out their tongue again and gazes adoringly up at me through their lashes.

Now I push into their mouth, imagining the wet heat of them on my cock and reveling in the visual of making them choke on my length. Jordie moves to take me right to the back of their throat. They swallow me down with an eager ease that has me turned on as hell.

They make the most deliciously sinful sounds when I bottom out and start thrusting, using their mouth as requested. Making them take it, lapping up every one of their needy moans while they go down on me like they're starving for my cock. They grab my ass, fondling me and pulling themself as close as possible as I thrust in deep.

It's good. Really fucking good. I haven't been getting as wet as before hormones lately, but my t-dick is a throbbing beacon of horny need under the dildo's base. Every thrust transfers through the silicone, a taunting tease of what I want to do with Jordie.

This might not be enough to get me off, but I still take my time enjoying the foreplay. The way Jordie's lashes seem so long when they're gazing up at me from their knees. How soft and luscious their curls are under my hands. The way their chest jiggles the barest bit now when I thrust harder. I love playing with their tits and their breathy moans when they press into my hands and let me lavish attention on their sensitive nipples.

Jordie takes me to the base, nose nestled against my groin. I just really need to be inside their ass now. Need to feel their body spread open under me.

"I want to fuck you so bad, Jords. Need to be buried inside

you." I urge them up to their feet, tugging on their curls.

Jordie lets my cock slip free of their mouth. Fuck, my t-dick twitches at how hot my strap-on dick looks glistening with their spit. A string of saliva connects me to their mouth and drips from the tip like precum. It would probably be weird to reach for my phone to take a picture, but I try to sear the details into my memories.

Jordie smiles up at me and licks their lips in a way that makes me want to shove them right back onto my dick. They reach for the lube from earlier and grab my hand, easing it off their head and turning it palm up to squirt lube into my palm. Then they guide my hand to my dick.

"Stroke yourself while you watch me finger the hot little hole you're about to come inside."

I shudder at the mental image of filling Jordie up with my cum. Actually ejaculating might have to remain a fantasy, but I like the dirty talk. A lot. Jordie kisses my neck, then goes to kneel on my bed. They present me with a perfect view of their gorgeous ass as they reach back to finger their hole with more of the lube.

I forget to stroke myself, hand still on my dick as I watch raptly. Jordie parts their own plump cheeks, two fingers disappearing inside of them with a sinful squelch and a breathy moan. They stretch their pretty pink pucker open, their skin glistening from the lube.

"Ready for a third finger. Want to help me?" Jordie winks at me over their shoulder and nods toward a disposable glove they set down on the mattress beside them. I scramble closer to get my hands on them, pulling the protective latex over my fingers. I massage the soft globes of their ass and wiggle a finger in alongside theirs. Jordie moans and arches back onto my digit.

"Mm, just like that. Feel how hot and tight I'm going to be around you, sunshine. Gonna milk the jizz right out of you." Jordie teases, rocking onto me.

"Crise. I need you, Jords. J'ai envie de te baiser."

"Yeah? Then fuck me, sunshine. Parle sale a moi, I fucking love it."

"Dis-moi des cochonneries? Unless you mean literal dirt?" I suppress a snort of laughter at their attempt to translate the idiom.

"Sure, call me your little piggy. Whatever gets you off." Jordie winks over their shoulder at me. It feels good to get to share even this part of myself with them. No need to be self-conscious over which language I'm using, and to know that they trust me with their fumbling beginner French.

"Maybe I'll make you squeal like a little piggy," I tease as I slip another finger inside of them, relishing the silky heat of their body.

What would it feel like for them to hug my flesh and blood cock like this? Maybe someday I can find out, but I'm not ready for that kind of surgery right now. Still, just imagining it is enough to have my t-dick straining under the strap-on.

"Think you can?" Jordie challenges me. "Better ditch the glove and wrap your cock so you can try."

"Yeah, that works." I pull my fingers free, taking the suggestion as an invitation to get inside of them. Mindful of the precautions we've discussed for anal play, I invert the glove as I peel it off and drop it in the trash beside my bed.

I can't wait to sink between Jordie's plump ass cheeks as I reach for the foil packet they brought out of the washroom with them. It's a surreal feeling to roll the latex over myself instead of a partner. I take a minute to savor the sensation, stroking more lube along my length. "You ready?"

"Mhm, so ready." Jordie wriggles their delectable ass. I get back in position behind them and line up my tip with their hole. Teasing them with a light touch, pressing against their rim, then pulling back. Jordie groans and rocks into me, taking the tip.

"Oh!" I gasp as I watch myself slotting into their body. "Mmm, look at you taking me, comme ma bonne petite saloppe." As the words slip out, clearly feminine, I worry that might not be the right tone for this, but Jordie just moans and fucks back onto my cock. Guess they liked it. And they said to err on the side of femme terms for French, so I'm going to go with what makes them moan for me.

"Mhm, fuck my slutty hole, sunshine. Need it so bad."

"Yeah, you do. Need me to fill that sloppy wet pussy, huh?" I thrust into them experimentally, and they move to meet me with another breathy moan. It's so good, I can't help but tell them how incredible they make me feel. "Tu me fais me sentir si bien."

"Mm, angle up a little more?" Jordie squirms under me and

I reach down to adjust myself and get the angle just right for them. I thrust again. Jordie sighs. "Mhm, just like that. Fuck me, Ray."

I hold their hips steady and fuck into them again, working up to firmer strokes. It feels so good to take them, to thrust in and stake my claim on their body. To make them shudder and shake with breathy little pleasure sounds falling from their lips. It's a raw primal sense of myself that makes me feel more whole than I ever have during sex.

Their fists clench in my sheets as they ride me. I need more stimulation, and I need to fuck them over the edge. I toggle on my cock's vibration feature as seek their p-spot and the perfect buzzing pressed right against my t-dick while I fuck into them is exquisite. So is the squeal they try to muffle in my pillow before babbling softly.

"Mmmff. Ohhhhh. Ray. Fuck. Fuck me. Nngh."

Pretty sure I found the right angle. I rub their back, thrusting into them and loving the way I'm making them come apart for me.

"Juste comme ça. Parfait. Ma parfaite petite cochonnette." I pound into that spot, driving them wild as I cling to my restraint, desperate not to come too soon. The vibrations are perfect and the fact it's Jordie I'm fucking into incoherence and just, everything about this is bliss and I never want it to end.

I snap my hips, driving my dick into them, every move a revelation. This is what it's like to be the one doing the fucking, to burrow inside of my love and find my home in their heart. I love it. And I love them. I'm so glad I saved this moment to share it with someone who will understand the hot tears running down my cheeks at the sense of completion I'm feeling as I merge our bodies, rocking into them. How supremely masculine and myself topping them like this makes me feel.

I can't go back to only ever showing the world pieces of myself, and now I don't have to. The thrumming buzz of the vibrations and the fulfillment of being able to be with my love in this way is indescribable. I'm panting for breath, clinging on to my control by a thread. Then Jordie lifts onto their elbows, changing the angle as I thrust in deep, and smiling over their shoulder at me, their face a revelation as they grunt.

"Oh, gonna... can't... I'm coming," Jordie says, voice breaking as they do just that.

Jordie on a normal day is gorgeous, but they're stunning, coming with me balls deep inside of them. I've had plenty of good sex, but nothing compares to tipping over the edge of bliss right behind them.

It's never been this good with anyone else. For all that my dick is made of silicone and covered in a condom, I've never had so little between me and my past lovers. A physical barrier is nothing compared to the invisible walls guarding my heart and distancing me from everyone else who has come with me.

Sex has never been this vulnerable, and real. Never before have I come with my lover crooning about what a good *boy* I am, and how hot my dick is. Before, there was always a part of me braced for the jarring reminders I was hiding a huge part of myself from my lovers. The unwitting misgendering.

With Jordie, there's nothing to hide. Nothing to hold back. I can make love to them with my whole being and I get to see the whole of them in return. It's gloriously freeing in ways I didn't know I needed before having it.

They make everything seem so much brighter. Simpler. Their total acceptance gives me hope I can be as open about myself and the version of myself I show the world as they are. They gave me the courage to open up to my family. Now that I've done that, I have no more doubts that I can face anything the world has to throw at me.

I cling to Jordie as I come, willing the moment to last. When I look at them, they're what I want as my forever. We can figure out what happens after they graduate and which country to live in and all the details together. It's all trivial as long as I get to spend the rest of my life making love to them and sharing all my big moments with them. I can only hope they feel the same.

Chapter Twenty-Three

Jordie

"Hey," Celeste pokes her head in my door at the same time she's knocking on the frame. "Got a minute?" The concern on her face catches my attention.

"Yeah?" I shove my headphones off my ears and turn my desk chair to face her.

It's not like I can focus on the textbook in front of me anyway. I need to study for finals coming up in two weeks. It's hard to keep my mind where it belongs when studying French conjugations only makes me think of Ray and our perfect weekend away. And the way reality crashed back onto my shoulders as we drove back into Boston and reached campus.

When Ray told his family, he blazed right past the last barrier, keeping him from fully embracing his identity. So what more does he need me for? The more I listened to him spinning out his vision of the future, the more it felt like he didn't. He talked about seeing his family again for the winter break and not having to hide any part of himself.

All the way home, Ray was brimming over with plans for the

future and I just—I couldn't see room for myself in them. He's in the country on a student visa, so when he finishes his degree, where would that leave us? Nowhere. Not an us. Not that he explicitly left me out of his dreaming out loud, just, it felt too much like he'd already outgrown his need for me. Like our road trip was the last hurrah. The last thing he needed me to shepherd him through to get his legs under him as a fully out and proud trans person.

And then Mom sent me a picture of the giant envelope from my top choice law school that was waiting for me on the kitchen counter at home. She asked if I wanted her to open it for me, but I already know the answer waiting inside the full page-sized envelope. I got accepted. My future is waiting for me here in Boston. So where does that leave me and Ray when he goes back to his family in Canada? He has no reason to stay in Boston now that they know about him, right? He told me that's why he chose Northeastern. So he can be himself. That reason is obsolete. I'm obsolete.

So I tried to force a smile as he talked about getting his name and gender marker changed on his ID documents. He shared the intricacies of how that might impact his student visa paperwork. I bit my tongue on the bitter suggestion that if he goes home to finish his degree, that won't matter. Instead of venting my fears at him, I tried to smile sympathetically as he dreamed aloud. My heart breaking more with every mile as he extolled how much of a relief it will be to have his actual name on his diploma when he graduates. Even though his every hopeful musing was like another boulder piled on my chest, making it impossible to catch my breath.

Every word about being out to the world now felt like him telling me he truly doesn't need me anymore. I dropped him off at his dorm with a plastered on smile. When he invited me to spend the night with him, I wriggled out of it by telling him I was planning to spend the night at my folks' place. I had to drop off the car I'd borrowed from Dad.

It wasn't entirely an excuse. Dad usually uses the car for his morning commute. And I caught a ride back to campus with him this morning. But it was still an excuse to avoid emotions I'm not ready to face. I could have come back to campus last night to see Ray again. Or I could have stayed when Ray invited me and swung by Dad's office to give back his keys today. It wouldn't have been the first time he took public transit to work.

"What's up with you?" Celeste asks.

"Huh? What do you mean?" I ask, totally disingenuous.

Celeste shrugs, sidling closer to me.

"Well, Pixel and I noticed you didn't come home last night. We figured you two were still all loved up and schmoopy. Until Ray was moping into his tacos at dinner about how you ditched him in front of his dorm last night. He says you haven't responded to any of his texts all day." Celeste arches an expressive brow at me, daring me to come up with an excuse or try to slip a lie past her finely honed bullshit detection. "So, what's up? You've been moping in here all afternoon, and Pix says you skipped your psych lecture. Did something happen on your trip? You never skip class."

"No. It went really well. Amazing even. He said he loves me and he came out to his family and they were great about it and so welcoming to me and..." I trail off, shaking my head.

"And?" Celeste crosses her arms and stalks closer, challenging me to excuse my weird behavior.

"And he doesn't need me anymore." It sounds ridiculous even as I say it, but that's the vulnerable, aching, wounded heart I've been nursing all day. I stand from my desk, shrugging it off like it's nothing to expose my fears to Celeste. I bend to fuss with my school supplies, lining them up on my desk before whirling to cross the narrow distance to my bed. I spin dramatically again to face my bestie.

"So?" Celeste taps her foot impatiently, waiting for me to get to the actual point.

"*So* why would he stick around?" I snap, and then slump onto the edge of my mattress, feeling shitty for getting angry with Celeste over this.

"Are you kidding me?" Celeste flounces dramatically onto my bed next to me and wraps an arm around my shoulders to shake sense into me. "That boy looks at you like you hung the stars. He likes *you*. Not what you can do for him. I had my doubts about you dating a first year, but he's been good for you, Jords."

"Technically, he's a sophomore transfer student." I stick my tongue out at her. Getting pedantic always makes her tease me about what an excellent lawyer I'm going to be some day. I need to break the tension. I've been marinating in my angst all day and it's exhausting.

Celeste clucks loudly, not taking the bait or letting me get away with distracting her. "That is *so* not the point, and you know it."

"I know. Just. Ugh." I tug at my hair, wishing that the sting brought me clarity instead of reminding me of Ray and making me ache over how much I care about him. "You really think so?"

"Mmm, do I think the guy who makes you smile more than I've seen from you since you started busting your ass studying for LSATs is good for you?" Celeste arches an expressive eyebrow at me. "You deserve to be happy, Jordie. So if Ray makes you happy, don't decide for him that he was only using you."

"What if he was?" I gnaw on my lip.

It's not like it would be the first time a newly out friend thought I was good enough to experiment with, but not enough to settle for. A test to be sure they were really queer, but too queer to stay with once they got their answers about who they were. I don't want to think Ray would throw me out like the trash he's done with. But I didn't want to think that about any of my other lovers, either. I breezed right past all the little warning signs with Nell for years.

Celeste shrugs. "Then dump his ass. But there's only one way to be sure. Go talk to him."

"Ugh, I guess." I heave a sigh. "I suppose you're right."

"Come on, Jords, you *know* I'm *always* right." She shoves playfully at my shoulder, then pats my back before she rises to grab my phone off the charger on my desk and shove it into my hands. "Text him back; you've made the poor boy squirm enough, leaving him on read."

"True. Thanks, Cel. I guess there's no time like the present." I grimace comically at her, not looking forward to the conversation I know I need to have with Ray.

"Exactly. Talk to him, tell him why you're wary. See what he says. You've got this." Celeste shoots me a thumbs up from the doorway, then pauses at the threshold until I obediently tap out a message and show her I've hit send.

Jordie: Hey, sorry I've been MIA all day. Kind of having a freak out. Can we meet to talk at Randy's?

The message flies into the ether. I stare at my screen, willing Ray to get it and reply right this second. As if he's been staring at his phone all day waiting for me to reply. I mentally roll my eyes at how unreasonable I'm being.

Is this how he's felt since last night? I texted to let him know I made it to my folk's place. He sent back a sweet goodnight, and I replied with a silly GIF. Since then, I've just been reading the message notification previews on all his texts to avoid technically leaving him on read. That feels like a shitty cop out now that the shoe is on the other foot.

Damn, I hope he hasn't spent his day this twisted up about the lack of reply. Guilt gnaws at me, and I can't just sit there. The little read notification updates to just past my last message. I hold my breath, waiting.

The animated 'the other person is typing' dots start and hope flares in my heart. It's not like we haven't gone more than a day without texting before. It's just that no matter how much I justified my cold feet to myself, I know the timing looks awful. We just got back from meeting his parents, our first big trip. We should be flying high on all the big emotions of declaring our love and sharing a sexual first. Instead, I disappeared from our usual running conversation and skipped our class and dinner. It looks as terrible as it feels.

I pace my room as he types. It seems like the dots indicating that he's typing are bouncing for an eternity before his reply comes through.

Ray: Did I do something?

Jordie: No. Not at all.

Ray: Cause we need to talk usually isn't a good thing? So, um, want to rip the bandaid off now if you're breaking up with me?

I swallow hard. This is going to be hard to discuss, but we need to get everything in the open. Time to be brave enough to stop burying the insecurities I've been hiding behind like a barricade.

Jordie: Sorry. I didn't word that well. You did nothing wrong, and this weekend was amazing. Too amazing, if that makes sense? I've got some baggage that I should discuss with you, nothing terrible or anything, just, easier to talk about in person, if you're up for it?

Ray: Am I up for late night poutine and pie? You know that's a silly question, babe :P

Jordie: I'm sorry I ignored you today.

Ray: Ah, so that was on purpose? It's okay. I figured you were either busy or you'd talk to me when you were ready. Maybe next time don't freeze me out though?

I wince.

Jordie: Yeah. Next time I'll talk to you sooner. Want to head to the diner?

Ray: Sure, heading out now.

Jordie: Me too.

I grab my wallet and keys. Celeste and Pixel are cuddling on the couch watching a movie as I slip past them.

"You getting your man back?" Celeste asks.

"Nope, getting my demi-boy," I correct her with a wink that's mostly bravado. "Wish me luck?"

"Oh, is that new?" Celeste tosses her long silky hair over her shoulder, all casual grace. She shrugs insouciantly. "Either way, get your love muffin. You don't need it, but good luck."

"Luck," Pixel echoes. "Open up your..." they pause suggestively and wink "... heart to him."

"Thanks." I wave as I let myself out and lock up behind me. At least whatever happens with Ray, the two of them will still be here for me.

***

There aren't too many people braving the blustery autumnal late evening streets now that rush hour is over. When I left my parents' place with Dad to head to campus this morning, the grass was coated in a layer of frost. A light smattering of freezing rain ran in melting rivulets down the windshield, not quite cold enough to turn into a dusting of snow.

I catch sight of Ray on the sidewalk ahead of me, a few blocks away from Randy's. Winter is on the way, and he looks adorable in the beanie he wore religiously before his haircut. He's chatting animatedly with Claude just in front of the diner. The two of them bonded over their mutual Francophone roots the first time Ray gravitated toward a familiar accent here at Randy's. It's reassuring to see Ray fostering more connections in the city. As if he intends to stay.

My heart clenches at overhearing him chatting away in French, gobbling up the little taste of the home he misses. Connecting with Claude points to putting down more roots in Boston. But Ray missing his language inflames all my doubts that he has any reasons left to stay here now that he knows he can be himself in Montreal with his family. Seeing him happy makes me smile even as my gut churns with the anticipation of a breakup I don't want.

I try to focus on the moment instead of letting my assumptions drag me into an anxiety spiral without even talking to my boyfriend first. His hat is cute with the shaggy tips of his hair poking out on his forehead. The colorful wool makes me smile. I love that it's a way of expressing himself now, instead of a crutch to hide a part of himself that made him uncomfortable.

"Ray!" I call his name and he whirls to face me. His confusion transforms into a beaming grin that melts my heart and shrinks all the worries I've been nurturing nonstop since last night.

"Hi! Just a second." Ray waves to me before he turns to face Claude and wraps up their conversation, urging them to go talk to their crush. "Va parler à Arlene. À bientôt."

"Ouai, je vais le faire. À plus tard. See you later, Jordie." Claude waves to us both before making a beeline to where Arlene is sitting near the dessert counter inside.

I'm tempted to follow them inside. Anything to delay this chat a little longer. And get out of the cold, but I'm afraid if I don't start this conversation, I'll just keep putting it off until it festers. Ray gives me a searching look. I need to tear off the bandage right now.

"So, you wanted to talk?" he asks.

"I don't want you to leave," I blurt as our eyes meet. I close the distance between us to hug him tight. Right there in front of the diner in the pale reflected glow of the pink and blue neon lights from within.

"Huh? Leave where?" Ray sounds completely at a loss to understand what I mean, pulling back enough to search my face for answers. I forge ahead.

"Boston." I swallow down my doubts and the fear that I'm not enough to keep him here. "I know you've been missing home, and you came here to create distance to explore who you are. And you don't need to hide anymore, so there's nothing tying you here. I know it's selfish to even ask when we've only been dating for a hot minute, but I want you to stay."

My words dry up, catching in my throat. I can't work up the nerve to put my deepest self-doubts into words. So I just meet his concerned gaze and hope that he can read how much this matters on my face. How much *he* matters to me. Enough to let him go.

Ray blinks at me, his brow furrowing. "You think I'm just going to, what? Drop you now that I'm out to my parents and siblings? Transfer schools and break up with you? Without even discussing it at all?"

He doesn't sound angry, precisely, but he gets louder and more incredulous as he talks.

I shrug, uncomfortable with how hurt he sounds. "This thing between us is new, I realize that. I'd understand if you got what you needed from it and need to move on."

I'd understand alright. And do everything in my power to hide my devastation. Maybe this broken heart will even be enough to get the lesson through my thick skull for good. No dating baby queers. No more being the stepping stone who they trample into the mud on their way to who they want to be.

Ray's face falls, his mouth hanging open for a long, shocked moment. Then he takes my face gently in his hands.

"Jords, I'm not going anywhere. I miss home, but I love Boston and university and our friends. I have every intention of graduating here in three years. And I hope that we'll still be together when it's time for me to figure out where to apply for grad school. Didn't you believe me when I said I love you?"

"Yeah. Sure. I just. I got into law school, here in the city and

I could apply to school in Canada, but I'm not sure about the legal side of moving there and—"

Ray cuts me off with a kiss. "I love you."

I'm so tempted to believe he means it. My lips part. Letting him in physically is so much easier than trusting the whole of my heart to his care. Ray cups my face between his hands and gazes into my eyes, like he can see right into my soul and read all my doubts.

"Je t'aime."

And that, in the language he's told me he uses for lovers, makes it even more real. He's offering me his heart, telling me with his entire self. I'm not part of some youthful semester abroad in the US to him, the way I've let my fears convince me I must be.

"Je t'aime," Ray repeats, apparently seeing the hope kindle in my eyes. He lets go of my face and rubs my upper arms reassuringly. "I want to be with you. You aren't just some convenient lay to me, Jords. You're the person I want to build my future with. I thought I made that clear yesterday in the car, but let me spell it out for you. You are who I want beside me when I graduate, and go to grad school, and start my own therapy practice. I want to cheer for you in the spring when you walk across the stage in your cap and gown. I want to hold your hand when you're nervous for your first day of law school. Be there by your side when you're studying for your bar exam. Where we do all of that doesn't matter to me nearly as much as getting to do it with you by my side. Unless you don't want that too?"

"No. I do. It's just that every time I've let myself think I might've found the one, it's turned out to be a lie. I—It's not that I don't believe you, or trust you, or want you. It's that I don't trust my own judgment when it comes to love, I guess. I fall too hard and too fast. And every one of my exes has basically turned out to be using me to explore their sexuality and I—" I shake my head, not wanting to accuse him of being like them in so many words because I can see he isn't.

Ray hasn't given me a reason to worry like this. I just can't block out all the past hurts to trust him fully. Not until I get this off my chest. I can't continue not knowing, second-guessing every milestone from meeting each other's parents to exchanging *I love you*'s.

"Shh, it's fine." Ray brushes my curls out of my face and rises on his tiptoes to plant a kiss on my forehead. "You have never been an experiment to me, Jords." He caresses my cheek, then kisses me tenderly on the lips.

"You sure?" I can't help asking, voice breathy with the effort of holding back tears. This is too much. This is letting him see past all my defenses, and it's terrifying.

"Beyond sure." Ray gazes into my eyes, like he can plant the truth of his love into the depths of my psyche. My breath catches in my chest at the intensity of his next words. "I love you and je t'aime. For all of you. For as long as you'll have me. And I'll tell you every day for as long as you take to really believe it and then every day after that. Okay?"

"Okay." I take a shaky breath and nod, then repeat it more

firmly, with all my trust. "Okay. Yes. I love you too, sunshine. Sorry I didn't respond to your messages today. I am so glad things went so well with your family, but seeing you happy and out with them scared me a little that you wouldn't need me anymore."

"I gathered that. I don't have to need you to want you, though. You don't have to earn anything from me; you're enough all on your own. Now, come inside. It's cold. Let's grab a shake and some fries and you can tell me more about your exes and this baggage with them. Sounds like there's a lot to unpack, and I don't want to inadvertently give you reasons to doubt my intentions again."

Ray wraps one arm around my waist and guides me toward the bright neon lights of the diner, shining like a beacon in the dark, cold night. I rest my head on his shoulder. The angle is a little awkward with our height difference, but it's worth the crick in my neck to feel diminutive and protected at his side.

Knowing for certain that all Ray's grand plans from the road yesterday include me by his side settles something in my chest. This chat goes a long way to putting my insecurities to rest. It's still early days, but knowing that he's all in on giving our love a chance makes me believe that I really can build a future with him, and damn, does that sound amazing. He makes me believe our love can find a way. True to his nickname, Ray makes every day brighter just by being here.

Stepping inside Randy's with my sweet ray of sunshine feels like coming home.

***

Thanks for reading! If you enjoyed Ray and Jordie's story, I'd love it if you leave a review. I hope you'll check out the rest of the Diner Days Series for more love at Randy's Diner.

For more contemporary trans romances from me, check out Table Topped, Summer of Adventures, and Merry Ex-mas. All of my series feature at least one trans POV character and important side characters, so if you're looking for more trans romance, be sure to check out my other books as well!

About the Author

Alex Silver (he/them) grew up mostly in Northern Maine and is now living in Canada with one spouse, two kids, and a lovebird. Alex is a trans guy who started writing fiction as a child and never stopped. Although there were detours through assisting on a farm and being a pharmacist along the way.

Visit me online at:

http://alexsilverauthor.wordpress.com/

Browse my entire book catalog at:

https://www.amazon.com/Alex-Silver/e/B07NPBW615

Join my Facebook group at:

https://www.facebook.com/groups/alexsalcove

Follow me on BookBub at:

https://www.bookbub.com/profile/alex-silver

Follow me on Twitter:

https://twitter.com/asilverauthor

Sign up for my newsletter for a free short story at: https://landing.mailerlite.com/webforms/landing/i2w6l7

And as always, consider leaving a review on Amazon or Goodreads if you enjoyed this book, reviews are of vital importance to independent authors, thanks!

Also By Alex Silver

Merry Exmas
Contemporary Holiday Romance
Christmas Carl (M/M) #1
Christmas Angel (M/X) #2

Table Topped
Contemporary Romance
Roll for Initiative (M/M) #1 Gui & Paz
Charisma Check (M/M) #2 Theo & Jude
Saving Throw (M/X) #3 Errol & Rene
Plus One Bonus (M/X) #4 Max & Si
Dump Stat (F/F) #5 Laura & Alice
Party of Three (M/M/X) #6 Pia, Emil, & Gregor
Balanced Party (M/M/X) #7 Pia, Emil, & Gregor

Summer of Adventures
Kinky Contemporary Romance
Dungeon Master (M/M)
Knotty Boy (M/M)

Service Call (M/M)

Picture Perfect (M/M)

Puppy Love (F/X)

Stud Muffin (M/M/M)

Hauntastic Haunts

M/M Paranormal Romance

Dan's Hauntastic Haunts Investigates:

Goodman Dairy *Book 1*

Hawk Lake *Book 2*

Ivarsson School *Book 3*

Joliet Asylum *Book 4*

Kapler Hotel *Book 5*

Free download links to the shorts are available in my FB group:

https://www.facebook.com/groups/alexsalcove

Drew's Haunted Hangout (*A Hauntastic Haunts Short Story 1)*

Rafael's Haunted Halloween (*A Hauntastic Haunts Short Story 2)*

Lee's Haunted Holiday (*A Hauntastic Haunts Short Story 3*)

Shift Work

Omegaverse MPreg Romance

Papa Bear (M/X)

Squirrel Trouble (M/M) (expanded edition)

Trash Panda (M/M)

Psions of SPIRE
Urban Fantasy
Shelter (M/M) Novella 0.5
Bright Spark (MMMM)Book 1
Bold Move (MMMM) Novella 1.5
Keen Sense (M/M) Book 2
Weak Link (M/M) Novella 2.5
Quick Fire (M/X) Book 3
Clear Sight (M/M) Book 4
New Look (M/M) Novella 4.5

A SPIREverse daddy kink standalone
New Ground (M/M/X)
Shared Universe Series
Super U - Superhero Romance
Super U: Rising Storm (M/X)
Final Days - Zombie Romance
The Willows (M/M GNC)
Anthologies
Playing With a Full Deck: Stories of Hope in Hard Times
All Amped Up (F/X hope punk)

Listen: The Sound of Fear
Haunt (M/M trans gothic horror)

Fix the World

<u>Upgrade (gay trans cyberpunk)</u>